Nia Taylor:
White House Memoirs

A NOVEL BY

M L LEWIS

Published by
Urban Concepts Publishing
1419 Bodmin Court
Saint Louis, Missouri 63129

A division of
The Urban Concept Group
1419 Bodmin Court
Saint Louis, Missouri 63129

Interior design by Sarah E. Holroyd, Sleeping Cat Books
http://sleepingcatbooks.com

ISBN-13: 978-0615723846

ISBN-10: 0615723845

First Edition

This book is dedicated
to my parents.
I thank God each and every day for
your unconditional love.

Acknowledgement

First and foremost, I would like to thank my wife, Falicia Lewis, and my mother, Joan Lewis. Your support was invaluable. Falicia, thank you for hanging in there and believing in me throughout the process. You are my rock. Mom, your encouragement and input were the only reasons I was able to see this through to completion. I couldn't have done it without you. Dad, I truly appreciate your support and for being the consummate example of hard work and dedication over the years—trust me, I absorbed it all. Buddy crew, Haley and Mickey, thanks for hanging in there with Daddy when the writing took me away from buddy-time. Melva Lavizzo and Wanda Lewis, thanks for believing in me the entire way through. Jonathan Wilkins, man, I can't tell you how much I appreciate you letting me bend your ear and for sharing your thoughts.

Table of Contents

Prologue

SECRET SERVICE AGENT RAFAEL CASTILLO STOOD IN THE WEST WING hallway, peering through a tiny, inconspicuous peephole which was embedded in the Oval Office's finely crafted door. Three other agents were stationed just a few feet away. Meanwhile, seven additional Secret Service agents were strategically located throughout the narrow, cream-colored West Wing hallway, which was adjacent to the north side of the Oval Office. Agent Castillo's chest rapidly contracted and expanded. His eyes darted back and forth, quickly scanning the Oval Office. He whispered into his tiny two-way radio transmitter, which dangled neatly against his lapel.

"I have Monarch in my view. I repeat. I have Monarch in view," he murmured. He was edgy, but collected.

"Roger that," Secret Service Agent John Roberts replied firmly on the other end of the two-way transmitter from the White House Secret Service room as he monitored the West Wing on a myriad of monitors.

The agents who stood near Agent Castillo made eye contact with him. Each nodded subtly. Silence filled the air and the only movement that could be found in the corridor was the pounding of the agents' hearts.

"Stand by," Agent Roberts ordered. Castillo, once again, nodded at his agents. He glanced up towards the small, cut-glass chandelier which hung directly above him from the West Wing's surprisingly low ceiling. He then closed his eyes and mumbled a few words of prayer.

"Go!" Agent Roberts shouted into the radio. "I repeat, go. Get Monarch out of the Oval Office!"

Castillo and the agents standing watch burst into action. The shuffling of their shiny, black dress shoes scuffing against the glossy, marble floors echoed loudly. Castillo lowered his shoulder and rammed into the Oval Office door. A boisterous thud reverberated as the screws popped away from the hinges and the door folded.

Agent Roberts stood frozen in the Secret Service office holding a two-way radio in one hand and a cellular phone in the other, completely transfixed by the Oval Office security monitor.

The 11 agents scattered about the Oval Office in perfect chaos. Castillo dove at President Davis.

"Are they in? Are they in the Oval Office? Did they get Monarch out?" the White House chief of staff screamed into the ear of Agent Roberts.

Tap—tap—tap—tap! Nia Taylor pecked away at the keys of her laptop, which rested on her lap as she sat comfortably in her pajamas in the center of her bed. *It's been a crazy ride. No one's going to believe half the things I've been through,* she reflected as she took a break from proofing her memoirs.

Chapter 1

TAP—TAP—TAP—TAP! THE TAPPING OF HEELS AGAINST THE PAVE-ment, coupled with the constant buzzing of cell phones, created an almost rhythmical sound which could be gently heard just below the women's quiet chatter. One humid mid-July morning, seventeen of the most powerful black women in the world had gathered on the front steps of the United States White House. *ESSENCE Magazine*, the world's leading black women's magazine, had assembled the largest collective group of black women ever to have graced the Executive Branch for a historic photo shoot, which would be featured on the cover of their August 2009 issue.

These influential ladies elegantly waltzed about the White House's broad, iconic, white columns exuding the very confidence that had propelled them to their prestigious positions. The group of black female powerbrokers included prominent government officials such as the U.S. director of the Office of National Drug Control Policy, the deputy chief of staff, and the counsel to President Davis. These ladies had arrived in Washington via a wide array of backgrounds—several had come from corporate America, others were suc-cessful entrepreneurs, while some were already seasoned government offi-cials—but they all had one thing in common; they had been handpicked to be members of the Executive Branch by the United States of America's *first* black President, Michael Davis.

Although Nia Taylor had already officially started her new role as White House deputy chief of staff, the tumultuous journey which lay ahead of her had just begun.

As the *ESSENCE Magazine* crew worked diligently to complete individual interviews with the women, Nia Taylor stood a bit misty-eyed, chatting with her close friends U.S. director of public liaison Beverly Harris-Moore, and the CEO of the popular advertising firm CogniShift Communications, Valerie Foley.

Valerie Foley and her ad firm were the driving force behind this momen-tous *ESSENCE Magazine* photo shoot and feature article. Nia Taylor, a child-hood friend of Valerie's, had helped her orchestrate the event. It had been a tricky task to synch up the schedules of so many busy U.S. officials, but Nia was thrilled with the idea of helping to document history, and needless to say, to assist her lifelong friend.

Valerie and Nia had grown up together on Chicago's gritty Southside. The two ladies attended school together from second grade through high school. The entire time they constantly competed for the number one spot in their class. This competitive nature and tremendous academic prowess eventually landed both women full academic scholarships to the historic Spellman University in Atlanta, GA.

It seemed to be the ideal scenario for both, but at the last minute Valerie was offered an internship at the corporate offices for Black Entertainment Television (BET) in Washington, DC. Meanwhile, Nia went on to attend Spellman University. After being thrown a curve ball by Valerie's abrupt, last-minute change of heart, she found herself rooming with an interesting Atlanta native, the eventual U.S. director of public liaison, Beverly Harris-Moore.

Beverly and Nia had instantly clashed. Beverly was a sarcastic, self-proclaimed southern belle, while Nia had a straight-edged, all-business Midwestern demeanor. Contrary to Nia, Beverly maintained a dry wit, which caught most people off guard and immediately rubbed Nia the wrong way.

"I'll never forget when we first met, Bev. I was telling you how excited I was to be at Spellman and you said, 'Ain't this just berries?!'" Nia snickered as she reminisced. "I was like, what did you say? And you said, 'I said, ain't this berries…can't you hear, or did all them noisy factories up in Chicago ruin your hearing?'" The three women chuckled.

"And all you could talk about was what Atlanta didn't have and what Chicago did have and how we pronounced everything funny. That used to drive me crazy," joked Beverly in her thick southern drawl. "It took me the entire four years of undergrad to get you to stop saying *pop* in that nasally Chicago tone and finally call it *soda* like everyone else at school. But when you left your job at Sam's Seafood early for me that day…"

"Oh my God, not Sam's Seafood… I was *so* glad when Rothschild and Smith Financial hired me on as an intern," Nia interrupted, shaking her head and then rolling her eyes.

"Yes, Sam's Seafood, which I vividly remember would have you coming home *every* night smellin' like fish. Had them boys on campus thinking something was wrong with you," Beverly joked, causing the women to laugh.

"Anyway, when you left work early and got in trouble with Sam to let me in after I locked myself out of our dorm room, I knew then that you were going to be a friend for life and we got along like sisters from that moment on," said Beverly with a lump in her throat.

After graduating from Spellman, Beverly and Nia had once again roomed together, this time at Harvard Business School. After graduating from Harvard, they moved back to Atlanta, and once more shared an apartment.

Although Nia and Beverly's personalities were completely opposite, they complimented one another. Beverly kept Nia loose with her witty sense of humor, while Nia helped to keep Beverly focused. In fact, Nia kept everyone in line. Just about the entire West Wing staff loved her, but also made sure to stay out of her path. If Nia liked you, she would fight for you to the end; but if you crossed her, she'd give you hell. She was *hell* on *heels*!

"I still can't believe we're here together. I never dreamed we would be in this position," Nia commented.

"I'm not surprised that you are," said Valerie. "Bev, I remember one time when we were just in fourth grade and our political science teacher Mr. Wilson was bragging about how great President Reagan was and Nia said, 'President Reagan is great alright, he should win an Oscar for his performance as President.'" Valerie giggled.

"I can't believe you still remember that, Val."

"Yes. His face turned beet red! Then he responded with, 'Ms. Taylor, with that attitude you will NEVER be a good political science student and definitely won't make it in politics.' Go figure," Valerie said with an eyebrow arched. "And then you snapped back with, 'No, with my attitude I will NEVER be a Republican!' Then strutted away like a *little* diva."

"I can just picture her," Beverly chimed in. "I can just hear the *little* diva theme music playing in the background as she walked away. 'IIII'mmm eeevery woman...whoa, whoa, whoooaaaa,'" Beverly whispered Chaka Khan's classic song as the three ladies leaned in closer to contain their laughter.

"You are *so* crazy, Beverly," Nia sighed softly, grinning.

"It's not me, you know it's true; and you haven't changed a bit," replied Beverly, shaking her head.

Nia didn't just possess a witty tongue; she was sharp from head to toe. Her tall, curvaceous body was always draped in the sharpest designer suits— BCBG, Louis Vuitton, Gucci—you name it. And her sassy, shoulder-length layered haircut always sat neatly tucked under her chin—if it wasn't pulled back into a tight bun—perfectly complimenting her chocolate skin tone and high, sculpted cheekbones. Nia was beautiful. But she didn't possess your typical runway model–like beauty; her full lips and wide hips provided more of an everyday *'around the way girl'* kind of beauty.

Nia and Beverly were different in a lot of ways, but they were definitely the same in one—they were both razor-sharp sisters who were not to be toyed with.

Valerie was called away from the ladies by an *ESSENCE* staff member.

"Anyway, this is an incredible moment, isn't it, Beverly?" Nia said as the sunrays glistened off of her all-black Prada sunglasses.

"Yes, I must admit, I am a bit awestruck by this moment. Seventeen *black women* in the Executive Branch? And one of them happens to be my best friend? Incredible...it's kind of surreal..." Beverly said, and then the two women embraced with a warm hug and a smile while fanning their faces in an effort to fight back tears.

"Okay, ladies, we're ready for you! If we could have you all line up right here in front of this column!" the *ESSENCE Magazine* photographer shouted. Then the diverse group of women, who came in all shades, shapes, and sizes and who were all impeccably dressed in upscale contemporary business outfits, began to form a long line descending from tallest to shortest that angled diagonally down the White House steps.

"Hey, Ms. Caldwell, you can stand right next to me. It's the only way I'm going to hold you still long enough to chat," Nia said with a smile while lightly tugging at Senior Advisor Kimberly Caldwell's arm.

"Don't try it, Ms. Taylor. *Some* people are far too busy these days to even have lunch with an old friend," joked Kimberly in her typical soft voice and stoic demeanor, and then flashed a subtle smile.

The First Lady, President Davis, and Kimberly Caldwell were perhaps the only people in the White House who Nia revered. There was also no one else in the White House—other than the First Lady—who was as close to President Davis as Kimberly Caldwell. She was a small-framed 55-year-old woman who sported a conservative look, which perfectly matched her conservative personality.

Kimberly had met Michael Davis when he was fresh out of Harvard Law School. He had migrated to Atlanta, Georgia, by way of Milwaukee, Wisconsin, to work as a legal activist in the inner city. At the time, Kimberly was one of the city's most influential business people. She owned a very successful construction company and an assortment of other local businesses. She also had deep local political ties in the Atlanta area—she was pretty much responsible for the nomination of Atlanta's longtime mayor Peter Weiss.

When Kimberly first met Michael Davis she was immediately impressed with his intellect and smooth demeanor—she felt in many ways it was like looking at a younger, male, version of herself in the mirror. She took him under her wing right away, becoming his unofficial mentor, eventually introducing him to everybody who was somebody in the Atlanta area, including the future First Lady. Kimberly and Michael would sit at her kitchen table sipping on coffee and chatting for hours. He would frequently express to her his longing to help people. She knew she was molding someone special, but had *no* idea that he would eventually become the President of the United States.

"Okay, ladies; give me a big, beautiful, *executive* smile!" shouted the *ESSENCE* photographer. The ladies then all paused and smiled. The camera snapped, and in an instant the historic moment was frozen in time forever.

As remarkable as the occasion was, this highly important group of female leaders was only able to bask in the glory for a moment. After all, they did have a country to run—the most powerful country in the world and one that was under severe distress. The economy had been tanked by the previous presidential regime and was steadily worsening in the face of a looming global recession. The new administration had clearly inherited a barrage of problems: war, damaged foreign relations, an explosion of home foreclosures, the highest U.S. unemployment rate in decades, and a bevy of frustrated and confused citizens.

As soon as the photo shoot ended several White House aides quickly swooped in and whisked the women away. Amidst the dispersion, a young aide emerged and grabbed Nia's hand, virtually yanking her off of her feet, and then quickly pulled her into the White House. Nia was late for a meeting with President Davis and the White House chief of staff in the Oval Office.

Back when Nia had first arrived to the White House she had been a little intimidated by the fast-paced, overcrowded, and surprisingly dilapidated West Wing, but now she thrived in this environment. The two dashed through the West Wing's busy first-floor lobby, nearly stumbling as they rounded the corner and passed by the Cabinet Room.

As Nia approached the Oval Office she paused for a moment to compose herself before entering. *Whew!* she sighed, a bit out of breath. As she reached for the Oval Office door it suddenly flung open.

"Mr. President, it was a pleasure meeting with you," said Sam Goldberg, the founder and CEO of the world's most popular social networking site, The Social Hub.

"The pleasure was all ours," said Chief of Staff Tanner Long eagerly.

"Yes, it was great to see you, Sam. Thanks for stopping by," President Davis chimed in.

"Hello," the technological genius greeted Nia and then quickly whisked by. *Whoosh.*

By the time Nia entered the office President Davis had already found his way back to his desk, where he sat erect as a young boy in military school. Tanner Long slumped down in a chair that was positioned directly across from the president.

"Good morning, Mr. President," Nia said, smiling with a bit of hesitancy. Then she turned and nodded at her immediate boss, Tanner Long.

"I'm glad you could join us, Nia," Tanner said, reeking of sarcasm. Tanner was the sort of person who would try to make someone else look bad just to make himself look good.

"I'm very sorry that I'm a few minutes late. The *ESSENSE* photo shoot and interview lasted longer than anyone anticipated."

"No problem. How did the shoot go?" President Davis asked with a warm smile as he stood and walked from behind his desk, then leaned back against it with his arms folded.

"It went well...very moving experience."

"Have to make sure to let the wifey know. She really wanted to be there."

"I'll be sure to fill her in, sir," Nia replied as Tanner inconspicuously rolled his eyes out of President Davis's view.

"Sir, I was really surprised to hear you tell Sam Goldberg that he was basically making a mistake to let Klein Schultz invest in The Social Hub." Tanner shifted the subject.

"Honesty is always the best policy. Right?" President Davis asked rhetorically and then shifted the subject himself. "Okay, let's get down to business. How are we going to approach this issue in Libya?" he asked. "Our intelligence is telling us that this revolt is definitely going to happen and it's not going to be pretty. They're saying that the entire Middle East is brewing with the potential uprisings."

"Sir, I think we have to remind the world who has the power and might," Tanner said, clenching his fist as President Davis listened patiently. "We should immediately send our forces into Libya and take out Gaddafi before this thing starts buzzing all over the media and we look *weak*. That's the last thing we need and it'll send a message to the entire Middle East."

"I would be cautious with that approach," Nia interjected. Tanner turned and glared at her as she went on with her explanation. "Our military is already spread thin and the American people may not react too kindly to us utilizing more of our resources in the current economic environment."

Nia glared back at Tanner and continued. "Plus, the general public isn't very familiar with the situation and they'll want to know more detail about why we're doing this long before we act. I think that's the key—informing the public as early on as possible. It's pretty obvious they're spreading their message through social media and we know if they generate enough attention on the Web the media will eventually jump on board and run wild with their own version of the story like they always do. I think we may want to bring the situation to the public ourselves and get the drop on the media, so we can better control the public's perception of this situation."

"Good point, Nia. I tend to agree with you," President Davis replied in acceptance, as he slowly nodded his head and scratched his chin. "Also, Nia, you know I've been meaning to mention to you that I'd like for you to start attending our daily intelligence briefings. I think you'd be a valuable asset to these meetings."

Each day intelligence meetings, known as National Security Sessions, were held in the White House Situation Room to brief the president on all the intelligence issues threatening the United States. The invitation was a tremendous compliment to Nia; the meetings were typically reserved for senior government officials and elite members of the CIA.

Tanner leaned back, clutching the arms of his chair tightly, and continued to glare over at Nia with disdain in his eyes. "Sir, with all due respect, do we *really* want to start inviting *staff* members to, perhaps, our most critical and highly secured meetings? And what about our other deputy chief of staff? I guess next are we going to start inviting her to our Thursday afternoon one-on-one briefings with the CIA director, too?" Tanner swiftly fired with an appalled look on his face.

Tanner didn't take kindly to being outshined in front of others, especially not the president, and he seemed to specifically have it out for Nia from day one. However, what meant more than anything to Tanner was *privilege*. And one of the most *distinguished privileges* in the world was being privy to the most highly-secured, confidential information on the planet and having input on the security of the country.

"Tanner, I couldn't agree with you more, I *would* like for Nia to sit in a time or two on our one-on-ones with our CIA head," President Davis responded while inconspicuously giving Nia a wink and a devious smile.

President Davis knew that Tanner truly relished the unique role of being his foremost gatekeeper, and he also enjoyed ruffling the man's feathers a bit from time to time. Nonetheless, President Davis had been genuinely impressed by Nia and wanted to continuously keep her challenged. He also knew that this process tapped into Tanner's deepest insecurities, and likewise, would keep him challenged and primed for growth.

"Tanner, did you tell Nia about her assignment this coming Monday?"

"No, sir, we haven't gone over it yet," Tanner responded smugly.

"Nia, tomorrow afternoon I'm going to announce that Rosa Chavez will be appointed as our nation's first Hispanic Supreme Court Justice, and after her latest comment in the media, as you can well imagine, things are going to be chaotic...she'll be bombarded by the press. We're a little worried about the situation getting out of hand, but not if we get you out there. So, I'll need you in New York on Monday, and at least through to Wednesday." President Davis smiled proudly.

"Sir, I can't wait," said Nia in shock.

"It's just for a few days and light work. I was thinking it'd be like a mini-vacation for you."

Wow, what a nice treat, she thought. *He's something else. Shopping! I can't wait. Maybe I can hook up with Val while I'm there. Too bad all the girls couldn't get together there, but I know it's too last minute. The only problem is I have so many things on my plate right now. Shoot, I really can't afford to be away from the West Wing, but I don't have a choice, do I? Oh well, guess I'm just forced to shop!*

"Thanks so much, sir! What a wonderful treat," Nia said with a warm smile.

"You got it, Nia," President Davis replied with an equally warm smile, and then flashed a fatherly wink. "Okay, what's next on our agenda?"

"The healthcare campaign," Tanner responded anxiously. "Do we have all of the cities lined up yet, Nia?"

"Yes, Sarah should have the schedule completed this afternoon."

"What's taking so long? My goodness, Nia, this should have been completed by now!" snapped Tanner.

"Let's hustle to get that completed so the press secretary can get that out ASAP," added President Davis.

"Sure, no problem, sir, I guarantee it'll be completed on time." *This is exactly why I can't afford to be gone right now and ughhh, now I have to work my butt off to be sure all my work is caught up before I leave. Tanner will be looking for anything he can use to make me look bad while I'm gone and something always pops up.*

"Nia, we should get together with the press secretary this afternoon to help him formulate exactly how we want to position this thing...*IF* you get the schedule completed. Let's try to meet in my office at about 5 PM," said Tanner.

"Will do, and the schedule *will* be completed," replied Nia. *Oh shoot, Terrence is going to kill me for canceling at the last minute on another event,* Nia thought. She not only had to routinely cancel on her fiancé Terrence Richardson, she also had little time to spend with him in general. As soon as the meeting came to a close, Nia went to her office and phoned her fiancé.

"Hi, sweetie, I just wanted to let you know that I won't be able to make your office event tonight—"

"I know...of course, you have to stay late for a meeting," Terrence interrupted with attitude in his voice.

"Yes, and I'm sorry, but *you know* how my job is," Nia replied in a point-blank manner.

"I figured something would come up...don't worry about it. As usual, I'll just go by myself, but *PLEASE* make sure you block out October the fifth for the firm's anniversary party. If I'm ever going to make partner, I need you there for that one."

"Okay. I am so angry right now that I could scream."

"Let me guess...Tanner?"

"Of course, he was grandstanding as usual," Nia griped. "Anyway, the good news is POTUS wants me to go to New York next week. It's almost like having a few days off. I'm going to give Val a quick call to see if she's free. Thanks for letting me vent, sweetie. I'll call you later." Nia tapped the speed dial button on her Blackberry phone.

"Hey, Val!"

"Nia, I was just thinking about you."

"Hey, girl, I'm not going to keep you. Of course, I have a zillion things to do, but I have to be in New York Monday through Wednesday. Are you going to be in town?"

"No, I have to be in California the entire week."

"Shoot. I wanted to see if we could hang out and maybe squeeze in some shopping while I was there," said Nia as she simultaneously glanced at her email's inbox. "That's it; I'm going to set something up for us all to get together. All of the girls."

"Just let me know and I'll make it work."

"I have to be in Atlanta in a few weeks. Maybe we can do a weekend together. I'll check with Bev and Carla and let you know."

Nia's exuberance over word of President Davis's little treat was short lived. As she continued to sift through a barrage of emails, she quickly realized several problems had reared their ugly heads in just the few moments she took to speak with Terrence and Valerie.

Nia scanned through an email. *I don't have time for this right now; I have to get those cities lined up for the president's healthcare initiative. I swear it's always something around here.*

There was only one thing that was for certain in the West Wing—no two days were the same. The West Wing's frenetic pace made it difficult to focus on any one task and see it through to completion. To call it *multitasking* was an understatement.

That night, Tanner, Nia, and several other staff members worked until midnight, which was actually very typical. Tanner decided to invite them all out for drinks to say thanks for their hard work. He routinely treated his staff to after-hours drinks, and even dinner, out of his own pocket, but while these seemed like generous gestures of appreciation, the reality was he would spend whatever amount necessary to impress.

The staff met up at their favorite local spot, Old Joe's Bar and Grill. Old Joe's was a historic local bar founded in 1872 that had maintained its "Turn of the Century" feel with its rich Victorian décor. It was located in walking distance from the White House, just around the corner at 650 15th Street Northwest, neatly tucked away across from the U.S. Treasury Building. Old Joe's wasn't just famous among White House staffers because of the staff's fondness for their tasty grilled burgers; over the years it had been frequented by numerous presidents such as Roosevelt, Taft, and Truman, and an almost endless barrage of government officials.

Nia loved a good burger from Old Joe's as much as any other White House staffer, but dreaded the whole *"let's stop after work for drinks"* thing. But she knew she had to be a team player and at least show her face. Nia had stayed behind for a while continuing to work, so by the time she arrived at Old Joe's the staff had already thrown back a series of shots, with Tanner leading the shot session.

As soon as Nia entered the bar, she found Tanner hanging off the side of one of Joe's antique wooden bar stools, already in a drunken stupor.

"Come over here, Nia, and sit with me! What are you drinking?" Tanner asked with slurred speech.

"Thanks, Tanner, but I really don't want anything. You know I'm not a big drinker. And you know, maybe you shouldn't have any more yourself."

"Oh, come on, Nia, stop being so uptight…just loosen up for once. At least have a beer?"

"I'll just take a Diet Coke."

"Alright, fine, suit yourself, party-pooper. Anyway, you know…you're really great to work with, Nia," said Tanner, almost in a whisper, as he leaned in towards Nia.

"Oh really? I'm definitely surprised to hear you say that. I would have never guessed you felt that way. You sure don't treat me like I am," Nia responded with a dry smile, as she leaned back from Tanner, fanning away the smell of his breath, which sailed through the air like troublesome smog.

"Oh, that's just the image that I have to give off. Plus, I'm extra hard on you because you're so damn talented…just trying to make you better," Tanner said with eyebrows raised and head swaying from side to side.

Are you kidding me? Nia thought. "Wow, that's quite a compliment, Tanner," replied Nia in a lackluster tone.

"Damn right, and when I become president…I'm gonna make you my chief of staff. You'rrre bad ass, Nia! You know what you guys call it…a *diva!*" Tanner said, grinning from ear to ear.

President…hmm, interesting. "Oh, is that what *WE* call it?" Nia asked sarcastically. "Well, thanks…I guess. Anyway, I had no idea that you aspired to be the president someday…interesting, but what about POTUS?"

"I'm not talking about right now. I mean down the line. Let me ask you something, Nia…have you ever seen that documentary by that comedian Chris Rock called '*Good Hair?*'"

"What?" Nia asked with a look of confusion.

"You know, 'Good Hair.'" It's about black women's hair."

What the hell is he talking about? "What are you talking about, Tanner?"

"I just always wondered…"

"Wondered what?"

"Is that a weave?" Tanner asked with an inquisitive look as he reached out, trying to touch Nia's hair.

"Tanner, have you lost it?" Nia said, as she slapped his hand down. "Seriously?"

"The documentary did say you're *never* supposed to touch a black woman's hair…" said Tanner with a dopey facial expression. "I just always wondered. Looks real to me though. In the movie they did say you couldn't tell the difference with the really good weaves. Please, can I just touch it once?"

"I'm just going to ignore that question, Tanner. Like you said, you're not supposed to touch *any* woman's hair or ask them such personal questions," Nia snapped. "Anyway, so now what were you saying about becoming the president down the line?" *Just get back to the subject, you goofball,* thought Nia.

"Oh, yeah, between you and me, I've got some very influential people that want to see me running things," Tanner whispered with a devious twinkle in his shifting eyes, "and one of them is probably the most influential person in the...now where is that damn bartender? I know he sees my drink is low. Anyway, hey, Nia, you know I almost dated an African American girl once."

Oh my goodness, people with ADHD shouldn't be allowed to drink. "That's really interesting, Tanner, but please finish what you were saying."

"She was hot, too. Her butt was so damn round it was amazing!" said Tanner with a look of deep reflection on his face.

What the... "That's...well, I guess that's nice, but let's get back to the subject, Tanner."

"*Boy* it was big. Kinda reminded me of that popular rapper...oh, what's that girl's name?" he scratched his chin, as Nia glared at him.

Oh my goodness!

"Nicki Minaj! That's her name. Biggest butt I've ever seen. It was just like that and between you and me, it kind of intimidated me," he said with a look of amazement.

Unbelievable. "Tanner, back to the subject."

"What was I saying?"

Ughhh. "You said something about the most influential person."

"I don't know, but you know I would never do anything to hurt POTUS. This is all much farther down the line. They just see my potential, but who could miss it? You know me!" Tanner cackled.

Oh whatever! Now just what is this dirty little son-of-a-gun up to, and who are these influential people anyway? Nia thought. "Yeah, yeah, but who are *they,* Tanner?"

"Hey *buddy,* can't you see my glass is empty?" Tanner yelled to the bartender while looking down into his glass and swirling the remaining ice.

"Yes, you are *the man* around here, Tanner, aren't you?" Nia asked rhetorically, pumping more air into his already inflated ego in an effort to pry more information out of him. "So tell me more details about your presidential plans, and just *who* the heck are these influential people anyway?"

"Trust me; you know how connected I am, but this is down the line. I better shut up anyway...I'm probably talking way too much."

"Ah, Tanner, this is just between friends. I'm not surprised by what you're telling me because, like you said, I know how talented and connected you are."

"Rrrright. These people are just drawn to me for some reason. Like I said, if POTUS decides not to run for a second term, don't be surprised if I'm on the next presidential ballot alongside their guy."

"Really? So just who are *these* people and who's *their* guy?" Nia inquired once more, bright-eyed with eyebrows raised so high they were virtually buried under the hair which hung over her forehead.

"Well, between me and you, the head of—" Just as Tanner began to speak Nia's cell phone suddenly rang, interrupting him. Nia glanced down at her caller ID.

Damn it, Jimmy Coleman Jr. What the hell does this idiot want? And just when this other idiot was about to tell me what the hell he's up to. This better be an emergency.

"Let me grab this real quick, Tanner, but hold that thought, I *really* want to hear more."

"Hello, Congressman," Nia answered her cell with a tone of irritation in her voice.

"Hi, Nia, sorry to call you so late. Were you already tucked away in bed?"

"No, but it is awfully late to be calling. I'm assuming this is an emergency?" *If you thought I would be in bed why the hell would you call me so late for anyway? What a creep!* Nia thought.

"Sorry for the late call, but I figured you were probably just getting home from the West Wing. I need to talk to you about something *EXTREMELY* important."

"*Okay*, I can give you a call back tomorrow during normal business hours."

"Sure, but we can't talk about this over the phone...we need to talk in person. When are you free? Maybe we can do lunch next week?" Jimmy asked, as Nia rolled her eyes.

Now what is HE up to? "Jimmy, things are pretty busy right now."

"When isn't that true? Come on, I know you haven't gotten too big over there in the *West Wing* to accept a lunch date with the little people over here in Congress, and especially one of your old buddies from the ATL."

"Okay, yeah, sure. I'll call you back tomorrow when I have my schedule in front of me," Nia said, rushing Jimmy off of the phone.

"Tanner, where were we?"

"Uhhh, this room just will not stay still," said Tanner, swaying back and forth on his barstool and reaching out into air.

"Alright, you look like you've had enough. Let me get a cab for you. You need to go home."

"Ohhh, my stomach...I am sooo nauseous."

"Oh, God...come on, Tanner, let's get you outside to a cab and whatever you do, don't you throw up on me," Nia said in disgust, as she hooked Tanner's arm around her neck and hoisted him from the barstool.

Damn it...Jimmy had to interrupt right when Tanner was finally about to tell me!

Chapter 2

MONDAY MORNING CAME FAR TOO FAST FOR NIA. AS USUAL, SHE HAD worked from home the entire weekend and was hustling to get to the West Wing early in order to prepare for the chief of staff's morning meeting. Historically the White House chief of staff holds a staff meeting each morning to go over the day's agenda. Each meeting is fast-paced and packed with information. The list of issues that must be tackled in just one day in the West Wing is the equivalent to a month's worth of issues for a typical corporation. *Intense* might be the optimal word to describe these briefings, as well as the atmosphere in general around the West Wing; and this Monday morning meeting was no exception.

"Good morning, staff. Sarah, what's on the agenda this beautiful Monday morning?" Tanner asked his secretary while straightening his handmade, five-fold, Italian silk Salvatore Ferragamo necktie. As the secretary began to read through the first topic of the agenda, Nia quickly scanned her copy. She noticed that she had been assigned by Tanner to head a meeting at the exact same time as the upcoming National Security Session that President Davis had invited her to attend.

"Excuse me, I hate to interrupt, but, Tanner, the 10 AM meeting that you have me scheduled for is in direct conflict with our intelligence briefing in the Situation Room later today."

"As you well know, Ms. Taylor, those meetings are reserved for senior officials. Anyway, this is not the appropriate time to discuss that. Please go on, Sarah," Tanner said in a condescending tone.

"Sure, we can chat about this after the meeting," Nia snapped back as her internal temperature suddenly rose. You could cut the tension in the room with a knife, but the staff totally ignored the two because they were used to these kinds of little inconsequential spats.

"Like I said, Sarah, *please* move on."

At the close of the meeting, Nia immediately marched straight to Tanner's office. She entered his office only to find him distracted by a young, heavily tanned, blond-haired woman sitting across from him. The young lady sat perched on the edge of her seat with her legs crossed, back arched, and cleavage bulging out of a tightly fitted blouse.

"Nia, I want to introduce you to Heather Kelly, our newest intern."

"Yeah, very nice to meet you," Nia brusquely greeted the young lady. "Tanner, I need to speak with you."

"Well, that's fine, but as you can see, I'm busy at the moment," Tanner replied snippily. "Like I was saying, Heather…"

Has he lost his damn mind? I know he didn't just blow me off! "Uh, no offense, Heather, but Tanner and I need to speak privately. Please go take a water break or something and give us a few minutes. And why don't you bring a bottle of water back for us, too. I think I'm going to need something to cool me down here in a minute. Okay? Go on. Bye-bye," Nia said, curtly motioning towards the door.

The tall, long-legged, noticeably fit intern stood up, wearing a tightly fitted skirt that hugged her toned butt and thighs, and then strutted out of Tanner's office wobbling on four-inch stilettos.

"Is there a particular reason why I'm no longer scheduled to attend today's National Security Session?" Nia asked sharply.

"Nia, you know those meetings are reserved for senior officials and I have other things I need you to work on," replied Tanner with an apathetic expression on his face without ever looking up from his computer monitor.

"Well, POTUS actually requested that I attend this meeting and *ALL* other future briefings in the Situation Room. I'd hate to disappoint him. So I'll let Sarah know about the change," Nia said gazing down at Tanner. Tanner's eyes slowly rose from his computer screen.

"Oh, I wasn't aware of this. POTUS really needs to do a better job of keeping me in the loop with these types of matters. After all, *I AM* his *chief of staff.*"

"Hmmm, not sure how you missed it. POTUS made this recommendation…I believe Friday morning during our meeting. Oh, you must really be burned out to have missed that—you should really try and get some rest," Nia said with a grin filled with cynicism. "The next time we meet with POTUS together I'll be sure to remind you to mention that to him, so he can a do a better job of keeping you in the loop with these types of matters."

Nia, never short on moxie, loved giving Tanner and the rest of the good old boy network around the West Wing the business. Being a black woman was challenging enough in corporate America, but being a sister in the White House took the word *challenging* to a whole different level. But Nia got a charge out of these kinds of witty little verbal exchanges, which by the way, she typically won. She was the sort of person who you hate to face when they're on the opposing team, but love to death when they're on your side.

"Look, first off, I have so many important things to worry about it's easy for insignificant ones like this to get by me. Second, your cynicism isn't amusing or welcome around here, Nia."

"Cynicism? Why, Tanner, whatever do you mean?"

"Nia, I'm not stupid…you know what I mean and I'm sure there are plenty of cynics lined up in unemployment lines all around this economically challenged country right this moment," Tanner scoffed. Tanner hated to be disrespected. Although his dad was a well-connected millionaire, Tanner had been fighting all of his life for recognition—especially from his dad.

"That almost sounds like a threat...wow, and I thought I was going to be your *chief of staff* once you're elected president," Nia said calmly, leaving Tanner speechless and his face flushed.

Heather entered Tanner's office clutching two icy water bottles.

"Thank you, Heather. Great job," Nia said in a condescending tone. "Tanner, I think you picked a real winner here."

"Oh, thank you. I just want to help in any way that I can," Heather responded in a soft, almost adolescent-like voice.

"Good for you. Keep up the good work." Nia rolled her eyes while turning to exit Tanner's office, virtually bumping into senior staffer Ted Thompson as he attempted to enter.

"Good morning, Ted," Nia said.

"Good morning, Nia...Tanner," the senior staffer said. Then he noticed Heather, once again, perfectly perched on the edge of her seat. "Who is this gorgeous young creature?"

Creature...gross! Ugh, how creepy. Who says that anyway? Nia thought, as she walked out of the office with Tanner immediately closing the door upon her exit.

Whatever! Two weirdos. Anyway, I can't believe I snapped at him and mentioned that conversation at the bar about him running for president someday. Now I'll never find out what he's up to and who these so-called influential people are he was talking about that night. SHOOT, me and my big mouth!

Chapter 3

NIA SET OUT TO ARRIVE AT THE SITUATION ROOM EARLY FOR THE National Security Session. As she walked down the narrow mahogany-paneled hallways of the West Wing basement, she felt her heart begin to race when she approached the heavy wooden door that bore an oval-shaped gold emblem engraved with the words, "The White House Situation Room." This room was somewhat mysterious even to White House staff members, but as Nia reached for the thick gold door handle, her veins weren't surging with adrenaline because she was nervous or afraid about attending her first Situation Room meeting. Instead, Nia felt more like a professional athlete preparing for a big game—nervous, no; anxious and ready for action, yes. She entered the 5,000 square foot pressure cooker 15 minutes early, which in West Wing time was extremely early, with her eyes wide. In the West Wing, staff members were never late for meetings, but also far too busy to ever be early for them.

The Situation Room is a group of rooms utilized by the National Security Council 24 hours a day to monitor crises and gather vital intelligence throughout the world for the president and his advisors. The president and his advisors also routinely hold meetings there to communicate with intelligence agencies all around the world. Only a select few are invited to attend these meetings. Highly secure information flies around this room like radio frequencies in the air.

President Davis entered the room with Tanner and Kimberly Caldwell. The president and Kimberly spoke to everyone individually, including Nia, but Tanner completely ignored her. Five-star general Sherman Schultz was displayed via closed-circuit television on one of several flat-screen monitors which hung neatly on the walls. Several high-ranking senior U.S. government officials and CIA members sat around a large oval conference table situated in the center of the room. As President Davis began to sit at the head of the conference table, he was immediately passed a small glossy loose-leaf navy blue binder by the director of the CIA.

"Mr. President, here's your PDB."

PDB stands for "President's Daily Briefing." This book contains a daily overview of the most pressing and up-to-date issues and intelligence information. The book also provides tactical and strategic elements, which include forecasts of potential future issues—both short term and long term. This book and meeting are critical to the president's decision-making process for the United States' national security.

"So, what's going on in Libya, General?" asked President Davis, as he flipped open the PDB.

"I think the rebels are about to make a serious attempt to overthrow their government. The information that we've been getting from the ground is that they're almost ready to make a move. I think the question *is* what type of role we need to play in this situation?" the general responded.

"So do you think he'll put up a big fight?" President Davis asked.

"Absolutely!"

"The real question here is do we swoop in and take him out ourselves as soon as this thing breaks?" Tanner boldly interrupted. "And I say, yes, we do! And we do it sooner rather than later...as soon as the fighting breaks out." He scanned the room for approval.

"Yes, that's something we'll have to consider. Thanks, Tanner," President Davis said in a patronizing tone, glaring at his chief of staff as if to say *who asked you anyway*. "General, I'd like for you to hear Nia's perspective on this thing. She's brought up some good points," he said, as Tanner sat with a look of disbelief. "Go ahead, Nia, please share your thoughts on this situation with everyone."

"Well, we know the entire Middle East is brewing with potential uprisings, but the U.S. public isn't very familiar with this issue yet. However, thanks to the growing popularity of social media and its ability to proliferate a message exponentially in minimal time, the insurgents and their supporters are online spreading the word like wildfire," Nia said with poise, while the general listened closely.

"Egypt has been utilizing social networking sites to gain followers by the thousands each day. As we all know, this has spurred rumblings of uprisings in other nearby areas like Libya. And we all know that once this thing gains a certain level of interest on the Web, the news media will swoop in and pounce on this story and put their own spin on the situation, painting *us* in whatever light they choose," Nia continued to explain her perspective as Tanner rolled his eyes and squirmed in his seat like an impatient five year old boy.

"So, I was, more or less, suggesting to President Davis the other day that we might want to get a jump on this thing before the media runs wild with it. Perhaps *we* should get out ahead of them and be the ones to inform the public about the widespread brewing of rebellion throughout the Middle East and let them know exactly where we stand before this thing picks up too much steam. This way we can beat the media to the punch and begin to shape the public's opinion ourselves ahead of time, as well as to let the public know that we're on top of this thing."

The general nodded in agreement, and then senior advisor Jack Chase, a close friend of Tanner's father, attempted to come to Tanner's rescue. "Thanks, Nia, but getting a jump on the media isn't exactly rocket science. Like Tanner said, the real question *IS* do we take him out ourselves before the *real* fighting begins or just sit back with our thumbs stuck up our butts waiting for this thing to unfold." As Chase spoke Tanner sat by his side with a noticeable smirk.

"We're already spread thin," General Schultz said. "Trying to go into Libya and snatch him out sounds easy to someone that doesn't have a clue about real combat scenarios and that has never been in the heart of Libya, but trust me, it's not that simple. I think Nia has a good point. I say we bring together our allies and have everyone prepared to surge on the area when the time is right."

Chase turned his nose up and sat stewing in anger. Senior advisors hate to be disrespected in front of their peers, or anyone else for that matter. They often clash with military higher-ups. Most military officials don't fear speaking their minds to anyone when it comes to anything combat related. General Schultz in particular was known for speaking his mind; when it came to military strategy he had no filter. Chase, like many senior advisors, felt like his opinion was superior to most *anyone* on *any* subject and believed he possessed some sort of Yoda-like wisdom which everyone should adhere to.

"General, that's debatable," Conrad Roth, the secretary of the Department of Homeland Security, interjected in support of the senior advisor and the chief of staff, "and I would beg to differ." Roth never fretted sharing his opinion even though he was one of only three Republicans in the Cabinet.

"Roth, what the hell do you know—"

"Okay, that's enough on that topic, let's move on, guys," said President Davis in a stern tone, abruptly ending the heated debate. "We'll finish this discussion when James is back with us next week." James Oberto was the secretary of defense. Accordingly, he was also the most well-respected official in intelligence and President Davis typically relied heavily on his opinion for *all* of his military decisions.

As the meeting moved on, Chase, Roth, and Tanner all sat noticeably quiet for the remainder of the session. At the close of the meeting, Nia strutted confidently past the three officials, grinning widely on the inside. When she arrived back at her office, before she was even able to take a seat, she immediately received a call from Kimberly Caldwell.

"Nia, great job in the Situation Room. You know, the president has really been impressed with your work. Let's try to get together soon so we can chat for a while."

As confident a person as Nia was, she loved praise, and compliments coming from Kimberly Caldwell were extra special.

Shortly after speaking with Kimberly, Nia received a call on her cell phone from Jimmy Coleman Jr. As she glanced at her caller ID, Nia thought, *Oh shoot...Jimmy! I forgot to call him back. Ughh, I really dread answering this call.*

"Hello, Congressman, I hadn't forgotten about you."

"Surrre, Nia. I don't think you realize just how important the information that I need to share with you really is."

Yeah right. Nia didn't know exactly what he wanted, but she knew Jimmy was always up to something. Once, Jimmy had run for mayor of Atlanta. In an effort to knock out the race's frontrunner, Atlanta's current mayor Peter Weiss, Jimmy and his mother Joletha had the ingenious idea to use the race card and accuse Weiss of being a racist. But what they hadn't realized was that Peter's deceased wife of 10 years was in fact African American. This was typical of Jimmy and his mom. They were opportunists and always trying to pull a fast one.

"I'm sorry that I didn't get a chance to call you back, but I've got my calendar right in front of me now. How about we do lunch at Old Joe's this Friday?" asked Nia.

"Sounds great!" Jimmy replied eagerly.

Just as Nia was ending her call, Conrad Roth and Tanner shuffled past her office. *Now what are they up to?*

Chapter 4

FRIDAY BEGAN FOR NIA WITH THE TYPICAL CHIEF OF STAFF MORNING meeting. As usual, a barrage of new issues had arisen overnight. As Nia pounded through the most pressing challenge, her Blackberry buzzed with a schedule reminder.

I almost forgot about meeting with Jimmy. I've got so many things I need to accomplish today. He's such a pain in the butt, Nia thought.

Nia reluctantly met the congressman later that day. She knew he was about to try to manipulate her in some way, but she also knew it was part of her job and that Jimmy really wasn't a whole lot different than any other politician in Washington...*always* up to something.

"Hey, you!" the short, well-dressed member of the House of Representatives, who sported a perfectly shaped, dark brown dyed mini-fro, said loudly to Nia, grinning from ear to ear as she approached. Jimmy then waived Nia over from one of Old Joe's corner booths where he sat anxiously tapping his foot against the glossy parquet hardwood floors.

"Looking beautiful as ever, I see," said Jimmy as he stood up while scanning Nia from head to toe. He then planted an inappropriately moist kiss on her cheek while giving her an equally inappropriate warm hug, pressing his body firmly against hers.

Gross! Who kisses and grinds up on somebody on a business date like that? thought Nia.

"Thanks for taking time out of your busy schedule to meet with me, Ms. Taylor, or should I say, Mrs. Taylor?" Jimmy asked knowing Nia wasn't married yet, as they both sat down. He had been trying to get with Nia since the day they first met. As a matter of fact, Jimmy had tried to get with almost every attractive woman he had *ever* met.

"No, it's still Miss Taylor. And how is your beautiful *wife*?" Nia fired back.

"Oh, she's fine...doing great, in fact. You know she's an independent little thang—too independent for me. She spends most of her time back at our home in Atlanta. We're both so busy we rarely have time to spend together. Might as well say it's like a marriage of convenience, but that's how we have to work it...you know how it looks for government officials to divorce...the standards we're held to are just ridiculous, aren't they? But I'd get divorced from her in a heartbeat *anyway* to be with a beautiful woman like you, Nia," Jimmy said with a devilish grin.

"Congressman, I know you didn't drag me away from my busy schedule saying you needed to share some *extremely* important information with me just to give me some lame pick-up lines. And just to be clear, even if you and I were both single, I think it's pretty obvious that our chemistry strictly lies within the lines of politics, and *NOWHERE* else," Nia snapped flashing a cold, lifeless smile.

"Damn, you're brutal as *hell* and cold as *ice* all in one…and I love it! Anyway, you're right, let's get down to business. Let me ask you something, Nia. What are your career goals?"

"Congressman, my focus right now is strictly on doing the best job that I can to support President Davis and my country."

"Nice politically correct answer, but what about after his term is over…then what? If I recall correctly, when you were in Atlanta I seem to remember a bright, ambitious young woman who had aspirations of taking over corporate America," Jimmy said with confidence while sucking on a toothpick. "I remember on a few occasions while you were vice president over at Rothschild and Smith Financial you mentioning to me that you aspired to be their CEO someday."

Nia was an extremely private person and astute enough to know that the more someone knew about you the more they could manipulate you. She immediately felt uncomfortable with Jimmy's line of questioning and couldn't believe that he remembered about her CEO aspirations from just a few brief casual conversations they'd had way back when they were working together on President Davis's campaign. Jimmy was the last person to make this sort of mistake with. He was the sort of person who would use *anything* he could against you to get what he wanted.

"Yes, I may have mentioned that a time or two, but what's your point?"

"I believe that it's important to follow your dreams."

"Okay, great, thanks for your advice. Now, my time is limited—"

"I know, I know. I'll get right to the point," Jimmy said, cutting Nia off mid-sentence.

"Please do."

"I know you're a no-nonsense kind of woman, which by the way is one of the *many* things that I love about you…nothing sexier than a strong, assertive black woman," Jimmy said sliding the toothpick from his mouth and licking his lips, "but anyway, here's the point. You know how Washington works, it's a town of favors and I have some *very* powerful people that are tugging at me right now."

Nia sat expressionless as he began to lose her attention. *When is he going to get to the damn point, I've got a zillion things to do today. Ugh, look at MY nails. This polish looks terrible…I knew I should have used a different color.*

"I'm sure by now you've heard that Klein Schultz recently invested two billion dollars into the search engine-slash-social media giant The Social Hub," Jimmy said quietly while shiftily looking around the room.

"Yeah, sure I heard about it…and?" Nia asked as her patience began to wear thin.

"Well, when they invested in The Social Hub instead of The Social Hub's rival Sharebook dot com it shocked the world. The Social Hub's valuation is expected to be almost 115 billion dollars. This has changed the entire online landscape forever, Nia. Let's just be real. You know as well as I do that in a lot of ways Klein Schultz controls most of the world's currency. They have their hands in everything—all of our major financial institutions. You know the CEOs of Prime Bank, Charles A. Schmitt and Associates, and even Bank of U.S. all came from Klein Schultz."

"Jimmy, of course I know that, but what's your point?"

"Let's not forget about the fact that many of our recent U.S. secretaries of the Treasury also came from Klein Schultz. Let's face it; they got their hands deep in America's pocketbook."

"What's your point, Congressman?"

"Anyway, the big boys are involved in the Internet world now, and they have to have The Social Hub be successful. Well, there's some privacy legislation floatin' around Washington right now that could potentially jeopardize their success and billions in profits. So, that's why I wanted to meet with you today. The Social Hub's lobbyists want your help, Nia."

"Me? In what way and why?" Nia looked puzzled.

"Nia, first off, they are crazy about you. Second, they know how strong your relationship is with President Davis. They just want you to help ensure that the president is on their side with this one. This is big, Nia. They'd like to have you get in his ear," Jimmy said in a whisper, leaning in towards Nia.

"Jimmy, I believe you'd be better served calling Tanner."

"No, Nia, they know how strong your influence is with the president and who wants to deal with that jackass Tanner anyway?"

"Like I said…"

"Just wait a minute, let me finish. This would be *very* beneficial to your career and ultimately your pocketbook, Nia."

"Congressman Coleman, thank you for meeting with me. You have a wonderful afternoon," Nia said abruptly, as she began to stand.

Nia wasn't sure what Jimmy was up to, but as soon as he started insinuating that money would be exchanged in return for her assistance she knew it was time to shut him down.

What the hell is he trying to pull this time? And he wants me to sit here and listen to this in the middle of Old Joe's so somebody can hear this nonsense and think I'm up to something shady with him. He's crazy…I'm out of here!

"Wait a minute, Nia. Don't shoot the messenger," Jimmy said, but Nia completely ignored him. She then slapped a fifty dollar bill on the table to cover the meal, grabbed her purse, and exited Old Joe's Bar and Grill in a huff with Jimmy scurrying alongside trying to return her money while also pleading his case.

"Wait, let me explain. Of course, they chose you because of your relationship with President Davis, but also because they're anxious to build a relationship with you, Nia. They think that you have unlimited potential. Like I said, you already know Klein Schultz has influence in almost all of the world's major financial institutions, even your ex-employer Rothschild and Smith Financial."

"Of course I know that, Jimmy," Nia barked, as the two stood at the corner of 15th Street Northwest and G Street Northwest waiting for the stoplight to change to cross the street.

"And of course you know now that makes them one of the richest firms in the country. They know all about your career, and of course, are aware of what kind of impact you made as a VP. It's that experience coupled with the immeasurable experience you're gaining right now in the White House that has them drooling over you. And this is why they envision you being Rothschild and Smith's CEO someday in the *VERY* near future."

Nia continued to walk, but Jimmy had struck a chord. One of the toughest decisions Nia had ever had to make was leaving Rothschild and Smith Financial to work in the White House. At the time of her departure from Rothschild and Smith Financial she was a rising star in the organization, but when President Davis asked her to join his staff, she knew she couldn't pass up on the once-in-a-lifetime opportunity to work in the White House and for the country's first black president.

"I guess you're forgetting the fact that they already have an outstanding CEO, Andy Muller, who is also a friend of mine."

"When is the last time you spoke with their CEO, Nia?"

"It's been a while. I've been extremely busy, but I consider Andy a close friend."

"Well, I hate to be the one to inform you, but Andy was diagnosed with cancer," Jimmy said with a somber look, as Nia instantly came to a halt.

"Oh my God, that's terrible. I have to call him right away."

"You should, but he's fine now. They caught it early enough to treat. He's still decided to step down though. He wants to take it easy and spend some time with his family. They're anxious to find his replacement and, Nia, you're their number one candidate."

Chapter 5

IN DOWNTOWN DC, JUST BLOCKS AWAY FROM THE WHITE HOUSE, NIA'S fiancé Terrence was trying to make his own moves at leading the locally based law firm McLoughlin and McLoughlin.

Terrence had been employed with the firm for just over a year and he was already trying to position himself for partner. He had gotten the position at the firm through one of Nia's contacts when they first arrived in Washington. It's a non-official tradition that various influential people in Washington help White House officials' spouses, and mates, gain employment when they move to town.

After graduating from historic Morehouse University in Atlanta, Terrence received a law degree from John Marshall Law School. He then worked several years for a small African American–owned firm in Atlanta prior to the big move to DC with Nia. Terrence was qualified for his position, but Nia's influence clearly had gotten him on with the firm.

McLoughlin and McLoughlin was a small firm, but very powerful and prestigious in the DC area. The father of the firm's present chairman Blair McLoughlin, who had passed away years ago, started the firm in the early 30s. It had a rich history and impeccable reputation. Terrence's outgoing, likable personality made him well-known around the firm. Terrence had lofty goals. He thirsted to make partner. He knew that making partner would ordinarily take many years to achieve at a prominent upscale firm like McLoughlin and McLoughlin, but he also knew having the deputy chief of staff for a fiancée changed the rules.

That afternoon, Terrence stood outside of Blair McLoughlin's office anxiously awaiting his secretary's return.

The hell with that, they aren't going to just use me for my connections. I want partner and I want it now! Terrence thought.

Blair's secretary returned, surprised to find Terrence waiting. "Hi, Terrence, what can I do for you?"

"If possible, I really need to see Blair for a moment."

"Let me see if he's available." Of course, Blair's secretary knew her boss was in fact available, but called to verify if the firm's chief desired to have this unscheduled meeting.

"Sure, send him in," said Blair to his secretary.

"Go right in, Terrence."

As Terrence entered Blair's office, he once again reassured himself that he was making the right decision. *Let's go "T," let's make it happen. Don't let them take advantage of you.*

"Hi, Blair, do you have a moment?"

"For you, Terrence? Of course. Come on in and have a seat," Blair said. Blair was tall with broad shoulders and an intimidating stature. He added to this intimidating appearance by speaking loudly.

"So, what's on your mind, Terrence?" said Blair, as he leaned back in his large, handcrafted, leather chair nibbling on the end of a fat, unlit Cuban cigar.

"Blair, I just have a few things I'd like to discuss with you."

Chapter 6

NIA WAS BLOWN AWAY TO HEAR THAT ANDY, HER OLD FRIEND, EX-boss, and the current CEO of Rothschild and Smith Financial, had been ill. She was happy to hear he had recovered, but shocked that he was stepping down, and even more shocked to hear that she was Rothschild and Smith Financial's number one candidate.

I'm sure glad Andy is okay. And I can't believe he's stepping down. I'd have that company running like a top, but I don't trust Jimmy as far as I can throw him.

"Well, I'm just glad to hear Andy is okay. I'll have to give him a call," said Nia, as she began to walk again.

"Nia, they think you're perfect for the job."

"It doesn't sound like it to me. If they thought I was so perfect for the job, they wouldn't be including any sort of stipulation," Nia said without giving Jimmy eye contact.

"Nia, it isn't a stipulation—it's just business. That's how things get done in Washington. We all know that here. I'll be honest with you. I'm getting something out of this. I stand to gain something if I can get you on board." Nia momentarily cut her eyes at Jimmy with a slight snarl.

"Don't look at me like that, Nia. You know I'm am honest guy. Look, I'll even tell you. I'll tell you what I stand to gain. Between me and you, they've promised me a future Senate seat. And trust me, they have the power to make it happen. This is serious business. Hansen even asked about you himself," Jimmy said with conviction, catching Nia's attention.

Paul Hansen was an elite hedge fund manager and the ex-CEO of Klein Schultz. It was said that he and his cohorts still controlled the financial behemoth, as well as the rest of the financial industry. His power and reach were unimaginable.

Although Nia didn't let on to Jimmy, she was shocked to hear that Hansen was interested in her. She knew that much of Jimmy's gibberish was true; Klein Schultz did in fact have their hands *deep* in America's pockets. Moreover, Klein Schultz was so powerful many considered them to be the primary cause of the country's recent economic meltdown. Klein Schultz was said to have created and sold bad mortgage investments to foreign banks, pension funds, and insurance companies. The rumor was that they secretly intended these investments to fail because they then bet *against* these investments and reaped tremendous returns. While Nia despised what Hansen stood for and had done, she also knew that the wicked truth of the matter was that he held the key to her future in the private job sector in his hands because he and his allies essentially controlled all of the big banks in America.

"Do you *REALLY* realize what kind of influence Hansen and Klein Schultz have on our government?" Jimmy asked, but was met with silence as Nia began to once again march down 15th Street toward Pennsylvania Avenue.

"I know you know this, Nia, but let's go back to the fact that Paul Hansen is one of four out of our five most recent U.S. treasurers that were all formerly high-ranking Klein Schultz executives. And we know that if this president wouldn't have bucked the system, we probably would still have an ex-Klein Schultz executive as U.S. treasurer. And let's not even talk about the Federal Reserve," rambled Jimmy, as he scrambled alongside Nia in an effort to keep up with her vigorous pace.

"Of course, I'm aware of that, Jimmy."

"Let's not forget about how many ex-government officials are now working for Klein Schultz or at one of their affiliate crony banks as a high-ranking executive. Ralph Kelly, Aiden Barnes, Art Hines, and the list goes on. And don't forget, these ex-government officials aren't just getting measly six-figure salaries either," Jimmy said with a wink, but Nia never gave him eye contact.

"No one is looking down on them for building their résumés in the White House then taking executive positions in the corporate world."

"Congressman, I said I am *not* interested." Nia sighed deeply, as she stopped at the corner.

"I understand," Jimmy said, huffing as he tried to catch his breath. "Look, the bottom line *IS*, The Social Hub's key lobbyist is asking me if they can have your support on this one and also to have you help them win President Davis's support on the issue. It's as simple as that. They know your track record and talent. When you're finished at the White House, or maybe even sooner, the CEO position at Rothschild and Smith Financial could basically be yours as long as you ride with them on this one. Do you know what a person with your experience can command in salary for a CEO position with a prestigious firm like Rothschild and Smith Financial? It could be a camouflaged eight, nine, maybe even a 10 million dollar signing bonus, not to mention a seven-figure salary plus year-end bonuses. You know how much the average Fortune 500 financial institution CEO earns? Look, Paul Hansen and their key lobbyist want to meet with you to personally explain in more detail," Jimmy suggested with his southern drawl growing stronger by the moment, which typically happened when he was wheeling and dealing. As the words *"Paul Hansen wants to meet with you"* rolled off of Jimmy's tongue with his southern twang blaring, Nia's jaw dropped and her legs involuntarily ceased to move as she became confounded in disbelief.

Chapter 7

BLAIR SAT REARED BACK IN HIS LARGE, BLACK LEATHER CHAIR WITH a fat, unlit Cuban cigar tucked in his mouth like a pacifier.

"Sit down, Terrence. How are you?"

"I'm well. How about you?

"Same here. So, what's your mind?"

"Just wanted to see if you were going to make it to the Boys and Girls Club charitable golfing event that Nia and I invited you to?"

"Always up for a round of golf, and of course, to help the underprivileged."

"How about the wife, Blair, is she coming out?"

"Hell no, I *DO* want to enjoy myself!" Blair said, as they both laughed.

"Well, thanks for your support. There'll likely be some good networking opportunities there for us too, Blair."

Blair leaned even farther back in his chair. A large grin surfaced on his face as he removed the cigar from his mouth. "I was hoping you'd say that, Terrence. We like the way you think. So how's your future wife doing over at the White House?"

"She's doing great. Everyone loves her in the West Wing. Nia's a networking machine. That's how she got where she is today and why we make such a good team," Terrence said with his chest poked out, as he pushed his trendy, black-framed glasses up on his nose with his index finger. "That brings me to my next question, Blair. I think I have a lot to offer this firm."

"You've done a fine job, Terrence. We like you a lot."

"But I believe that I can offer much more. Blair, I'm out at these incredible events with Nia all the time meeting with foreign diplomats, political figures, CEOs, and just about anyone that you could imagine. And saying that I'm only an associate with the firm just doesn't hold any weight with these influential types. They almost look down at me when I give them my title. Flat-out hurts my opportunity to land new business for the firm. I'll cut to the chase. Blair, I'd like to make partner."

Chapter 8

NIA STOOD MOMENTARILY FROZEN. *PAUL HANSEN WANTS TO MEET with me? Wow, I can't believe that. Jimmy must be serious, but I still can't trust him.*

"Jimmy, I don't know what you're up to, but I don't want any part of it. Like I told you, I am here in Washington to work hard for President Davis and the people. That's it. Nothing more and nothing less," Nia said and then quickly pivoted and continued back to the White House.

"I understand, but I just want you to keep two last things in mind. The average term of a chief of staff and most deputy chiefs is only two years, Nia. Everyone knows that…burnout isn't just a figure of speech in your position, it happens to everyone—it's inevitable. So the expectations *are* that it's almost time for you to move on anyway."

Damn it, Jimmy's got a point, people in my position rarely make it a full term and Lord knows I am getting burned out. And a 10 million dollar signing bonus does sound…what am I thinking? This is Jimmy and I know this idiot has to be full of it, Nia thought, as Jimmy went on pleading his case with the precision of a high-priced defense attorney.

"I know this is a lot to throw at you all at once. Why don't you meet with their lobbyist, so you can hear it straight from the horse's mouth?"

I really wonder if he's on the up and up with this.

"Lastly, just think about you and your family's needs…your grandmother, and especially your brother."

How does he know about my family!

"…and with that type of money, you could take care of them both for the rest of their lives. Just think about it, Nia." Jimmy had struck a chord just as they arrived at the White House gates where an unmarked government agency car awaited Nia to escort her back to the West Wing. As Nia pulled away in the back of the government vehicle, she stared out of the window, thinking of her family.

There was nothing in the world more important to Nia than her family. When Nia was just 11 years old, her mom was killed by a drunk driver in a car accident that also left her younger brother Eric paralyzed from the chest down. Nia had been devastated. She was extremely close to her mom and brother. After her dad left when she was just three years old, the three of them did everything together. As Nia reflected on the moment that her grade school principal gave her the news that her mom had passed away, Nia's throat became full. She vividly recalled telling her principal that God wasn't fair for taking her mom away and injuring her brother. Fortunately, Nia's grandmother stepped in and raised her and Eric, but her grandmother struggled both physically and financially. Not only did her brother's doctor bills mount out of control from a variety of surgeries, her grandmother had also successfully fought through a difficult bout with breast cancer. Eric and her grandmother were now living together in Chicago and Nia shouldered the financial burden of taking care of them.

Chapter 9

"IS THAT RIGHT?" BLAIR REPLIED SMUGLY WITHOUT FLINCHING.

"I can bring in business that no one else in this firm can. Not Harry, Aaron…anyone. When I'm out networking with Nia, if I was able to represent the firm with a more prestigious title, I guarantee I'd be able to pull in a ton of business. The bottom line *is* the bottom line, isn't it, Blair?" said Terrence with an eyebrow arched high.

"You know, Terrence, McLoughlin and McLoughlin was built upon certain values…principals…we're well respected because we have the highest quality attorneys in the DC area. We believe that making partner here is a tremendous accomplishment…one that has to be *earned*," Blair replied and then leaned back in his chair, continuing to nibble on his fine-quality cigar. Silence filled the room. Terrence gathered himself for a moment, contemplating the appropriate comeback.

"That being said, Terrence, you make a valid point. An attorney that can bring in high-quality business does add a certain value to the firm…and does deserve consideration." Terrence tried to fight back a grin as he listened carefully. "Let's get back together on this after the firm's anniversary party. Nia *IS* coming to the event, isn't she?"

"Of course."

"There're going to be some very influential people there and I think Nia's attendance would definitely be welcome. And perhaps she can also see to it that I'm added to the guest list of a few major events over at the White House, as well. I think these are the types of things that lend themselves well to what you're trying to accomplish here today, don't you, Terrence?" Blair asked, with his eyes squinted and glaring squarely into Terrence's eyes.

I have to set a date or he'll take advantage of Nia's connections and string this thing out forever, Terrence thought. "Yes, they do, but perhaps we need to come up with a timeline for this?" countered Terrence.

"Sure. We can do that…after the anniversary party and once we've gotten to know each other a bit better at some of those White House events you'll have Nia invite me to," Blair responded in a firm tone, as if to say *touché*!

"Yes, that sounds fine, but I think we should at least set a date to reconvene?"

"As I said, after the anniversary party and once I'm able to attend a few White House events so that I am better able to see all of the benefits this relationship may bring. Anyway, I know my schedule is booked for several months…*right*, Ann?" Blair asked his secretary after tapping his speakerphone.

"Yes, sir, you are absolutely right, you aren't free for several months," his secretary replied in perfect tag team fashion.

"Well, Terrence, I'll have her give you a call this afternoon to let you know a good time once I'm able to get together with her to review my schedule."

He is so full of shit, but he'll never turn down the opportunity for more business.

"Sounds good, Blair. I'm glad we were able to *agree* on something," said Terrence and both men countered one another by flashing a devious smile.

Chapter 10

NIA COULDN'T RID HER MIND OF JIMMY'S INSANE OFFER. EVEN though Jimmy was known to be a bit shady, Nia knew he wasn't intelligent enough to make up such an elaborate story. Yet still, Nia would have ordinarily dismissed Jimmy's pitch to begin with, but she couldn't help but think about an offer of this magnitude. Ordinarily Nia was as honest as they come. She was the sort of person who would return *cash* to the lost-and-found, but this offer not only included her lifelong dream of becoming the CEO of a Fortune 500 financial firm, it also included millions of dollars which she desperately needed to care for her family. And although she knew that this sort of *"you scratch my back, I'll scratch yours"* arrangement was what politics was unfortunately built upon—especially in Washington—this situation still presented her with quite a moral dilemma.

Damn it, why did Jimmy have to drop this in MY lap. I can't believe that offer. It's a loose, loose situation—if I took advantage of the opportunity I'd be wrong and if I don't take the money I'd be letting down my family.

Nia was faced with the type of moral dilemma that everyone faces at some point in life, but at an incomprehensible level. Life's minefield of moral dilemmas unexpectedly surfaces, presenting us with tricky, unforeseen forks in the road, but when money is at the root of the ethical conundrum, the decision on what direction to take suddenly becomes even more complicated. Money truly is the root of all evil and the millions of dollars that were perhaps about to be thrust upon Nia had the needle of her soul's moral compass fluttering out of control.

It's wrong, but it really is just a part of politics and I could do so much good for my family and countless others with that kind of money and power. How can I say no? On the other hand, that damn stipulation is just flat-out BS and feels wrong, but damn it, if I don't take the offer I'd really be doing a disservice to my family. It's a lose-lose situation.

Nia shocked herself because she couldn't readily stop her mind from running wild.

This is crazy, a multi-million dollar CEO offer. I know I should just let this go, but I've gotta talk to Terrence about this situation.

Nia really didn't want to share this offer with anyone, but it was eating away at her and she felt compelled to talk it through with someone to at least get it out of her head so she could move on. She and Terrence always vented back and forth about work to one another. Terrence loved to talk. He was raised by all women—his mom, grandmother, and aunt. He possessed a unique quality to somehow relate to women; not as a girlfriend like many gay men do, but more like a man who was in tune with a woman's needs.

"What? They're trying to offer you 10 mill plus and a CEO position! Are you serious? That's a no-brainer, sweetie. We have to take that offer," Terrence said, practically jumping out his skin.

"Terrence, I'm kind of surprised at you. You seriously would do something like that?"

"Surprised at what? Yeah, I would do it in a heartbeat and I think you should consider it too. Nia, you're the one that explained to me that the average deputy chief of staff only lasts for about two years anyway. Besides, you know that's just how things work in Washington. I don't know why you're in denial. They're not talking about any kind of straight forward quid pro quo—they're just saying they're interested in you. Hell, you're the damn deputy chief of staff and ex-VP of a Fortune 500 investment firm, so you're definitely qualified. And the cause is harmless. The privacy issue with social media; are you kidding me? Corporate America sells our information without our permission already anyway," Terrence said adamantly.

"Terrence, you know I don't like to play games, especially unethical ones."

"I know. I know you better than anyone. It's about them more or less promising you the money and position in return for you backing them, isn't it? That's what's bothering you. You worked hard for POTUS on the campaign and he rewarded you with the position, *but you deserved it*. And more importantly, you were qualified. It's the same scenario—they want you to work for them on their behalf and then they want to reward you, but the key is *YOU ARE QUALIFIED*. Look at your girl that used to be the White House social secretary...she got let go from her position and still got a CEO position in the corporate world because she was *qualified*, Nia, just like you."

I am qualified, Nia thought.

"How do you think people at that level get their positions anyway? You know that, Nia. Plus, you're beating your head against the wall over an issue of *online privacy*? Seriously, Nia? What the hell kind of ethical dilemma does that present? You wouldn't be doing anything wrong. It's not like they want you to shoot down some legislation that would close some chemical plant that's giving little kids cancer."

"Don't use that as an example, Terrence."

"Look, like I said, it's *online privacy*. Hell, cell phone companies have tracking devices that track our every move anyway. If you don't like it, don't have a cell phone. And if you have a problem with online privacy, don't be online."

He does have a point; people don't have to use these technologies...they do have choices, thought Nia, trying to fight the temptation of buying into Terrence's persuasive argument.

"That's not the point, Terrence. It's an ethical issue on my side if I take the money and the position. Plus, why are they lobbying President Davis so hard? You know how that works…most lobbyists are concerned with Congress. You know that…they go after them because they have more long-term collective control."

"You poor, little, sweet innocent girl, you. That's why I snatched you up when I had the chance!" said Terrence condescendingly with a snicker.

"That's not funny, Terrence. This is serious," Nia said, as she gave Terrence a piercing stare with her nostrils flared.

"Come on, Nia, The Social Hub isn't your traditional corporation with long-term goals. These Internet companies are short-term to begin with. These geeks build up these start-ups for about two to three years then they sell and make millions…even billions."

"Again, what's your point, Terrence?"

"Think about it. They're all based on trends anyway. The day they are no longer hot with the public they dry up and fade away forever and the next company or technology steps in."

"Terrence, the Internet will be here forever in some shape or form, it's not going anywhere, so if you're insinuating this decision is no big deal because The Social Hub won't be around forever, you're wrong. This decision will still affect the other companies and this country for years to come."

"What? You are so dramatic. This decision won't have an impact on society. They aren't tracking people and invading their privacy to do harm. They just want data to sell to corporate America…big-money advertisers. That's it. So, the privacy issue is overrated. The Social Hub doesn't give a damn what some 40-year-old, stay-at-home mom is talking about online. Like I said, if you don't like it, don't use a cell phone or the Web. But you know that won't happen. People will always sacrifice their privacy for convenience. History has proven it. You want an example? I don't see anyone choosing not to own a home in DC because the District of Columbia makes the name and address of every property owner, as well as how much they pay in property taxes, available on DC's Office of Tax and Revenue website. Like I said, people will always sacrifice their privacy for convenience!" Terrence rebutted loudly, shaking his head.

"Calm down, Terrence. You're getting all worked up."

"Yes, I'm getting all worked up because you're talking about walking away from millions, and a career opportunity of a lifetime! Look, what I'm trying to explain to you is that that's the nature of that kind of business. It's the only industry in the *world* where you can make billions, that fast, and that's why they're not just lobbying Congress. They're lobbying President Davis too because they need *short-term* support to make that fast money. They can't afford to let legislation slow them down. All they care about *IS* the next two or three years. So they don't care about throwing a few hundred *million* around *now* because in just two or three years they'll sell The Social Hub for a few hundred *BILLION*! And that's also why Klein Schultz invested so much in them," Terrence said, smirking, with his shoulders hunched and palms up.

"I see your point...I do see your point...," Nia said clearly pondering Terrence's argument, "...but it's still a moral issue for *me*." Nia explained her perspective while jabbing her index finger into her chest.

"Nia, I'll say this, and then I'll leave it alone. Didn't Klein Schultz give POTUS campaign money?"

"Yes, you know they did, Terrence," Nia snapped.

"I rest my case," said Terrence, shaking his head.

"So what does that mean, Terrence? It's not like he could turn it down. It's not his fault that they wanted to contribute to his campaign. When you're a politician you have to work for everyone."

"Yup, exactly," Terrence said with a smile. "Like I said, I rest my case."

"What? What are you talking about? 'I rest my case.' Thanks, Terrence. Great, I think I'm even more confused now," Nia said as she rolled her eyes. Nia initially thought talking to Terrence would somehow organize or even clear her thoughts and make the decision easier, but instead, sharing her dilemma with him had only made her more confused.

Nia made her way back to their kitchen and began to load the dishwasher. The sound of dishes clanking together echoed loudly throughout the apartment, as she rammed them into the dishwasher rack. *He was a big help!* she grumbled.

"By the way, don't forget about the anniversary party," Terrence reminded Nia.

"I haven't forgotten. That shouldn't be a problem, and if it is, I'll make it work." Nia's reply was accompanied by a noticeable tone of attitude in her voice.

"No, you don't get it. *WE HAVE* to attend it *TOGETHER*. Nia, it's extremely important that I make a good impression at this event...they want to make me partner."

"Oh wow! How come you didn't tell me?"

"I just talked to Blair about it yesterday."

"Congratulations, sweetie!" Nia said, changing her tone as she was genuinely excited for Terrence. "Why didn't you tell me?"

"I am now. That's why you *HAVE* to make this event!" Terrence said.

"I'll make sure I'm available," Nia replied, as she entered the date into her Blackberry.

"Good, I'm just excited about this opportunity."

"And I'm so happy for you. You deserve it."

"And you deserve your new opportunity too, sweetie. Just think; you have an opportunity to become the CEO of a Fortune 500 company…just what you've always dreamed of!"

Yeah, thanks, Terrence. That's a big help.

Chapter 11

AS THE TWIN-ENGINE 737 JET TOUCHED DOWN IN ATLANTA'S HARTS-field-Jackson Atlanta International Airport early Saturday morning with the orange glare of the rising sun glistening, Nia, Valerie, and Beverly simultaneously exhaled with a sigh of relief. The stress of the White House and the East Coast was behind them for the moment. Nia had arranged for the ladies to get together in Atlanta for the weekend and the plane touching down signaled that the *weekend with the girls* had officially begun!

It was the first time in months that the ladies were going to all be together at once. To complete the quartet of BFFs, later that morning the three ladies were meeting up with fellow Spellman alum and Atlanta resident Carla. In many ways Nia's position in the White House had somewhat isolated her from many of her friends, but she knew she could let her hair down with her girls. Excitement filled the air.

After checking into a hotel near the airport, the ladies headed over to the popular restaurant the Flying Biscuit Café to meet Carla for brunch. Carla had selected the restaurant chain's Buckhead location near her home. The posh, high-profile Buckhead area was known for housing Atlanta's celebrities and elite, and Carla fit in perfectly.

Carla worked for the popular national television network NBN as an up-and-coming correspondent on the number-one rated morning show, "This Morning Show." She had begun her career as a news anchor for a leading cable network that was based out of Atlanta. A natural-born social butterfly, in no time Carla had quickly schmoozed her way to the cable network's top local anchor spot. But when NBN, the country's second-largest television network, purchased the local cable network, it catapulted Carla's career to another level. Now she had become a bona fide celebrity.

Carla had met Nia and Beverly while attending Spellman, but was three years younger. Carla was a petite little thing with a cute Halle Berry–like haircut and similar shade of skin tone. Her fair complexion and fine hair grade had clearly been drawn from her father's DNA. He was Creole, born and raised in Louisiana with an eclectic mix of ancestral roots, which included Caribbean, European, and Native American descent. On the other hand, Carla's mom was a Georgian peach with a gorgeous, russet-brown skin tone. While Carla hadn't inherited her mother's beautiful dark brown skin color, she had inherited her sexy little figure, which she typically made sure to accentuate with a flimsy and often revealing outfit.

"Hey, Carla!" the three ladies said in virtual unison.

"Hey, ladies! How have you been? Out there doing your thing in New York and DC...running off leaving your girl here all by herself in this crazy town," Carla said with a momentarily sad face, and then flashed her brightly bleached smile. As the four women exchanged heartfelt hugs, the warmth they shared with one another seemed to permeate the room.

"Trust me; all we've been doing is working our tails off, girl!" replied Beverly, as they sat down at the table.

The four BFFs had an interesting dynamic. Nia, of course, was strong, sharp, and somewhat sassy. Beverly was witty, laid back, and a constant instigator. Meanwhile, Valerie was somewhat quiet and possessed extreme poise and an elegant grace. But she was also quite judgmental. And Carla was just a flat-out firecracker always ready for a good time.

"Is this place really that good, Carla?" asked Valerie.

"Trust me, this place is a triple The Social Hub *Like*. The French toast is off the chain! Oh, and the biscuits are the bomb dot com! I don't even need to see the menu," Carla responded, as she flipped out her shiny new white iPhone and began to tweet to her fans. Carla was a Twitter addict, amassing more than one million followers. The chatter amongst the ladies was almost non-stop. Then Nia's phone rang.

"Hello. Hello. Hello..." Nia said and then hung up. "There's Terrence's phone calling me again."

"What? Is Terrence already trying to track you down since you're away with the girls? Probably thinks you're down here dippin' off with some old college boyfriend," said Beverly laughing.

"He always does that...he dials me with his cell by accident. I guess it happens in his pocket...drives me crazy. Anyway, Carla, what's been going on at NBN?"

"OMG! Things are *POPP-ING*! As a matter of fact, I have some good news to announce!" Carla said, shrill in her excitement. "Guess what? Now, it's not official yet, so don't tell anybody, but I just got offered my own show!"

"Congratulations!" said Valerie.

"I am soooo happy for you! What kind of show?" asked Nia.

"Daytime talk. It's kind of like a hipper version of 'The View.' It's going to be called 'Real Talk,'" Carla said, lowering her tone to a whisper.

"They already have 'The Talk' and 'The View,' aren't you afraid that might be kind of passé?" Valerie said with a look of contemplation.

"Yeah, but those shows don't have your girl hosting them. Trust me, it is going to be *POPP-ING*!"

"So how does Steve feel about it?" Nia inquired.

"Oh, that's a whole other issue. We're getting divorced," Carla replied bluntly.

"Oh no, why didn't you say anything to us?"

"We've been having issues for sooooo long…I am *SO* over him. Totally a faint memory in my past," responded Carla, rolling her eyes and turning her lips up.

"What kind of issues? Did he cheat, girl?" Beverly interjected with her southern twang heightening as she leaned in towards the group of ladies.

"Yes, and it wasn't the first time. I found out he had been cheating almost the entire time we were together."

"What? Who was he messin' around with?" Beverly asked nosily.

"You'll never guess who. It was somebody that we all know."

"Who?" Nia asked.

"He had the nerve to have two different girlfriends, at least that I know of, and one of them was Monica Davenport!"

"I'm not surprised," Nia added.

"She always did have whorish ways, didn't she?" Beverly said in a blunt manner. "I remember when she slept with Stephanie's man while Stephanie was away at Hampton. Y'all remember that, don't you? Now were you givin' him enough at home though, Carla?"

"What does that have to do with anything?" Valerie interrupted.

"A lot."

"Beverly, please!"

"I'm just sayin'."

"So how'd you find out?" Valerie asked.

"Sheila Carmichael. She still lives around my mother's house and I see her sometimes when I go home to visit. She stopped me one day and asked me if we were divorced, and I said no, why? She said because she kept seeing them together."

"How did you react, girl?"

"I flipped! I called Monica's ass up and of course she denied it all, but when I asked him, he didn't."

"Bold little rascal, huh," Beverly said.

"Oh yeah, he got real bold after I caught him. Told me our marriage never meant anything to him and it was my fault."

"That's crazy," Nia said.

"Was it the sex? I'm tellin' you, you gotta satisfy these boys in a marriage. That's what I keep tryin' to tell Nia about Terrence," Beverly interjected.

"Beverly! Please."

"I'm just sayin'."

"He actually did try to use that excuse and said he didn't get enough sex and attention, and blah, blah, blah. Plus, he said I cared more about my career than him."

"Typical...full of excuses. He knew when you got married that you had a demanding career. It didn't stop him from driving that new BMW," Nia said, rolling her eyes. Nothing irritated Nia more than a man who stood in the way of a woman's career.

"I am so surprised at him," Valerie said.

"I'm not," Beverly said. "He was a pretty boy...he looked like the playboy type. He wasn't on the *down low* too, was he? Wearin' them tight-fitted jeans all the time. I never trust a man that wears jeans tighter than mine," she added with a devilish smirk.

"Anyway, who was the other woman?" Nia asked.

"Some chick from his job."

"Job...what job?"

"He was trying to become a writer, so I had got him a job with Black America Web dot com."

"At his job, huh? Should have known. They always get caught up with someone from their job," Nia said, as her cell phone rang again. "Ugghhh, I am so sick of him and this phone." Then she quickly clicked the End button on her phone.

"Do you ever try to listen to what Terrence is doing when that happens, Nia?" Beverly asked. "Perfect time to find out what's going on with your man."

"No...please, girl. I can hear him jabbering and I just hang up."

"I'm surprised you don't listen...like I said, perfect time to check up on him. And I hope y'all checkin' ya man's emails and especially their Social Hub pages too?" asked Beverly.

"No. Are you serious, Beverly?" Valerie replied, shaking her head.

"Well, when you *get* a man, Val, you better," said Beverly, taking a jab at Valerie's severely depressed love life, which earned her a stern glare from Valerie. "I'm serious, girl," Beverly continued. "Y'all think I'm crazy, but nowadays it all starts online. These boys be meetin' up with old girlfriends and even new women on The Social Hub all the time. You gotta keep an eye on them... these women don't care if they're married and them boys just *love* the attention. I'm tellin' you, you just gotta give 'em attention and keep them boys satisfied. It ain't complicated. They're such simple creatures. You gotta let 'em have a little bit of that good-good regularly, girl. Trust me, Darren loves when I stuff all this voluptuous, chocolate, full figure into a little, skimpy piece of lingerie."

"Good-good, Beverly...really? Uh." Valerie responded with disdain in her voice. "How can someone be so articulate and intelligent when they have to be and then be so *ghetto*? Who would ever think you work in the White House?"

"I'm just keepin' it real. I'm tellin' you it's a psychological thing...an ego thing...you have to make a man feel like a man...they like that. Hell, they just like sex. I'm just sayin'. Y'all all know that old southern saying; to keep a man happy *all you gotta do is feed 'em and f—"*

"Alright, Beverly, we all get the picture," Valerie interrupted and then Beverly smiled and calmly continued to sip on a mimosa.

"Bev, can you ever be serious for one moment? *ANYWAY*, are you okay, Carla?" asked Nia.

"I told you...I am *SO* over Steve. This happened months ago. I told him to *keep it movin'*. Girl, I already have a new man and he is *SO* hot!" The ladies shrilled in laughter like a group of teenage girls.

"Are you serious? Who?"

"You'll never guess. It's someone from NBN."

"What? Is it someone that actually appears on television?" Nia asked.

"Yup!"

"Who? Just tell us!" Nia asked emphatically.

"Jeff Conley," Carla said, finally letting on.

"Jeff Conley from 'This Morning Show?'" Beverly and Valerie asked simultaneously.

"Yes! I told you... *SO—HOT!*" Carla responded.

"Are you serious?" the ladies all screamed again. Then there was an awkward moment of silence.

"Uhhh...isn't he married?" asked Valerie with a perplexed look.

"Yes, but he's going through a divorce," Carla responded nonchalantly.

"Girl, you fallin' for that old trick?" Beverly commented with her lips turned up.

"No, he really is."

"I don't know if that's a good idea. He's STILL married, Carla. I'm really surprised at you," Valerie scoffed at Carla, sounding like a disappointed parent.

"But they've been separated for months," Carla said, trying to defend herself.

"That's what they all say," Beverly fired back.

"Ughhh...I knew I shouldn't have told you all," Carla huffed with her hand pressed against her forehead shaking her head from side to side.

"I just wonder why you picked him. There's so many other single men out there—" Nia began to question.

"Not in Atlanta," interrupted Beverly.

"Bev, please. What are people going to say?" Nia asked.

"It just happened and nobody knows."

"Yeah, what a coincidence that it *just* happened right around the time NBN offered you your own show, huh?" Beverly interjected sarcastically.

"Whatever, Bev. Obviously it's going to help my career, but I got that offer on my own. I know what you all are thinking, and to a certain degree, you might be right. Anyway, I'm sorry, but when you're a celebrity, it's just easier dealing with someone else that's on your level...somebody that can complement your career. Look at Jay-Z and Beyonce, Will and Jada, or David Bowie and Iman. Power couples doin' it!" Carla insisted.

"David Bowie and Iman? Huh?" Beverly asked cynically with a shrug of her shoulders.

Then Nia's phone rang and it was once again one of Terrence's arrant phone calls. She immediately pressed the End button to terminate the call. *I really wish he would take his phone out of his pocket!* Nia thought.

"I just don't think it's a good idea until the divorce becomes official. This man has a wife and family at home," Valerie said in disgust.

"I'll be honest, Carla. I have to agree with Val. Think about if the shoe were on the other foot and it was your husband," Nia said.

"It was."

"Whatever you do, just be careful," Nia added, as Carla ignored her advice and continued to blissfully tweet away.

"So just how did this whirlwind romance begin anyway?" asked Beverly with a devious grin.

"Well, it was crazy!" Carla began to explain with the look of a kid sharing a big secret. "We were at a Grammys after-party that had live performances by all the big artists…Beyonce, Lady Gaga, and on and on. And there were a bunch of little dressing rooms backstage. Seemed like there must have been at least 25 of these little 12 by 12 rooms. And girl, Jeff was walking by with his ex-wife backstage near the changing rooms and I was back there talking to Tyrese when the three of us bumped into each other—"

"Emph…you were with Tyrese's FINE chocolate ass and you were thinking about Jeff Conley? Girl you're crazy!" interrupted Beverly.

"Wait, I'm confused. I thought you said they had broken up?" asked Valerie.

"They are, but they have to make it look good for the media."

"Oh, that makes perfect sense," Valerie replied sarcastically.

"They weren't even living in the same house."

"Just finish the story," said Beverly with a grin, while Valerie sat with a look of disgust.

"Girl, when I gave him a hug he whispered, 'I want you…right this moment,' in my ear, then kinda grinded against me and he was as hard as a rock. It was so loud and crowded that no one else even noticed. Then he looked down at his cell phone and told his ex that a big story had just broke and we both needed to call the network ASAP. He looked around and said we needed to find a quiet place to call into the network. He told her to go back into the party and as soon as we were finished he'd call her on her cell to find out where she was.

"Before I knew anything he had grabbed my arm and pulled me into one of those little changing rooms and slammed me down on a dresser. Before I could ask him what he was doing, my dress was up and I just happened to be letting my *kitty kat* out to get some air that night."

"Gross, you and this no panties thing," commented Valerie.

"Have to let her breathe sometimes, girl. You should try it sometime," replied Carla with a smirk.

"*Anyway*," responded Val.

"Well, that was the first time he'd ever gotten so physical…so rough."

"And you liked it," Beverly added, smiling.

"Girl, please. I loved it!"

"I thought you said this was how it all got started? Has to be more to the story," said Nia with a curious look.

"Well, we had been innocently flirting for a little while before this. That's how it really all started."

"I know what you call innocent, Carla," said Valerie.

"No, seriously, it all started off innocently."

"How did it build?" asked Beverly.

"All kinds of little flirtatious situations. Like at our meetings we'd always manage to sit next to each other and he'd do little sexy stuff like run his fingers on my leg and I'd do stuff like take my shoes off and run my feet up his leg. Then it just progressed from there."

"How?" Beverly asked.

"At work, Carla? Come on, girl," interjected Valerie.

"It was just kind of exciting. I'd do stuff like wait until it'd be a critical moment in the meeting and start messing with him just for the fun of it. Get him all worked up. Do something like start stroking his—"

"Okay, we get it," interrupted Valerie. "I thought you said *we* started *innocently* flirting with each other? Grabbing the man's genitals doesn't sound so *innocent* to me, and it sounds like you were the main one doing all the flirting."

"Oh, he did things too…trust me."

"Like what, girl?" Beverly asked with her chin resting in the palm of her hand and her eyes dancing in delight.

"We get the point," said Valerie.

"Well at least finish the Grammys story," requested Beverly.

"Oh, so like I was saying, he slammed me down on a dresser with his hands clinched up under my ass. Then he whipped my legs apart and—"

"We get it. You all screwed on some filthy little table in some dirty little closet in the middle of the Grammys, with another woman's husband, and oh yeah, while she was in the building. Come on, Carla, you're better than that. You know he does this with all the women," said Valerie.

"It just happened."

"So what happened with his wife that night?" asked Beverly.

"Nothing. He just found her later that night and everything was fine."

"Wow, Carla. That was a bit much. Val has a point; he's probably slept with so many other women at the studio *alone*, that she's numb to it all," Nia commented.

"Yeah, but it's different. We're actually dating. Our situation wasn't just a one-night stand. We have a relationship."

"Come on, girl, don't you think all of the others thought the same thing?" Valerie asked.

"I know he isn't a saint, but what man is? He just did what any other men in the same situation would do. All those women knew what they were getting into."

"And so do you," Valerie fired back.

"Val's right, Carla," added Nia. "You pretty much know going in what to expect from this situation. It's loose, loose. I hate to see you set yourself up to get hurt…that's all."

"Trust me, I know the situation, and I'm good. You all need to loosen up some. We're grown women and all those fantasies about finding the perfect man and situation are just that…fantasies. The reality is, there is no Prince Charming out there waiting for us."

"Well, I got my Prince Charming. Darren does it all for me, girl. Like I told you earlier, if you had pulled some of them dressing room tricks with Steve maybe he wouldn't have cheated," Beverly commented calmly while swirling her drink.

"Well, that's good for you, Bev, but that is a one-in-a-million situation. And your situation is a fine example; Darren did his dirt once upon a time, and I'm sure Terrence did too, Nia."

"I'm sure they did, but we can't worry about that," replied Nia.

"And he wasn't married before he and Nia started dating," interjected Valerie.

"Val, I hate to say it, but that's why you're still alone, girl. You have to stop being so damn picky, otherwise you're going to end up a lonesome, little, old, horny lady someday."

"If you're happy, I guess we're happy, but just be careful, Carla. We're just worried about you," interjected Nia, trying to cap the growing tension.

"Okay, enough about Jeff. Tell me, what's going on in Washington?" asked Carla.

"I want to get you guys' opinion about something. I've got this crazy situation going on at work that I really have been wanting to run past you guys," said Nia.

"Really, what's going on?" asked Valerie.

"Well, I met with Jimmy Coleman Jr. last week and—" As Nia began to speak her Blackberry chirped with an appointment reminder. The girls were scheduled to get their hair done at Élan, a hair salon, which was also located in Buckhead just blocks away on Peachtree Street. Nia was somewhat relieved that her cell phone's notification had interrupted her because she was still unsure if she wanted to share the *big offer* with anyone—not even her closest friends.

I guess that was a sign. Wow, I almost let it slip, Nia thought.

"That was my reminder for our appointment with André. We better get out of here; you know how angry he gets if you're late for an appointment."

"Okay! Crabby little man," added Beverly, as the four women hustled out of the restaurant.

⤳

André was a flamboyant, well-known, local hair stylist and the owner of the swank Buckhead hair salon Élan. The girls had known André for years. They entered André's salon and were immediately met with hugs and chatter. André's shop was chic and contemporary. Bright colors covered the walls of his upscale four-chair salon. Several high-end, wire-framed silver chairs lined the sitting area. André had a private room in the back of his shop just for his celebrity clientele. Two large glass doors, which opened to the inside, separated this area from the rest of the salon.

"Hey, you power bitches! How have you girls been doing? You look gorgeous...*except* for your hair!" said André, laughing loudly and also causing a loud roar of laughs from the girls.

"We're good. How are you, André? You look like you picked up a few pounds...makes you look good though. Are those *love* pounds?" Carla asked André.

"Honey, yes! Let's just say I'm still a bitch, but now I'm somebody else's bitch!" replied André with an eyebrow arched and rolling his neck like a 14-year-old girl. "But I do gotta knock some of these pounds off though, cause, honey, I got a new reality show comin' out on Bravo this year!"

"What? Congratulations, André!" all the ladies said in unison.

"Yes, honey, gonna be the hottest thing on TV!" André explained as he walked the ladies to the back of the salon into his private room, where three more silver chairs lined the wall.

"Do you have a title for it yet?" asked Carla.

"Yes, of course. It's gonna be called 'Unbeweavable!' Honey, I'm gonna go all around this country on a crusade tryin' to save women with bad weaves!" André said, laughing along with the girls.

"Ms. Valerie, are you finally gone let me put some perm on that dry little TWA?"

"Don't start with me, André!" Valerie snapped back.

"Oh, fine. I'm gone start with Ms. Nia today anyway. Come on, Ms. Nia, and have a seat. Come on, girl, hustle. You know time is money. There's water and champagne in my little fridge in the corner. Help yourselves. So, how they treatin' you in the White House, girl?" André asked.

"Life is hectic, but good."

"So what's it like? Girl, you're not just a Black person dealin' with all those pompous, little white men, you a sista too…I don't know how you do it."

"Everybody is pretty fair, or *almost* everybody," Nia said with a devilish grin.

"Almost? I know they givin' you hell, girl! But they messin' wit the wrong sista! A *diva*, honey!" André said with his lips turned up.

"André, you know I can handle myself," Nia replied with a snicker.

"I know…but, girl, I don't know how you do it. What y'all really need in the White House is a real *queen* like me callin' out all those closet freaks workin' in there…I know it's a bunch of undercover drag queens runnin' around in there, honey. I'll put 'em in they place!" André said boisterously, as he whirled around Nia effortlessly snipping away at her hair in his skinny jeans with the sleek, red soles of his pony-print Louboutin pumps flashing with every step. The ladies laughed hysterically. When André cut hair it was also like a performance.

"So, Ms. Nia, please explain to me what is really going on with the economy? I can't have folks out of work doin' they hair in they kitchen," André fussed as he shook his head. "Just what the hell is the problem?"

"Ugh, not you too?" Nia rolled her eyes.

"No, honey, I'm not complaining. I know y'all got a lot on your hands. I know y'all walked into a mess."

"Thank you," Nia huffed. "People have no idea what President Davis had to deal with as soon as he entered office. And one of those things that people completely overlook is the fact that this is the first presidency that has to contend with a global economy. That's probably the biggest underlying issue."

"That's right. The Internet has changed the world," Valerie chimed in.

"Exactly. We are truly one big economy and when he entered office the entire world was impacted by it."

"Honey, you know I hate that damn Internet. I tell people all the time it ain't nothing but the devil," André complained. Nia chuckled in a patronizing manner.

"No, I'm serious, girl. Think about it. The Internet is infinite and uncontrollable. You can laugh if you want to, but I'm telling you it ain't nothin' but the devil."

"Well then why are you on Twitter, André?" Carla asked, oozing with sarcasm, provoking a thunderous laugh from André.

"Oh, you just shut up, you little heffa you," André snapped back with a giggle.

"I've got you, André. I see where you're going," Nia smiled.

"Speaking of hate, girl, why are they so damn *hateful* of President Davis? Oh, wait, honey, I don't even know why I asked you that question, because I already know the answer. They just so *prejudice*," André said smacking his lips as he twirled his neck in disdain.

"André, you have no idea. President Davis receives more death threats and hate mail than any president in the history of this country. Actually, he receives three times as much hate mail as any president has ever received," Nia said and then took a deep breath.

"Girl, that is so sad," André responded. "You just be careful, Ms. Nia. Just be careful."

"Oh, don't worry I am, André."

As André continued to snip away at Nia's hair, the other three ladies sat scanning through a myriad of women's magazines, which lay spread neatly across a stylish glass coffee table, and then Valerie said, "You really did this place up, André."

"Thanks, girl. It's all about the ambiance, honey. I got some ideas from that cute, little Nate Berkus, honey. You ever checked that show out?"

"No, I can't say that I have. I rarely get a chance to watch television."

"I bet I know why you watch it, André," Beverly grinned.

"Oh, honey, yes, he *is* fine, but his show is so good. If you ever need decorating ideas you need to check it out. He has some really good tips. And I found some great thrift shops around here. You ever checked out 'Thrifty Interior' on the Eastside? Oh, girl I keep forgetting you're not from Atlanta."

"Nope. Now, you can find some really nice thrift shops in Chicago."

"Child, please. Y'all don't know real style in the Chi."

"Oh, we know style in Chicago, André."

"Nah, I know Chicago is pretty trendy, but it can't mess with the ATL. What part of Chi did you grow up on, Nia?"

"I grew up on the Southside, but went to a high school just west of downtown, Whitney Young High School."

"Honey, I know the Southside. I used to date a guy that lived right off 79th and Cottage Grove," André explained. "Nothin' but a brute…a little thug."

"I thought you liked the thug type, André?" asked Carla.

"I used to, but he was just too *rough*, honey. Knuckles all bruised up and ashy from fightin'. Plus he was broke! Now I just date RICH men with *soft*, manicured hands. Are you familiar with that 79th Street area, Nia?"

"Yes, my grandmother lived not too far from that area. And *by the way*, she and my mom were actually originally from Atlanta," Nia smiled and then gave a slight roll of her neck.

"Emph. Is that right? Now just how did you meet these three heffas?" asked André with a giggle.

"Well, Val and I grew up together on the Southside. As a matter of fact, we actually met just a few blocks down from 79th and State in a little store-front church on 79th and Union called Abundant Gift of Love, Fellowship, and Worship Church. Val's mom was our Sunday school teacher. Uh, she was *so* strict."

"Are you serious? Girl, I know where you're talkin' about and I don't know if you been back in a while, but that ain't no little storefront church no more."

"I knowww. I can't believe what they've done to it. It's beautiful."

"Now what about those two hookers," André asked pointing the comb he was clutching in the direction of Beverly and Carla.

"Oh, I met Bev and Carla in undergrad at Spellman," Nia responded.

"Yes, I remember when we first met Nia. She was so damn serious," said Carla.

"I was just focused—my grandmother didn't play. I had to produce, and Carla, you hit the campus partying." Nia laughed.

"I still got the grades though. My parents didn't play either. You don't understand; I couldn't do anything when I was growing up. No boyfriends, and I don't just mean boyfriends as in dating either—I mean no male friends, period. But trust me, I still managed to have a few daylight rendezvous when they were at work though. So by the time I got to college, I was all about having a good time."

"Well, my grandmother was strict as far as grades, but she gave us free-dom. But let me tell you, that freedom came with a price…responsibility. If I couldn't handle what she felt was important—which pretty much meant doing *everything* around the house and maintaining straight As—she would shut us down in a heartbeat. So I just learned to handle a lot at one time and not play games with my time."

"Now if you want to talk about culture and style," Valerie commented, "Chicago was it! Hyde Park, 87th Street, downtown, Garrett's Popcorn, Giordano's Pizza…you guys have no idea."

"But notice she came down to Spellman to have some *real* fun," joked Carla.

"And that was the only mistake Nia made. She should have gone to Howard with me," Valerie snapped back, laughing.

"I thought Chicago was so ghetto when I used to visit," said André.

"Just like any other big city, it has its bad areas," Valerie answered, "and I must admit the gangs were pretty bad too, but it was just such an eclectic mix of people. Black folks in Chicago were just on top of their game long before Atlanta was popular. I think we had more great black entrepreneurs come from the Southside during the 70s and 80s than anywhere in the country.

Companies like Johnson Publishing were founded in Chicago. And remember, *Ebony* and *Jet* were *the* black magazines during the 70s and 80s. And we went to school with these great business people's children."

"It's true. I wouldn't trade growing up in Chicago for nothing in the world," added Nia.

"Come on, sit your little narrow bourgeoisie butt down, Ms. Carla. It's your turn. Wait a minute, before you sit your little self down, turn around and let me see you. Look at that little booty! Oh my goodness, you need to get some meat on those frail bones. Now what made you pick Spellman, Ms. Nia?" asked André.

"I picked Spellman primarily because it was my mom's alma mater. Don't get me wrong, I love Atlanta and it's like home too."

"And, Val, you missed out on all the fun we had," said Carla.

"Oh, Howard was way more fun and much more progressive than Spellman," Valerie replied.

"She's just saying that 'cause she got to work at BET while she was there," Carla snapped back.

"Oh, that's right, you did work for BET. I bet that was fun. What'd you do there?" André asked.

"And you know she got to the top by sleeping with Diddy when he was at Howard with her," joked Carla.

"Diddy wishes he could have got with me. And he wasn't even there when I was there. You are so silly," Valerie replied, rolling her eyes with a smile. "And to answer your question André, I was their chief marketing officer."

"Why'd you ever leave?" André asked.

"I left because they were going in a different direction than I was."

"Tell the truth, you had to be disgusted that you didn't get the CEO position when Bob Johnson left?" asked Carla.

"No, I actually like the direction they're going now versus when I was there, but it was just time for me to leave."

"So how's your ad firm going?" André asked.

"Well—"

"Honey, I need you to do some marketing stuff for me," André interrupted Valerie.

"So what new projects are you working on, Val?" asked Nia, trying to fill the momentary silence, as Valerie ignored André's request for marketing assistance.

"I actually just picked up the WNBA. Did you know they had a black woman as their new president? We both came up together in New York's marketing scene. We did a ton of pro bono work together back in New York. When she landed the job she gave me a call right away."

"Oh, that sounds interesting," replied Nia.

"Now we gotta talk about who's doin' you girls' hair…ugh…I ain't Houdini, damn it. I can't keep workin' magic like this. We need to find a way for me to do y'all hair more often. And is Craig still doin' the First Lady's hair?"

"Yes, to my knowledge he is," Nia replied.

"I'm not going to bad mouth him, 'cause he does a pretty good job. She always has herself together…always looks so pretty. But you let her know, if she ever wants to step her hair game up…tell her call me!"

Chapter 12

AFTER A REFRESHING WEEKEND WITH THE GIRLS, NIA FELT PHYSI-
cally revived, but internally her thoughts continued to roil with *the big offer*. The dilemma had gone on far too long. It was out of her character to let
something sit this long without making a decision. Nia always believed that
life and business were all about making decisions—whether easy or difficult.
As she drove down Pennsylvania Avenue in her shiny new silver BMW 1
Series M Coupe and approached the White House, she couldn't take it anymore.

*Just to be clear and to keep my name out of this, I better call Jimmy right now
and let him know that I'm not interested in his offer*, Nia thought.

She called Jimmy but got his voicemail. As she listened to his greeting she
thought, *I don't need to incriminate myself in any way. I need to be clear that
I'm not interested, but very vague about the details.*

"Hello, Congressman, this is Nia. I just wanted to be *very* clear. I am *not*..."
As Nia began to leave a message on Jimmy's voicemail she heard a click. It was
Jimmy calling her back.

Shoot! I shouldn't even answer this. Oh, forget it. "Hello."

"Hi, Nia, I saw that you just called."

"I was actually leaving you a voice message when you called."

"What's up?"

"Jimmy, I just wanted to give you a call to clarify that I am not interested in
any kind of job offer or any other sort of offer." Nia felt a sense of relief.

"No problem." It seemed like Jimmy had heard nothing she had just said.
"Are you coming to the *DC Post*'s event tonight?"

"Yes, I'll be there. Tanner desperately wants me to attend for some reason."

"Great! I'm co-hosting the event, and so is the Klein Schultz lobbyist Ethan
Miller I've been telling you about."

Did he hear anything I just said? "I had no idea that you or *this* lobbyist was
involved." Nia's posture folded. She slumped down in her car seat and shook
her head. "Well, I guess I'll see you and this lobbyist there, but, like I said, I'm
not interested in any kind of offer."

Jimmy, once again, completely ignored Nia's statement. "Great! We're having the finest caterers in the DC area to cater the event. And of course, the
finest wine. It's going to be a blast! I look forward to seeing you tonight, Nia!"
Jimmy said, as giddy as a kid on the eve of Christmas.

When Tanner had asked Nia to attend the *DC Post* event, she'd had no
idea that it was going to be co-hosted by Jimmy. She couldn't believe that this

never-dying ethical dilemma was back. Just like any difficult decision, a simple yes or no is rarely the solution.

⌒

That evening, Nia and Terrence chatted as the GPS system in Terrence's behemoth all-black 2009 Infinity QX56 SUV guided them down George Washington Memorial Parkway alongside the Potomac River en route to the *DC Post*'s event. The event was being held at the home of the *DC Post*'s owner Stan Wagner. The *DC Post* was the largest and most powerful newspaper in the DC area. Wagner's home was in McLean, Virginia, which was located on the other side of the Potomac about 25 minutes from the White House and just 20 minutes from Nia's apartment in Georgetown. As a result, McLean was also home to numerous high-ranking government officials and diplomats.

"Thanks for coming with me, sweetie…I just want to make a quick appearance…maybe stay for 30 minutes or so, and then we can leave. Did I tell you that this event is being co-hosted by Jimmy and that lobbyist that he's been trying to connect me with?" asked Nia.

"No, that's great news. I can't wait to meet this guy," Terrence responded, eyes wide.

"Good news…are you kidding? I was trying to shut that whole situation down, but it just doesn't seem to want to go away," said Nia shaking her head.

Nia and Terrence finally arrived at the Wagner Estate. They pulled up to a small gatekeeper's booth which sat at the entrance of the estate. They gave their names to the guardhouse attendant and were admitted to the estate grounds.

Terrence and Nia slowly ascended the estate's winding cobblestone road, which was lined by trees. As the path continued to curve the large estate eventually came into full view. The two were a bit surprised by the sheer size and magnificence of the home.

"Look at this home! It makes the houses on 'MTV Cribs' look tiny. What would you say it's worth…eight, maybe 10 million dollars?" Terrence commented with excitement in his eyes.

A large water fountain sat in front of the home, surrounded by a circular path that led to the home's front entrance.

"It is beautiful…but let's just get in and get out," Nia said, uninterested in the fabulousness of Wagner's massive home. After Terrence maneuvered his SUV around the fountain and reached the entrance, a valet attendant took their keys and directed them to the home's entryway. As soon as the two strolled through the two oversized doors and entered the 19,000-square-foot home, they were immediately greeted by Jimmy Coleman Jr.

"Hi, Nia! Thanks for coming," Jimmy said eagerly, giving Nia a warm hug.

"Hi, Congressman. You've met my fiancé Terrence."

"Sure, I remember Terrence. Good to see you, big guy," said Jimmy.

"Good to see you, Jimmy," responded Terrence as he shook Jimmy's hand and gawked at the large, brightly glistening chandelier which dangled overhead. The chandelier perfectly complimented the all-white foyer which was elegantly lined in gold trim.

"I've got some people that I'd like for you to meet, Nia," said Jimmy anxiously as he whisked Nia and Terrence away from the foyer area down a long hallway. At the end of the hallway they reached a large crowded room with a 16-foot cathedral ceiling. There Jimmy introduced Nia and Terrence to Stan Wagner, the owner of the *DC Post*.

Stan Wagner was one of the most powerful men in the Washington area. He had amassed his billions through a variety of successful online media companies. The short, balding billionaire was soft spoken, but flat-out uppity.

"Stan, I'd like for you to meet Nia Taylor, deputy chief of staff, and her fiancé Terrence Richardson."

"Hello. Thank you for coming," Stan said as he provided a limp hand in response to Terrence's outstretched hand. "I've heard a lot about you, Ms. Taylor," Stan said to Nia in a snobbish tone.

"Hopefully all good things, Mr. Wagner. Likewise, I've heard a lot about you, as well," Nia responded with a smile, as Stan lifelessly shook Terrence's hand.

"Nice to meet you, Stan. I'm with McLoughlin and McLoughlin law firm," Terrence said in a serious tone, as he whipped out his business card with his chest poked out, just falling short of saying *bam*!

"How nice." Stan sighed with a blank expression, as he accepted Terrence's business card and tucked it away in his pocket without so much as glancing at it.

"I noticed that you have 18 holes out back. You must be quite a golfer?" Terrence asked.

"I'm not too bad," Stan once again responded curtly.

"I'd love to hit a few balls with you someday and tell you more about McLoughlin and McLoughlin," Terrence said with a gleam in his eye.

"Yeah, sure...I have your card," Stan responded without making any eye contact with Terrence, and then quickly turned away to speak with other guests.

Jimmy pulled Nia and Terrence away and took them to the other side of the room. He approached a thin young man with blond hair, sporting a conservative blue suit, who stood talking with two other young men who looked like college students.

"Nia, this is Ethan Miller, the lobbyist that I've been telling you so much about." Jimmy introduced the lobbyist to Nia, grinning from ear to ear. Nia and Terrence were surprised that the lobbyist looked so young. He barely had peach fuzz on his chin.

"Nia, I've been dying to meet you. Everyone has so many wonderful things to say about you. We have a lot to talk about."

Nia took a deep breath and sighed quietly. Meanwhile, Terrence was beaming.

"Please let me show you around Stan's house. I'm sure he won't mind," Ethan said as he began to escort Nia and Terrence through the home.

"Let's stop in his study. This is the perfect place to get a little privacy," said Ethan as he opened the door to the large study. The entire room was crafted with the finest cherry wood: the floors, the shelving—which was built into the walls—the paneling, and of course, the desk and chairs.

"Nia, I know Jimmy has filled you in on what we're trying to accomplish here," Ethan said.

"Yes, he told me a little bit about what you're trying to achieve," Nia responded.

"Well, the first thing that I want to explain is that Klein Schultz thinks that you are an incredible talent. They flat-out think that you'd make a tremendous CEO for an organization. That being said, I know that you're familiar with the legislation that they're trying to prevent. It's simple, nothing complicated or harmful. The privacy issue is just one that can drastically hinder earnings," the young blond-haired lobbyist explained with the precision of a veteran lobbyist. "We'd like for you to be on our side with this issue and also help President Davis understand our view. And Nia, more importantly, they'd also be interested in discussing the opening for CEO at Rothschild and Smith Financial."

Nia sat shocked at his forwardness. The last thing she had expected him to do was hit her with the CEO position so quickly.

"You did an excellent job there as a vice president and you are very familiar with the organization. This, coupled with the experience that you've gained as deputy chief makes you an ideal fit."

"What kind of salary are we talking about?" asked Terrence, as Nia gave him a sharp nudge in his side.

"I would have to guess that, all together, the first year's total income would be in the neighborhood of 20 to 30 million dollars. That's, of course, including a healthy signing bonus. There may also be stock options that could possibly run that total up significantly to as much as 40 million."

As Ethan explained nonchalantly Nia and Terrence sat in disbelief. Although Nia was used to being around others with enormous wealth and had made a wonderful living herself, she'd never anticipated an offer of this magnitude at this stage of her career. The numbers she had just heard were staggering. Her mind raced with thoughts.

As much as 40 million the first year! This is crazy! After just one year I'd be set for life. After three or four years I could be sitting on 100 million dollars. There's so much that I could do to help my grandmother and brother with that kind of money. And I know I'd be successful because I know Rothschild and Smith Financial better than anyone. Oh, Nia, come down. You still haven't heard from anyone over at Rothschild and Smith Financial. How do you know this offer is legitimate? Nia thought.

"Now, they know that President Davis's term has a ways to go, but Rothschild and Smith Financial need someone now with Andy's upcoming retirement. So, their offer would be for the very near future," Ethan said calmly. "So does this offer sound of interest to you, Nia?"

"I think that's an outstanding offer, Ethan! What about a chauffeur and limousine, and maybe a private jet?" Terrence interjected. "That's pretty common these days for CEOs of Fortune 500 companies." Terrence was so excited he could barely contain himself. As he eagerly spouted off a series of questions, Nia gave him a cold stare.

"Anything is negotiable, Terrence," Ethan answered with a cocky smirk. "In the meantime, the key is for us to continue to build a relationship and work on this legislation together. Nia, I've got someone I'd like for you to meet."

Ethan then slipped his cell phone from his belt clip and made a call. "Send him in," he said, as Nia and Terrence sat clearly overwhelmed by the meeting.

When the door to the wood-paneled room opened, their jaws dropped. As the average-looking, slightly balding man entered the room, Nia was speechless. She couldn't remember the last time she was at a loss for words, but after the man in his mid-50s stepped into full view and she was able to clearly identify him, she became completely dumbstruck. It was a surreal moment. Not because she was in awe of who was standing in front her—after all, her boss *was* the President of the United States—but because his presence cleared any doubt about the validity of this implausible offer.

"Nia, I'd like to introduce you to Paul Hansen," the lobbyist said.

She could hear the words coming out of the lobbyist's mouth, but it seemed like a dream, or perhaps a nightmare.

I can't believe Paul Hansen is actually here to meet with me, this thing just became serious.

"Hi, Nia, it's a pleasure to meet you," Hansen said.

"Likewise, it's a pleasure to meet you, as well."

"I can't tell you how impressed I am with your career. Nia, you have quite a future ahead of yourself."

"Why thank you, Paul. I just try to work hard and earn my keep," Nia replied with a humble smile.

"Well, whatever your formula, from what I've been hearing you're a hot commodity. That being said, my friends over at Rothschild and Smith Financial are very interested in you. And I'm sure by now you've heard that Andy's stepping down."

Nia nodded.

"Nia, if you do decide to move back to the private job sector, and maybe even as Rothschild and Smith Financial's new CEO, feel free to call me. I've got a little bit of experience in the financial world and could probably give you some decent guidance," Hansen said, flashing a captivating smile. He handed Nia a business card and left.

Nia took Hansen's card and mentally sought to find a place in her purse where she knew it wouldn't be misplaced.

After Hansen left the room the lobbyist immediately moved in again. "Nia, so what are your thoughts?" Ethan asked.

"Wow, this has been quite an interesting conversation," Nia began, but was cut short.

"I'm glad we have your attention, but there's one more person I'd like for you to meet."

Just as Nia had begun to compose herself from the lobbyist's first guest, he again gave a jolt to her equilibrium. Ethan, once again, slid his cell phone from the case that was attached to his belt. "Send him in."

The anticipation was killing Nia. She had already been wooed by the most powerful man in the financial world. Who else could they possibly throw at her?

As the large wooden door began to open, Terrence inconspicuously squeezed Nia's hand in excitement. The moment Nia saw the tip of the gentleman's nose, she knew who it was. Her heart sank. It was her ex-boss and the present Rothschild and Smith Financial CEO, Andy Muller.

"Andy, what a pleasant surprise," Nia said.

Nia immediately rose and the two shared a warm hug.

"Nia, how are you?"

"Well, Andy. How are you?" Nia asked in a sincere tone.

"Better. Much better."

"I'm so happy to hear that," Nia replied, gripping her ex-boss's hand firmly.

"So I'm sure Ethan has shared that I'm moving on, Nia."

"He did."

"So, that means Rothschild and Smith Financial is in search of a new leader. Nia, I think you'd be an ideal fit."

"Well that's quite a compliment, Andy."

"And to tell you the truth, I wasn't thinking about a replacement. I've kind of been in my own little world over the last few months. Your name had been thrown around while I was out, and of course when I heard, I endorsed the idea 100 percent."

"I'm flattered, Andy, but…"

"I told them it wasn't going to be an easy sell. Well, I'm not here to sell you, Nia. I just stopped by to say hello and give you my vote of confidence."

"Andy, I'm so glad you did. It's so wonderful to see you."

"Same here. Nia, don't make a rash decision and turn the offer down without really thinking it through. Take your time to think about it. It'll be a few months before I step down. Take your time and think about it, but at least come meet with us at Rothschild and Smith Financial to hear us out. If you still decide you're not interested, we'll understand. Just give me a call when you have time to meet," Andy said.

"Will do, Andy," Nia replied with a warm smile.

↬

The ride home that night seemed like an eternity for Nia. Terrence couldn't stop talking about *the big offer*. His constant chatter only added to Nia's already overwhelming internal turmoil and deep reflection on the proposition. She felt like she had made the correct *strategic* decision by politely fending off Ethan's feverous pitch earlier that evening, but it was a tricky situation and a draining experience.

The precondition accompanying *the offer* made Nia feel like she would have possibly been putting herself in harm's way if she had openly entertained it. Yet, she also knew it was important not to offend Hansen and the financial world.

This is truly a Catch 22 situation and I wish Terrence would just shut up already! He's only making this worse.

"Forty million dollars…I can't believe it! How can you pass that up?"

"Terrence, please don't start talking about that damn *offer*."

"Why not? You're going to have to deal with it and make a decision sooner or later, Nia."

"My goodness, we just left the party."

"Yeah, but you don't want them to move on to the next candidate."

"My goodness, Terrence, we just left."

"Yeah, but they move fast. Look at how fast they've been moving thus far," Terrence responded, but was met with a deaf ear. "Nia, they brought in *Paul Hansen* to recruit you! Who brings in the top financial guy in the world to recruit somebody? Who does that?"

Yes, he's right…who does that?

"Yeah, it makes you wonder what their motives are."

"Motive—the motive is landing a highly qualified CEO. That's the motive."

"If there wasn't a motive, Terrence, they wouldn't have added that precondition, and I don't think that's their only motive. There's more to it."

"Oh my God, Nia, you always overthink things! Why can't they just be interested in you?"

"Because they want something in return."

"Everybody does in Washington. That's politics. It's an incredible offer and you'd be crazy to not at least consider it."

It is an amazing offer.

"Paul Hansen used to be our U.S. treasurer. You think he didn't have to deal with conditions? That's just the way they do business at that level. You know that, Nia," Terrence said, shaking his head.

He's got a point.

"Your lifelong dream is right in front of you, but it just comes with way more money than you expected. And all you have to do is accept it."

"You know it's not that simple."

"Why isn't it? Just go meet with Rothschild and Smith Financial and weigh all of your options."

I guess that wouldn't hurt, Nia thought.

"Alright, I didn't want to bring this up, but…"

"But what?" Nia asked.

"You know what I'm about to say."

"I know and I can't believe you'd bring that up!"

"Nia, don't get mad. I just want you to be realistic about this, and the reality is you have to think about what this would do for your family," Terrence said, shooting an intense glare at Nia.

"Pay attention to the road, Terrence. And that has nothing to do with this and I can't believe you'd go there."

"What do you mean? I know you hate to talk about it, but it's just the reality that we have to deal with. Your brother has needs and your grandma has a lot on her plate."

"Do you think I don't realize that? And you don't think I immediately thought about that when they made the offer? Of course I did!"

"Just think about all the bills from Eric's surgeries and your grandma's chemo treatments. Plus, she needs more help with him, Nia. This opportunity might be sent straight from heaven."

"Don't say that, Terrence. I don't know. I did think about how much I could do for them."

"I know it's been difficult for you ever since the accident…to see your brother in that wheelchair, and of course, losing your mom. And you've done a phenomenal job taking care of them, and Eric has become really independent, but like I said, they both still have *lots* of needs. This opportunity could take care of them both for the *rest* of their *lives*."

"I know. It would mean so much to me to know that they would be taken care of for the rest of their lives, but it's not that simple."

"It is and I hated to bring it up, but I had to do it. I love you too much not to and I know how much they mean to you."

"I don't know," Nia responded, as her eyes began to tear up. Terrence clutched her hand, resting it on the SUV's center console.

"Just face it, it's a blessing, and you can't always try to understand God's blessings, you just have to accept them and be thankful."

Chapter 13

"I'M SO BURNED OUT. I FEEL LIKE I'M RUNNING IN PLACE. I HAVE TO get more organized," Nia explained to her counterpart deputy chief of staff Gregory Connors in her office.

As days passed, the combination of the stresses of the West Wing coupled with Rothschild and Smith's *big offer,* which persistently continued to lurk in the shadows of Nia's mind, caused her to reach burnout.

In the midst of Nia's venting session with Gregory, White House intern Heather Kelly entered her office with another new young intern, Maria Lopez.

"Nia, you just need to find something to take your mind off this mayhem. You just need to come get a good workout with us after work," Heather said, with Maria nodding in agreement.

"Ladies, I wish it was that simple."

"Nia, do you remember Maria? She's one of the newer interns," Heather explained. Maria had just recently been brought on board as an intern. White House staff generally didn't have much time to mingle with interns. Most internships required long hours and bearing much of the grunt work, but Heather was Tanner's favorite. As a result, she had gotten to know Nia and the rest of the staff fairly well.

"Hi, Maria, hopefully things are going well for you," Nia said, shaking the young woman's hand firmly.

"Nia, like I said, I think you just need something to clear your head of this mayhem and exercise will force you to do that. When you're trying to keep a 100-pound weight from slamming down on your chest, your mind will clear itself pretty quickly," Heather said with a chuckle.

"Nia and a 100-pound weight…really?" Gregory joked.

"Be quiet, Greg," Nia fired back.

"We try to sneak in a workout at least four days a week."

"Did you tell her you were a certified personal trainer, Heather?" Maria asked.

"No, she didn't," Gregory interjected. "I'm impressed. Now I may want come."

"Oh, please, Greg. The first thing you need to do is trash that big box of Twinkies you have hidden in your lower left drawer." Nia laughed.

"Have you been going through my desk, Ms. Taylor?"

"Yes, I've been certified for a while now," Heather said.

"She used to compete, too. How many national titles did you win?" Maria asked.

NIA TAYLOR: WHITE HOUSE MEMOIRS

65

"I've won a few fitness titles."

"Wow, fitness titles? Damn, that's impressive. Those women are cut. Maybe I will hit the health club with you guys," said Greg.

I could stand to tighten up this big butt of mine and could definitely use some cardio. "Oh, calm down, Gregory. You just head home to your wife and kids. Chasing them around is enough exercise for you. Well, Ms. Kelly, you just sold me. I think I may take you up on that offer."

"We work out at the Fitness World a few blocks away. We'd love to have you join us."

"I just might join you guys tomorrow. I desperately need to release some stress before I lose it and ring Greg's neck one day," Nia joked, eliciting a chuckle from the two young women.

⌣

The following evening Nia joined the interns for a workout at the 24-hour fitness club Fitness World. It had been years since she'd actually been in a health club, so she was already a bit apprehensive, but once she saw the two young interns in their workout gear, she immediately felt uncomfortable. The two young women were in phenomenal shape. Although everyone around the White House believed that Heather's size 32 double D breasts were the result of a breast enhancement surgery, she was the classic tall, beautiful, busty, blue-eyed, All-American blonde and packed with lean muscle. The men in the White House drooled when she passed by. Many of them secretly referred to her as the *White House Clydesdale*.

Maria was also in excellent condition. The Georgetown student had played tennis for her school's team prior to entering the White House internship program. Her many years of tennis had created thick, toned legs and a full, perfectly round butt, which the male staffers often gawked at as she breezed past them in the West Wing.

The awkwardness Nia initially felt quickly faded once her competitive spirit kicked in. Nia hated to lose at anything, so she took everything she did seriously and was always committed. Her new-found interest in working out was no exception. She also found it to be therapeutic. Before long, she was hooked on fitness and the two interns had landed themselves a regular training partner.

The three ladies would squeeze in workouts whenever possible. Due to the demands of the White House, they would often find themselves at Fitness World in the wee hours of the morning. In doing so, they became very close. In many ways, Nia became like a mentor to the young women, providing guidance on every subject from careers to men. These late night workouts didn't always sit well with Terrence, so Nia even convinced him to join them. Although he didn't attend all of their workout sessions, his periodic attendance eased much of the tension that this new activity had created between the two.

Chapter 14

"THIS BETTER BE GOOD!" BILLIONAIRE ALEX STRAUS GREETED WELL-known political strategist Bill Adler and his two protégés from the head of a large conference table in a private meeting room at the luxurious Ritz-Carlton Hotel across from Central Park.

Bill answered proudly, flapping a thin booklet of paper in his hand, "Trust me, we've woven the best plan possible! This is what was missed in the last election."

"Well, hand it over," Straus ordered. Bill handed four copies of the booklet, titled "The Blueprint: Dethrone the Commander in Chief," to the billionaire and his three executives who sat alongside him.

"I hope you brought enough copies because almost everybody is coming today."

"Of course."

The political strategist opened his laptop on the conference table and connected it to the projector in preparation of unleashing what he thought was an ingenious promotional plan to oust the current president. Meanwhile, Alex Straus impatiently thumbed through the plan as he awaited the arrival of the rest of the members. He was impatient for a good reason. Alex was presumably about to invest millions of dollars in Bill's plan, but it wasn't the money that would be at stake that had the billionaire so worried—the thought of the plan failing was what had cost the wealthy businessman countless sleepless nights ever since President Davis took office. In many ways he had blamed himself for the Republicans' defeat in the last presidential election, feeling as if he hadn't done enough. But he was even more disgusted with the citizens of the country for voting the man into office to begin with.

Over the last decade, Alex Straus and his family-owned business had acquired billions in the investment industry, but when they launched the online discount brokerage e-Investments.com, his riches had expanded into the stratosphere. Although he had reached the top of the heap in the business world, even attaining a top 100 spot on Forbes' Richest list, his deep-seated hatred for the current president would not allow him to enjoy his fortune peacefully. So, instead of just providing financial support to the next Republican presidential candidate, he had decided to take matters into his own hands.

The affluent 71-year-old businessman had formed "Recapture Our Excellence," a new independent-expenditure–only committee, more commonly referred to as a super PAC. He had formed political action committees in the past, but thanks to two recent Supreme Court rulings, he and his newly formed group could now spend an *unlimited* amount of funds to independently campaign for the candidate of their choice. The rulings were monumental and had significantly changed the dynamics of campaigning.

Straus was so determined to influence the next presidential election, he didn't stop with just forming a powerful super PAC, which included other millionaires and billionaires; he had *personally* handcrafted a meticulous plan to oust President Davis. But he knew he would need someone with more expertise to hone his plan, and Bill Adler had been at the top of his list.

Bill Adler had been a successful political strategist for more than two decades, consulting for a long list of past presidents and presidential hopefuls. Nevertheless, he had failed woefully in the last election with the current president trouncing his client at the voting booths. Adler blamed his client, the opposing presidential candidate, for the loss. He claimed his client had refused to use a similar plan in that election, but Adler was determined to gain the appropriate backing and support to win this time around, or maybe even oust President Davis before the election season even arrived.

After Bill's laptop was fired up, he was eager to explain. "Okay, I'll just start by explaining the plan to you guys…"

"Hold on, Bill. Let's wait 'til everyone has arrived. No need for you to explain twice."

"Alright. I'm just anxious to explain exactly how we're going to take his arrogant little ass down."

Chapter 15

ALTHOUGH NIA'S NEW ADDICTION TO FITNESS HAD EASED SOME OF her tension, it didn't erase all of her problems. The *offer* continued to torment her. The conversations she'd had with ex-Klein Schultz CEO Paul Hansen and soon to be ex-Rothschild and Smith Financial CEO Andy Muller at the *DC Post* event played over and over again in her head. It was a very enticing offer. Nia also knew that eventually she'd have to move back to the private job sector and Paul Hansen and his cohorts would likely determine her job future, so completely snubbing the offer to be Rothschild and Smith Financial's new CEO by not at least meeting with them could come back to haunt her someday. Plus, she felt obligated to hear her ex-boss Andy out.

That's it; it couldn't hurt to meet with Rothschild and Smith and hear them out. Anyway, I almost have to meet with them to see what they're talking about, so I won't insult them.

Nia had convinced herself. She phoned Andy and set up the meeting.

Chapter 16

ONE BY ONE, MEMBERS OF STRAUS'S POWERFUL NEWLY ASSEMBLED super PAC filed into the Ritz-Carlton's private meeting room. Each member possessed deep pockets. Millionaires and even billionaires had flown in for the meeting with checkbook in hand.

Straus worked the room. He was somewhat charismatic, or at least he thought so, and no matter how many millionaires, or even billionaires, filled the room, he always considered himself the leader.

"I tell you, Jim, this country's falling apart," Straus vehemently expressed to fellow billionaire Kevin Finch. "What the hell were the American people thinking when they stepped into the voting booth two years ago? That's alright; if it's the last thing I do, we're going to fix this problem. We're going to take *our* country back."

The grey-haired billionaire diligently touched each person in the room, sharing his views one by one. In total, 25 billionaires were in attendance that day and Straus also had the support of eight more who were unable to attend. "Recapture Our Excellence" was truly a *super* PAC.

After thoroughly working the room, Straus had come full circle and stood beside Adler, firmly clutching his shoulder.

"Alex, I really think we can pull this off," Bill Adler told the billionaire.

"No, Bill, we *will* pull this off," Straus replied confidently. "And here comes our assurance. The troops have arrived." Just then, a drove of U.S. Congressmen flooded into the room—55 in total.

Chapter 17

NIA SAT RESTLESSLY ON A LARGE WRAP-AROUND COUCH IN THE BACK of a stretch limousine, which was en route to Rothschild and Smith Financial. She tried to prepare herself by going over every potential scenario in her mind.

If I know Andy, once he gets me in his home court, he'll go for the jugular and make a formal offer. I wonder how much they'll offer. And how soon would they want me to start? Nia shook her head. *What am I thinking? I can't take this job and I for damn sure am not going to take it with any sort of precondition.*

The Rothschild and Smith Financial headquarters came into Nia's view. The limousine swung around the circular driveway and arrived at the entrance. The driver opened the rear door of the limousine and Nia emerged from the massive luxury vehicle in her favorite pair of all-black Prada sunglasses, which fought off the blazing morning sunlight.

It's like déjà vu. I remember the day I first arrived here as an intern, Nia thought, as she strolled up to the building's entrance.

"Ms. Taylor, Mr. Muller has been expecting you. I'll have his assistant come right down," the receptionist greeted Nia.

As Nia rode up the elevator en route to Andy Muller's office, her mind raced with the possibilities. When she stepped out into the lobby of the floor which housed Rothschild and Smith's senior management team, she immediately noticed that a major renovation had been done. This level had always been posh and possessed a rich look and feel, but Rothschild and Smith had clearly stepped things up in the luxury department.

Nia carefully navigated the lobby area's glassy white marble floors, which matched the all-white décor. The only things that weren't white in the senior management lobby were the polished metal desk the receptionist was seated behind and the purple and red shield adorning Rothschild and Smith Financial's logo, which was neatly centered on the wall behind the receptionist.

As Nia followed Andy's assistant down a long corridor lined with a string of large offices, she noticed the assistant had passed Andy's office.

"Excuse me, but didn't we just pass Andy Muller's office?"

"Yes, Ms. Taylor. Your meeting was scheduled for one of our conference rooms, which is just around this corner."

They finally arrived at the conference room—which Nia wasn't readily familiar with—and proceeded to enter. When Nia entered the room, she was startled to see so many faces.

Chapter 18

THE PRIVATE ROOM IN THE RITZ-CARLTON REEKED OF WEALTH AND power. An ominous energy was present as the group mingled. Straus huffed and then glanced at his watch anxiously.

"Where the hell are they at? We have to get started! That's it, I'm just going to go ahead and get this thing going." The tall, grey-haired billionaire lumbered to the head of the conference table located at the center of the room.

Straus then began to kick off the meeting. "Good afternoon, ladies and gentlemen. Well, they screwed this thing up four years ago..." Straus bellowed to the large group, causing Adler to wince a bit as the billionaire mentioned his previous client's defeat.

"But we're not going to let that happen this time. We're going to *Recapture Our Excellence!*" Straus raised his voice even louder and then thrust his glass high into the air, causing his audience to do the same. The room rumbled. As Straus continued his kick-off speech, a handsome young gentleman burst into the room. The crowd's attention quickly shifted in his direction and silence filled the room.

Chapter 19

"I'M SO GLAD YOU COULD MAKE IT," ROTHSCHILD AND SMITH FINANcial's current CEO Andy Muller greeted Nia, along with several members of their board.

"Thank you for having me."

"Let me introduce you to a few of the members of our board." Andy introduced the seven men, who all stood with the exact same smile on their faces. Nia then sat down at the head of the oval conference table and the typical small talk ensued.

"So how's our faithful leader treating you over at the White House?"

"I have absolutely no complaints," Nia responded with a smile.

"Seems like he'd be great to work for."

"He is wonderful to work for and I can't say enough about the experience."

"Has to be invaluable," Andy commented with the board members looking on, still maintaining the same generic smile.

"Yes, it is."

"Nia, it's that *unparalleled* experience you've gained in the White House coupled with what we saw you do here at Rothschild and Smith that, quite frankly, has us completely enamored with you."

"Why, thank you," Nia replied humbly and a bit hesitantly.

"Now I know it was probably kind of awkward to discuss this opportunity at the *DC Post* event, but you've had some time now to think about it…so what are your thoughts, Nia?"

Chapter 20

THE ROOM WAS SILENT AND MOTIONLESS WITH THE EXCEPTION OF the handsome, wiry, young gentleman who had just entered. He quickly moved through the crowd and arrived at the head of the conference table, looking Straus squarely in the eyes.

"Well it's about time!" Straus said loudly, as he and Adler stood side by side with outstretched hands. The crowd roared. The man gave Straus and Adler each a firm handshake and then waved to the crowd, flashing a bright smile.

"Ladies and gentlemen, I'd like to introduce the *next* President of the United States, Jim Curry!" The crowd, once again, roared.

Jim Curry was a brash, new, budding political star. He had been handpicked by Adler. Adler felt he matched up perfectly against President Davis. His tall, square-chinned, JFK-like features were clearly presidential. He was also charismatic. These attributes were essential ingredients in Adler's formula for defeating the current president because his charisma, charm, and good looks were virtually unparalleled in the country's history of past presidents. Yet, Adler felt Curry's sharp tongue and aggressive style would likely be the most important ingredients.

Just as with President Davis, Curry's good looks, charisma, and intellect were perfectly offset by his modest beginnings. The youngest of 10 siblings, he was born and raised in Fort Wayne, Indiana. His dad was a carpenter and well-connected union member. His mom was a homemaker. Curry's hard work coupled with his dad's union connections had helped catapult him into local government. For many years he had worked diligently as a representative of Indiana's 3rd Congressional District, and eventually became a state senator, becoming somewhat of a local folk hero. And it was this local celebrity-like attention that had initially attracted Adler.

"Thank you! I appreciate your support," Curry spouted.

"Alright, let's get back to the business at hand. Unveiling the plan that will help to get Jim in office and *oust* that pathetic political figure *they* call our president," Straus said with a tone of hatred in his voice. "Bill."

The short, dumpy-looking political marketing guru confidently approached the desk-top podium. "Why thank you, Alex. Ladies and gentlemen, I am about to unveil a plan that will change all of our lives. But this plan won't work without a team effort. It will require the help of you all, in a monumental way. If we all work together, we can 'Recapture Our Excellence.'" Strategically, Adler once again uttered the super PAC's title. He then clicked the Enter key on his laptop, triggering the first slide in his presentation. One word appeared;

the word "Character" sat squarely centered in the middle of the page.

"The key to this plan is simple. The first thing we must do is dismantle... excuse me, I should say, expose President Davis's true character. He's likeable. Our fateful leader did a masterful job in the last election of giving the *illusion* that he was the perfect family man and this terrifically quality person, but we know the truth. We know it was nothing more than an act. And although like-ability is a slick way to win people over, at the very core, the American people ultimately make their choice for president based on the candidate's character. This country was built on character and deep in the American people's psyche, character is what really matters. Don't get me wrong, agenda is *extremely* important and statistics have shown that people choose candidates based on the issues, but how do you sway them if the opponent's agenda is in line with theirs? Character. You see, at the chore, character is what truly matters and it's what can swing the pendulum back in our favor. No one wants an unethical person running their country. So just how do we expose this *severely* flawed character?" Adler had hit full stride at this point. His chest was pompously poked out just past his round belly. Deviousness could clearly be heard in his voice and seen in the smirk he had to fight off as he spoke.

Adler tapped the Enter key on his laptop. "Step one—" Adler was interrupted by the sound of the meeting room's doors opening. A group of men burst into the room. The room became silent. The only sounds that could be heard were the gentle oohs and ahhs from many of the PAC members, whose jaws dropped.

Chapter 21

AFTER ANDY ASKED NIA HER THOUGHTS ON TAKING OVER HIS CEO position, Nia rapidly processed his inquiry, but maintained her typical calm, cool demeanor.

Now how can you ask me that when you didn't give me any kind of formal offer? Nia thought.

"Well, Andy, it's flattering that you guys have included me on your list of candidates, but I honestly couldn't put too much thought into an off-the-cuff interaction like that because I really didn't have all of the details to make a proper assessment."

"Fair answer and that's exactly why we wanted to meet with you...so we could really lay out our thoughts and hear yours as well," Andy responded smoothly, running his fingers through his sandy blonde hair, which had grown back even thicker than it had been after completely falling out due to his chemotherapy treatment. Smoothness was Andy's trademark. Nia knew she would have to be on her toes because Andy was shrewd and talking to him could often be like playing a game of poker—he was always trying to read her face.

"We'll get straight to the point, Nia. What would it take for us to steal you from the White House so you could take over Andy's position as CEO?" Chairman of the board John Clark cut to the point and asked in his scratchy voice.

"I'm extremely happy at the West Wing."

"Nia, like John said, today we really want to establish what it would take to get you to fill my seat," Andy said. "What we're going to do today is explain in more detail what we have to offer, find out your thoughts, and try to come to a happy medium. Does that sound good?" Andy asked a rhetorical, closed-ended question, simply seeking affirmation and setting the tone to control the conversation in classic *negotiation 101* fashion.

"Yes, sounds good." Nia had no choice but to respond *yes* to Andy's simple, but strategic, question.

"Look, Nia, beating around the bush isn't going to get us anywhere. So forgive us if we're overly aggressive here today, but as you can tell, we're very interested in you. So let's just get to it. Money is always the most important aspect of any discussion," the chairman of the board said aggressively.

Andy looked on, a bit agitated. "Yes, John's absolutely right," Andy said, hoping to regain control of the negotiation. Although Andy was leaving, he still had a vested interest in the company because of his stock and the fact that he was going to stay on as a board member. "First, let's lay out all of the possible ways you'll have to earn money." Andy then opened his iPad, propping it at an angle towards Nia.

"Of course, you'll have your annualized salary, the potential for a bonus, stock options that will likely be where the bulk of your income will come from, non-equity incentive compensation, which is another big category, and a host of other perks. We will also have a substantial pension package put in place for you. In total, we're looking roughly at an annual compensation of three point five million dollars."

That's it? You flew me down here and had me stressed out for all of these months for three and a half million. This is ridiculous, Nia thought.

Chapter 22

THE GROUP OF MEN IN BLACK SUITS SWIFTLY USHERED A WELL-dressed young man to Adler and Straus.

"Our secret weapon has arrived," Adler announced with his hand extended. "Welcome the newest member of our team and perhaps your future United States Vice President, Tanner Long!" The crowd applauded, but appeared noticeably shocked.

"Tanner has decided to walk away from his duties as chief of staff and join our team," Adler continued. A thunderous roar of applause ensued. Meanwhile, Tanner's close buddy Conrad Roth had slipped into the meeting without all of the hoopla.

"Alright, calm down everyone, so we can get everything in today," Straus said, motioning his hands downward at the crowd to cease the applauding.

No one but Adler and Straus knew that Tanner was joining their team solely to act as an informant—not even Tanner. They were equally as excited about his presence, but had no intentions of letting Tanner run alongside Curry as his vice presidential candidate.

Six months prior to this "Recapture Our Excellence" private super PAC meeting, when Adler and Straus had initially joined forces in an effort to oust President Davis, Adler had told Straus he thought he had an ideal informant.

"Alex, I've got a surprise for you. I've been working on President Davis's chief of staff and I think he'll do anything to make a name for himself. He's definitely not loyal to his boss," Adler said with a chuckle.

"Are you serious, Bill? This could be huge," Straus replied.

"Yes, I'm serious. I had some friendly conversations with him when he was running President Davis's campaign and I was campaigning for MacDonald. I could tell then he was trying to prove something, so I stayed in touch. He wants to be president someday, but feels like the powers that be in the Democratic Party are overlooking him."

"Are you saying you want him to be our presidential candidate?"

"No, Alex. I'm saying that's what he desperately wants and if we can just promise him that he's a future prospect, we might just have the informant we need to pull this thing off."

"Well how do you promise that?"

"Tell him he's not ready just yet to be a presidential candidate, but we'll let him run as the vice presidential candidate, making him the logical candidate for president the next time around. I promise you he'll fall for it."

"Are you saying we actually let him run alongside our guy?"

"Hell no; no way will conservatives vote for our guy with that clown on the ballot. Don't get me wrong, he's actually a bright kid, but he doesn't have a clue, and like I said, there's no way they'd vote for us with him on the ballot. But we can make him think he's running with our guy and drain him for information and then yank the carpet out from under him at the last minute. And we can still use his name strategically. Think about it…people would go crazy over President Davis's chief of staff unhappily leaving their party. Hell, we could even convince him to write a 'tell all' book or something right before the election. It'd be a classic move!"

"Damn it, Bill, how do you come up with this type of stuff? You're a genius!" Straus laughed. "Together we're unstoppable. Who the hell cares who gets in office, as long as it's one of our guys."

"Exactly. That's why Curry's perfect. He's another one that's thirsty for fame. We get him in and he'll do whatever we tell him. And best of all, we get that arrogant little prick out of office!"

Chapter 23

AS NIA SAT WIDE-EYED, PATIENTLY LISTENING TO ANDY EXPLAIN Rothschild and Smith's offer, she felt a bit insulted. It was hard to get something past Nia. She knew the *minimum* total annual compensation for a CEO at a firm with the kind of assets Rothschild and Smith possessed was in the $5 million range.

This is like an insult. Do they think I'm desperate, or even worse, stupid?

"Nia, how does this sound so far?" Andy asked with a confident smile and a shifty twinkle in his eyes.

Nia gave a deep internal sigh and sat quietly for a moment as she gathered her thoughts. Although she had come into the meeting a bit perplexed over whether or not to take the *big offer*, during her plane ride down she had convinced herself to simply meet with Rothschild and Smith out of respect and to keep her reputation intact in the financial community. She had even hoped they'd make the decision easier by completely letting her off of the hook and rescinding their offer all together. While they hadn't rescinded their offer, the proposed below-market salary should have been just as good of an out; however, whether they realized it or not, the insulting offer had, instead, ignited Nia's competitive spirit.

"First, let me thank you for the offer," Nia said with a coy smile, "but wouldn't you say that compensation package is s*everely* below what, I would think, the position of CEO at such a prestigious, *wealthy* institution as yours would command?" Nia scanned the members, gaining eye contact with each one by one. Her competitive juices had taken over.

"Well, you have a valid point, Nia. The last thing we would want to do is insult you," Andy responded more humbly.

You're damn right! Nia thought.

Andy glanced over at the chairman of the board and seamlessly got permission to unleash plan B without so much as uttering a word. "The compensation package that we just discussed was loaded on the base salary side which was one point five million dollars annually. The best way for us to increase your compensation would be to increase your stock options," Andy explained. "We could definitely afford to bump them up to a range that would be worth approximately six point five million, which would bring your total compensation to roughly 10 million dollars annually. Does this sound more along the lines of what you had in mind?"

Much better. Can't believe Andy would even try that with me. Now we're talking.

"Wait, before you answer, also keep in mind, we haven't discussed the various perks that we're looking to include."

I could care less about perks, Nia thought. "I understand. This definitely sounds *closer* to what the market is dictating," Nia said calmly.

Chapter 24

ADLER CONTINUED TO EXPLAIN THE PLAN. "STEP ONE IS TO PULL THE single most prevailing situation out of his past to define his character. That situation is what MacDonald wouldn't let me focus on in the last election; President Davis's ex-pastor," Adler said inciting a host of amens.

"That's right, Bill. MacDonald shouldn't have let that go last time around," said a member of the crowd.

"It was deplorable!" another shouted.

"Exactly. His former pastor denounced us. He denounced our country. Statements like '...not bless America...damn America.' President Davis followed this man and we let him off of the hook for this during our last election," Adler said, becoming preachy when a tall, balding gentleman surfaced at the head of the crowd.

"How does this prove he's got a questionable character?" the gentleman asked as he came into Adler's view.

"Paul Hansen, thank you for coming. To answer your question, his pastor—"

"Former pastor," Hansen interjected.

"...*former pastor* clearly represents his beliefs!"

"That's what you're banking on...that's the core of your strategy?"

"If you'd let me finish my presentation, Paul, you'd be able to hear our plan, in its entirety. And his former pastor did reveal something about his character."

"Bill, if you look at the situation much closer, his *former* pastor didn't center his discourse on this type of anti-America rhetoric. It was a comment that revealed something about that pastor's character, not necessarily the president's. The key word being '*not necessarily.*' If he routinely preached this sort of word, then you'd have a leg to stand on with this, but he didn't. And President Davis not only denounced it, but left his congregation. This is a worthless strategy. You'll fail," Paul Hansen declared bluntly. Hansen was outspoken and his power made others listen. While he wasn't the richest man in the world, he certainly was one of the most powerful because he controlled a great deal of it.

"Well, Paul, you certainly have the right to your own opinion, but we'd appreciate—"

"Look, no offence to anyone here, but the bottom line is I don't give a damn if a Republican or Democrat gets into office," Hansen interrupted. "All I care about is how the person who gets into office the next time around affects the things I need to do and the way *I make money.*"

Who the fuck invited you anyway? Adler thought.

The vast majority of the members of the meeting disagreed with Hansen and were clearly aggravated with his outburst.

"Paul, trust me, you'll get what you want in the end, but give Bill a chance to finish," Straus said to Hansen crossly, as he shook his head. "Then if you don't like what he says, say so. You are not locked into anything, but at least give him a chance to finish."

"*Like I was saying,*" Adler continued, "attacking shaky character is key. We'll feature an entire campaign themed 'Character Matters,' which will highlight the ex-pastor's comments with video and sound bites. The campaign will also highlight his support of gay marriage and abortion. These are issues which divide our country. We're not going to win over those who would never have voted for our side to begin with, but we can win back those that we lost and the ones that are on the fence."

Adler clicked the Enter key on his laptop and a layered graphic appeared. "From the ground up, this campaign has to be digitally charged. The new foundation for any campaign begins with its grassroots, and in today's world, grassroots is almost all digital. We have to infuse the message of his lack of character to the public via social media. The next layer is traditional public relations; talk shows, print, and so on must be saturated with questions about his character. We plan to enlist a well-spoken, intellectual, right-wing African American journalist to help pioneer this effort. There's a radio talk show host out of LA that may be the ideal fit. The psychology here is to mirror President Davis for the sake of the minority vote and to cancel out his underdog minority advantage.

"And of course, our guys here," Adler smiled at the group of congressmen in attendance, "are working on the voter ID legislation. The final layer is the mass media. Just as in any other presidential campaign, television ads will be a focal point. Visual images resonate and remain in the human memory much longer than any other medium. Clips of his ex-pastor denouncing America must be played over and over again. Meanwhile, our good friend Tanner Long here, will be providing us with a great deal of insight on President Davis's current campaign plans. Right, Tanner?"

Tanner quickly rose to his feet and took center stage. "Yes, I'd be happy to share my insights on the president's current plan, as well as my expertise on campaigning, in general…much of what got President Davis into office in the first place—" Tanner began to brag, but was quickly cut off by Adler.

"Thanks, Tanner. We're looking forward to those discussions. Now, let's get back to discussing the details of the plan. We won't lose focus of President Davis's ineffectiveness and this dreadful economy, either! He's failing. Nothing he does works. And he hasn't been too successful getting his initiatives through Congress either," Adler said, grinning, and then winked at several congressmen.

"And he won't be either," a congressman shouted.

"The day he first got in office, we said that we weren't going to let any of his hair-brained initiatives get through Congress and thanks to these congressmen," Adler paused and proudly scanned the group of congressmen, "he hasn't."

Chapter 25

"CLOSER?" ANDY SAID WITH A LOOK OF DISMAY. "IT SOUNDS LIKE these numbers aren't exactly what you were expecting." The board members' smiles quickly faded.

"Well, I actually didn't have any specific expectations. To be honest with you, I was expecting for us just to meet and chat about the potential opportunity."

"Nia, that's actually one of the things we wanted to discuss with you," Chairman John Clark said. "Andy was looking to step down from his position within the next two to three months. And before we dig too far into the numbers we need to know your availability," he said, looking Nia squarely in the eyes.

Nia's competitive spirit adrenaline rush quickly shifted to heart-pounding panic. *Me and my big mouth. When they initially low-balled me with their original offer, they gave me the perfect out. Then me and my competitiveness had to fight for more money. Shit! Now what do I do?* "Again, my initial expectations were to simply sit down and hear more about the opportunity."

"Okay, but now you know *our* expectations and our situation in general. *Would* you be available if we were able to work something out?" the board chairman once again put Nia in the hot seat.

"At this point, I would have to say two to three months is just too short of notice," Nia replied in a firm tone, staring squarely back into the eyes of the chairman of the board.

"I see, and can respect that, but I can't let you off the hook that easily, Nia," the chairman said with a smile. "Nia, we really want to have you run this company. You proved what you can do when you worked here and are further proving yourself over at the White House. We've heard nothing but good things about you from the highest level of this industry. Now, we do have a decent list of highly qualified candidates, but you're the number one candidate. The question for us now that we know you aren't immediately available is can we afford to wait and just how long would you make us wait?" the chairman asked with an exasperated expression.

Why didn't I just say no when I had the chance? "Well…"

"Wait just one minute, Nia! Before you answer that question, give me a chance to enhance our offer a bit. First, let me say, we think you're worth the wait. You just tell us how long you think it will take for you to come over and we'll figure out the rest," the chairman explained while Nia sat dangling in awkward suspense. "Second, I think we can figure out a way to increase that 10 million in total compensation a bit. What if we were able to add a bonus, bump up the stock options and non-equity incentive compensation, and arrive at 18 million dollars annually, which would put you in an elite class of CEO earnings?"

"That's—"

"Wait, I'm not done. Lastly, I know perks aren't typically a deciding factor, but this position will include personal access to our corporate jet, legal advice, financial planning, a car…if you like, we can arrange a driver. Nia, this is an unheard-of package for someone without any previous CEO experience. It's an incredible offer," the chairman said.

"It's an opportunity of a lifetime," Andy added.

"Nia, have we come to an agreement? I would have to think 18 million dollars would meet your compensation expectations, and since you can set the start date, I think we've ironed everything out. So how soon can we expect for you to come over?" the chairman asked, staring deep into Nia's eyes with a grin.

Chapter 26

ADLER HAD COMPLETED EXPLAINING THE DETAILS OF THE 54-PAGE
plan. The members of the super PAC and the congressmen in attendance were
excited, but a few had their concerns. Several pulled Adler and Straus aside to
express their concerns before exiting.

"Bill and Alex, while I think what you're trying to do is great, I don't know
if you have enough in that plan to pull it off," billionaire Texas oil tycoon Cole
Miller expressed, with two other members nodding in agreement.

Straus's eyes shifted quickly as he looked around and then proceeded to
explain. "Guys, look, I've known you for years. Now, I'm going to share something with you that you have to promise won't leave this room. As a matter
of fact, this can't go beyond the five of us. You can't even tell anyone else who
was in attendance today. Here's the thing—Adler and I realize this plan may
not be foolproof, so what you guys heard here today was just one of two plans
we've got lined up. The second plan isn't for the general public, or anyone else,
to know about, but trust me, it's pretty damn nasty. And I *guarantee* it will
take him out."

Chapter 27

NIA SAT IN THE MEETING WITH ROTHSCHILD AND SMITH FINANCIAL feeling overwhelmed. Just as she'd thought she had made her decision, she felt more confused than ever.

Oh my God, how can I say no? They just offered me 18 million dollars a year. My brother could get the best treatment money can buy. He and Granny would both be set for life. They'd never have to worry about anything again. It's so hard to turn this down. "I think you guys drive a hard bargain," Nia said with a smile, "but I do have one more issue with your offer."

"And what might that be?" Andy asked with a perplexed expression.

"Your lobbyist mentioned that this offer came with a precondition."

"Such as?"

"Apparently there's a certain piece of legislation that I'd be required to fight in order for us to move forward with your offer."

"That's not true."

"Well, this is what I was told by your lobbyist."

"Nia, it's not a precondition," Andy nonchalantly explained. "If you join our organization again, you'd quite naturally align with our agenda—especially in a role of leadership like CEO. In this case, that legislation is important to us and something we just can't have go through, so you'd have to fight it, as well. And being that you're in a position to influence President Davis, we'd obviously expect for you to do so. It comes with the job. Make sense?"

They almost had me, but that's a lot of nerve to sit here and try to pass this off as just another part of the job. You're not going to use me, and furthermore, that makes me not trust you. "Well, it seems like a precondition to me."

"How, Nia? We're not asking you to do anything until you accept the offer. At that point you'll be one of us. You'll be a part of our team—the most important part. Like I said, it'd just be natural for you to work in your organization's favor. Correct?" Andy asked with a look of puzzlement.

"Andy, I see your point, but that's putting me in a compromising position that I don't think is necessarily fair."

"I'm confused."

"I'd be using my position in the White House to do something for Rothschild and Smith Financial in return for something else. In some ways that could be construed as unethical. Perhaps even illegal."

"Wow, I think you're misunderstanding us, Nia. We want you aboard regardless of your influence with President Davis."

"But the offer still comes with a prerequisite."

"No. Like I said, that part is just business. Either way, if you join us, you'd have to align with our organizational goals."

"We can look at it from as many angles as you like, Andy, but it's still a precondition."

"Nia, I'm sorry that you feel that way," Andy explained, sharing a mystified look with the board members. "Look, don't make a hasty decision. After all, it's a big one—an 18-million-dollar plus decision. One that could affect your career for the rest of your life. Go back to Washington and think about it for a few days. I'll give you a call at the end of the week after you've had a while to think it through and you can let me know your final decision then. How does that sound?"

"Sure, we'll talk at the end of the week," Nia replied unenthusiastically.

Chapter 28

NIA ARRIVED TO WORK THE FOLLOWING MORNING AFTER HER MEETing with Rothschild and Smith Financial somewhat lethargic. She'd had a difficult time sleeping the night before. The entire day she fought to stay awake. Fatigue was a tricky proposition in the West Wing. Everyone knew exhaustion was inevitable and just a part of the job, but the expectations were still that you mustn't ever fall asleep or show fatigue during a meeting. Furthermore, you had to look and remain alert at all times so as not to miss anything, because almost all of the meetings were critical on some level.

Nia had become far too used to the grind of the West Wing, so she pushed through the day, hoping to leave early for a change, but was called into a last-minute meeting which included the president's senior advisors in the Cabinet room. At the close of the meeting Kimberly Caldwell inconspicuously pulled Nia aside.

"Hi Nia, can you stop by my office for a few minutes? I need to speak with you in private for a moment."

"Sure."

The two proceeded to take an elevator up to the second floor and headed straight to Kimberly's large corner office.

"Come on in, Nia, and close the door for me."

"Okay...sure," Nia replied with a slight stammer, as she closed the door. "What's going on, Kimberly? Is everything okay?"

"Everything is fine. You have been doing a wonderful job and POTUS is very impressed with your progress, but I just really want to caution you to be extremely careful of the pitfalls that exist out there for people in our position. Nia, this place is all about decisions. The right ones can lead you wherever you want to go, but making just one bad decision can ruin your entire career. And I know you know all of this, but every now and then you have to hear it from someone else."

"Yes, that does worry me, Kimberly. How do you handle avoiding the pitfalls without stepping on toes?"

"As silly as it may sound, by simply doing what I think is right...and if I hurt a few feelings along the way, oh well. All they can do is respect me."

"That's sound advice. I am *so* glad that you brought this up. Lately I've been finding myself always trying to please everyone and that's something I've never worried about doing before."

"Unfortunately, politics puts us in that awkward position, but at the end of the day you have to live with yourself. I'm not suggesting you burn bridges, just do what you think is right for *you*, and what's right in general. This business tends to make good people bend and eventually they bend so much that they become crooked," Kimberly explained with a warm smile.

Oh my goodness, she has to know! Nia thought nervously.

"Like I said, I know you're an intelligent, savvy business woman and I know you know all of this, but I think sometimes it's just good to hear it from someone else—especially someone that's gone through similar challenges. We are in such extraordinary positions and so much is thrown at us that I think we can very easily get pulled away from our center...our deepest truths...our core values."

Oh, that's it, she definitely knows.

"You're absolutely right, Kimberly. I find myself constantly being asked to bend. More than I ever have in my life. As usual, your words of wisdom have a way of centering me. You know you're my mentor, whether you want to be or not. Right?" Nia said, misty eyed, with a smile.

"I just sensed that you may have been experiencing some growing pains, which we all go through, and thought I would just share some positive words with you. Have to look out for my friends around here," Kimberly said with a wink and a smile.

"Kimberly, you can't keep turning down my request to be your mentee. I'm going to keep pressing until you give in someday," Nia said with a chuckle.

"Nia, I'm open to a mentoring relationship. You have enormous potential, but more importantly, you are a wonderful human being. But the only catch is, you know how busy we are around here, so it will be your responsibility to stay on top of it. That's not saying I won't do my part, I just want to be honest with you."

"Kimberly, you know I'll stay on top of it and it's too late now, I got you to commit! You are officially my mentor now." Nia grinned.

Nia left Kimberly's office in a bit of disarray. Although she was thrilled that Kimberly, the same woman who had mentored President Davis and the First Lady over the years, had officially agreed to be her mentor, she was equally as confused and worried that Kimberly knew about the offer from Rothschild and Smith.

That's it, I'm calling Andy right now and putting this nonsense to rest.

Nia swiftly made her way back to her office, closed her door, and immediately dialed Andy on her cell phone. "Hi, Andy."

"Nia, I'm surprised to hear from you so soon. This must mean we pulled it off. You're coming to join us."

Keep it simple, Nia. Don't give him too much, just let him know you're turning down the offer. She cautiously thought through her choice of words before responding. "No, unfortunately, it's just the opposite. I can't tell you guys how much I appreciate your offer, but I must respectfully decline," Nia responded confidently, but was met with momentary silence.

"Nia, are you sure? I would just hate to see you miss out on an opportunity like this."

"Yes, Andy, I am."

"I can't believe you'd turn down the opportunity of a lifetime. It really doesn't get a whole lot better than this—especially without any experience at the CEO level."

"It's a wonderful opportunity, but just bad timing."

"Timing? I know you're working in the West Wing and that's an incredible opportunity in itself, but unless you want to be a politician, you're going to end up right back in the private job sector. Unless you have aspirations to run for some sort of office, the West Wing is nothing but a stepping stone."

"True, but I just have a bit more to do in the West Wing for now." *If you all didn't have that damn precondition, I would be taking the offer! But don't bring that up, Nia. Don't drag this thing out any longer. Something just isn't right with this situation,* she thought.

"With all due respect, Nia, that's crazy. If you don't want to be a politician then, at this point, you're wasting your time. If you're not going to run for anything, then you're really just there to gain experience. Experience that'll help your career. Unless you decide to stay in politics, passing up on this opportunity is just going to set you back and is just *asinine.*"

"Perhaps."

"I know what the problem is. It's the fact that we want you to support us in fighting against that privacy legislation. Supporting what's in the best interest of your company just makes sense."

Here we go. "Andy, I appreciate your concern, but I'm going to stick with my decision. And you're partially right, I wasn't fond of the fact that the offer came with a condition attached."

"That's just business, Nia. I can't see how a savvy businesswoman like yourself just can't get that."

"Oh, I get it, but it just isn't the right situation for me."

"Doesn't make a bit of sense to me, Nia, but if that's what you've decided, then that's fine. You have to live with that decision, not me. But the board isn't going to be happy about this. Like I said, you're making a *big* mistake. I can *assure you,* they won't come knocking again and *won't* forget this, either. And don't forget, they have a *very* big influence on the *entire* financial industry," Andy said with bitterness in his voice.

"I understand and can appreciate that."

"Well, good luck. That's all I can say, is good luck."

"I wish you the best as well, Andy."

Thank God that's finally over!

Chapter 29

THE BURDEN OF *THE BIG OFFER* **WAS FINALLY OFF OF NIA'S SHOULDERS.** She was relieved and dying to move forward with her life, but knew Terrence wasn't going to be happy with her decision. Later that evening Nia explained her encounter with Kimberly and her final decision to her fiancé.

"I am so relieved. I told you the whole thing was shady. I just wonder how Kimberly knew."

"You don't know if she knew for sure, Nia. I swear. You just panicked and threw away that opportunity and all of that money."

"Is that all you can think of is the money?"

"How can I not think about it?"

"And she had to know something for her to bring it up."

"You don't know that for sure. It could have been a coincidence," Terrence said, shaking his head.

"That was too ironic. Either way, that was a sign to just say no and move on."

"Yeah, but you could have at least talked it over with me first, Nia!"

"What? It's my career and ultimately my decision."

"Oh, it's like that? It was *your* decision?"

"Yes, it was *my* decision."

"Damn, Nia, it's all about you!"

"Terrence, you act like I quit my job or something. Our life isn't changed one bit."

"Selfish…flat-out selfish!"

"Selfish? How is that selfish, Terrence?" Nia asked with a perplexed look.

"I quit my job and came all the way out here for your career and you don't even have the decency to consult me about your final decision first?" Terrence said, and then threw his hands in the air. "And I'm supposed to be your future husband? What else is that but selfishness?"

"Terrence, I'm not going to let you put a spin on this situation like that. You know this wasn't a typical job decision. If they hadn't put a condition on the offer, we would have had something to talk about. You know that was shady. And you know that's why I just couldn't have taken the offer—especially after Kimberly insinuated that she knew."

"It wasn't shady." Terrence pouted.

"Come on, now. We both know it was shady. If I'm patient and continue to do a good job, the same type of opportunity will come along again later, but with no strings attached," Nia said confidently, as Terrence continued to pout.

"I guess," Terrence replied, as he rolled his eyes and gritted his teeth.

Chapter 30

THE FOLLOWING MORNING, AFTER THE MORNING STAFF MEETING came to a close, chief of staff Tanner Long told Nia to meet him in his office immediately to discuss an important issue. Nia usually didn't think much of Tanner's last-minute requests. Last-minute requests in the West Wing were as routine as the morning sun. But something was different this time.

"Nia, I need to speak with you in my office immediately," Tanner requested.

"Tanner, I have a meeting with the press secretary in less than five minutes to talk about a press conference that is happening at noon."

"I'll take care of that. This is more important. We need to speak in my office ASAP." The two swiftly marched out of the second-floor conference room and onto the elevator. Nia could sense something wasn't right. Tanner appeared abnormally standoffish, not saying a word on the elevator ride down to the first floor.

"Come on in and close the door behind you," Tanner said in a cold lifeless tone, as he immediately grabbed his phone and dialed the press secretary. "Kevin, Nia told me that you guys had a meeting planned in five minutes, but we had an emergency arise, so she'll be a few minutes late. Thanks."

"What's going on?" Nia inquired with a look of trepidation.

"*Nia*, has Jimmy Coleman Jr. recently introduced you to anyone from Klein Schultz?"

"Yes, he did. Why?"

"Who'd he introduce you to and did this person offer you anything?"

Now how in the hell did he know? Nia thought. "Well, to answer your first question, one of their lobbyists. To answer your second question, he didn't offer me anything, but Rothschild and Smith Financial did. They offered me their CEO position. Why? What's going on?"

"Look, the Feds are investigating this Klein Schultz lobbyist. The most important thing is that we have to make sure to protect the president...right?"

"Of course," Nia replied calmly, concealing her anxiety. *What the hell is going on?*

"Have you discussed this with POTUS? Did you try to pitch anything to him?"

"No, absolutely not."

"Good. It could all blow over, but I just wanted to let you know what was going on."

"So now what? Should I go talk to POTUS and let him know about the encounter?"

"No, we want to protect him at all costs, so we have to keep him out of this. We don't want to give the Feds, the press, or any of those damned Republicans any reason to tie this back to him."

"Tie what back to him?"

"This situation, Nia," Tanner replied condescendingly.

Thank God I turned that offer down. "Are you sure we shouldn't just let him know what happened?"

"No, I'm telling you, we don't want him caught up in this mess. If you want to tip anyone off close to him, you may want to let senior advisor Adam Rubin know," Tanner said.

"I'd feel more comfortable discussing this with Kimberly Caldwell."

"Kimberly gets too worked up over these types of issues, so I definitely don't want us to get her involved. Adam, on the other hand, might be good to run the scenario by."

"Maybe I will," Nia responded with an arched eyebrow. *No way. I wish I would go talk to his buddy Adam. Something isn't right. Tanner's up to something and somebody needs to know.*

Chapter 31

NIA COULDN'T BELIEVE TANNER KNEW ABOUT THE OFFER FROM Rothschild and Smith Financial. She realized the situation went much deeper than she had ever dreamed. She couldn't figure out how or why Tanner was involved, and how this chaos all came together. The one thing she did know was that someone needed to know about Tanner. The morning following her encounter with Tanner, Nia arrived early to the West Wing. She immediately called Kimberly.

"Kimberly, I am so glad that I caught you," Nia said anxiously.

"Hi Nia, how are you? Is everything okay?"

"I'm well, but I really need to speak with you about something." Nia knew she couldn't discuss this situation over the phone, but didn't want to alarm Kimberly by telling her that directly.

"I have a few moments right now. What's on your mind?"

"It's somewhat of a long story. Probably be better if we met up in person."

"Sure, no problem. I have a meeting in a few moments and after that I have about a 30-minute gap between meetings that I was planning to use to catch up on emails, but if you want to come by then that's fine. I'll give you a call when I get out of the meeting."

"Wonderful. Thanks, Kimberly. I'll see you then."

∽

Nia could hardly wait for Kimberly's call. It seemed like an eternity before she finally received the call and anxiously made her way over to Kimberly's office. She closed Kimberly's door and apprehensively began to explain the scenario.

"So, what's on your mind, Nia?" Kimberly asked with concern.

"Kimberly, some strange things have been going on."

"Oh, like what?"

Nia's anxiety caused her to feel as if she couldn't catch her breath. She paused for a moment, trying to gather herself before she began to speak. "Well, I met with Jimmy Coleman Jr. a few months back…"

"Oh boy…"

"Yes…he tried to get me to influence POTUS on some online privacy legislation. He was speaking on behalf of Klein Schultz and The Social Hub. Basically, he said that they would offer me the CEO position with Rothschild and Smith Financial in return for talking to President Davis about shooting down this legislation," Nia explained, sounding as if she were out of breath, as

Kimberly leaned forward with a look of intensity. "Of course, I didn't really believe Jimmy, but then I met the lobbyist at the *DC Post*'s recent party and he actually made an informal offer right there at the party. They even brought in Paul Hansen and the current CEO of Rothschild and Smith, Andy Muller, to try and convince me."

"Andy was at Rothschild and Smith Financial when you were, wasn't he?"

"Yes, I reported to Andy directly."

"Bringing in Hansen and your old boss was a pretty slick ploy on their part. So how did you respond?"

"Well, I accepted their offer to come out to Rothschild and Smith, just to show my face and be respectful, but turned their offer down. I just told them I couldn't do it...not with that kind condition attached to the offer. And of course, Andy let me know I was making a huge mistake...insinuating that I'd be blackballed if I didn't take the offer."

"Well, you did the right thing. You can't even entertain that type of conversation, and can't worry about silly blackball threats either."

"Then Tanner calls me into his office yesterday morning asking all of these questions about the situation...saying he wanted to make sure that POTUS was safe. I'm not quite sure what's going on, but I have to be honest with you, Kimberly, I don't trust Tanner. Do you think I should say something to POTUS?"

"I don't think it's necessary. Things will work themselves out."

"I just don't want to see him blindsided by this mess."

"Oh, he won't be...he's been through this type of nonsense many times before. He can handle himself," Kimberly said with a confident smile, then leaned back in her chair.

"I just want to handle this thing appropriately."

"He'll come to you if he wants information. You'd be surprised, he keeps an ear to the ground. The main thing is that *you* did the right thing," Kimberly said.

Nia gave her a shaky smile, trying to conceal her nervousness. *Thank God I did the right thing!* "Thanks, Kimberly. That makes me feel more at ease."

"Any time, Nia. Trust me, it'll all work out."

Nia exited the office in a trance. By the time she arrived back to her office her head was spinning. Before she had a moment to reflect on all that had transpired, an aide tapped on her door to let her know that there was an emergency meeting.

⌒

Later that night, Nia arrived home at almost one o'clock in the morning, stressed out and exhausted. When she entered her Georgetown apartment, she found Terrence slumped down on the far end of their brown, Italian-leather sofa with his feet propped up on a foot rest, watching the news. The two hadn't spoken for more than a few seconds at a time over the last two days. Terrence had been away on a business trip and had just arrived back home himself.

"Hi, sweetie, it's been the craziest—"

"Shhh…be quiet for a moment, Nia. This is BNN live. Apparently, about three hours ago a story broke about the Feds' investigation into several Washington lobbyists."

"Oh great, just what I needed to hear right now," Nia said in disgust. They both sat in silence as they listened to the report.

"This is crazy!"

"Yes, and I'm right in the middle of this nonsense."

"Don't worry about it, Nia. You didn't do anything. You turned them down."

"No, you don't understand. Tanner pulled me in his office yesterday and talked to me about the whole situation. He knew all about the offer from Rothschild and Smith Financial and Klein and Schultz's involvement. It's a mess. The whole damn thing is a complete mess!"

"Are you serious?"

"Yes, and he was acting really strange. I don't know what's going on right now."

"How the hell did he find out?"

"I don't know…I'm telling you something really fishy is going on."

"Yeah, that's crazy! But like I said, you didn't do anything wrong anyway, so you're good."

"Thank God! I told you it wasn't worth it. You start messing around with these kinds of people and it only leads to trouble. And to think, I almost listened to you."

"You were right," Terrence admitted sheepishly.

"I would have ended up in some half-way house, listening to you."

"I'm so glad you didn't do it, but I promise you half of Washington is getting hooked up like this…why do you think they're investigating?"

"I'm sure they are, but you see now they're going to get pointed out. The federal prisons are filled with politicians," Nia said with a deep sigh.

"Yeah, but I bet only certain ones are going to be called out. The ones that are plugged don't have anything to worry about."

"Are you crazy? What is it that you don't get? This is serious stuff. I don't even know if any of my conversations with them were taped. Jimmy could have been wired, the room at the *DC Post* party could have been wired…hell, when I visited Rothschild and Smith Financial, *they* could have been wired." Nia's mind ran wild.

"Calm down, sweetie. You didn't do anything. They wouldn't have anything even if they had taped the meeting."

"I guess you're right."

"I know I'm right. Anyway, what are you going to do now?"

"I met with Kimberly this morning and she said not to worry about it. She said that I did the right thing and POTUS will be fine."

"See, nothing to worry about. You should just keep playing up the fact that you turned down millions. It actually makes you look good…you're like the hero in all this madness."

"Whatever, Terrence. I'm not playing up or down anything. You don't get it, I just want this thing to blow over."

"Have you told Beverly or any of the girls?"

"No, this is something that I don't want anyone to know."

"Good, don't tell those nosey bitches anything."

"Bitches, Terrence…really? Don't call them bitches. You're getting a little too crazy now."

"They just give bad advice and talk too damn much. Plus, Carla works for the news. So you know you can't trust her."

"I just said I wasn't going to tell them anyway, Terrence!"

"What about Heather and Maria? I bumped into Maria at the health club and she seemed to be acting kind of funny the entire time. Do they know?"

"I said I haven't told *anyone*. You didn't tell me you saw them."

"Yeah, I saw them the other day. Look, I'm just trying to keep you out of trouble."

"Terrence, I work in the White House. Don't you think I know how to handle confidential information? Especially when it's about me?"

"I'm not saying that. I'm just saying that you have to be careful."

"I know. You're right."

"Just be careful…oh shit!"

"What's wrong?"

"I just thought about the firm. I hope this thing doesn't get blown out of proportion and they find out you're involved."

"What? I can't believe that's what's on your mind! I can't believe you'd be that selfish."

"I'm not trying to be selfish, Nia. I'm just being realistic."

"I'm worried about my job—the job that got you in that firm in the first place—and President Davis, and all you can think about is making partner?"

"As usual, you're blowing things out of proportion."

"Whatever, Terrence. It is *too* late and I am *too* tired for this…I'm going to bed!"

Chapter 32

THE FOLLOWING FRIDAY AFTERNOON, AS NIA WORKED FEVERISHLY on a vital report that needed to be finished within the hour, she received a call from President Davis's secretary.

"Nia, the president would like to see you in the Oval Office immediately."

"Oh, okay. Sure, I'll be right there."

I wonder what's going on, Nia thought. She ordinarily wouldn't have been surprised by this sort of last-minute request, but the investigation had her on edge. She grabbed a pen and pad of paper and nervously rushed out of her office and then down the hall towards the Oval Office. She took a deep breath before entering.

Oh, come on, Nia, pull yourself together and just go in there, she thought and then proceeded to enter. "Hi, Mr. President. You wanted to see me?" she asked nervously.

"Have a seat, Nia."

Nia immediately noticed that there was no one else in the Oval Office, which was rare. Although President Davis had met with her alone in the past, protocol would have it that, outside of his family, the president was only left alone with one of four people: the chief of staff, his two senior advisors, or his personal assistant.

As Nia sat down, her body temperature surged. She tried to remain calm, but looked noticeably nervous. "Is there an emergency, sir?"

"No, I just want to talk to you about—" As President Davis began to speak his phone rang. He tapped the button for speaker phone. "Yes, Jessica."

"Mr. President, you have Attorney General Robert Holderman on the line."

"Thank you. Put him through." The line clicked, indicating that the caller was through. "What's going on over at the Department of Justice, Rob? By the way, I've got you on speaker phone. I'm sitting here talking with the deputy chief of staff, the lovely Ms. Nia Taylor," President Davis said with a smile.

"Mr. President. Nia."

"Hi, Robert," Nia said.

"Sir, I just want to talk to you about an investigation."

Gulp. Nia swallowed an air bubble that felt like it was the size of an apple. *Oh my God,* she thought nervously as another troublesome lump reemerged in her throat. The pit of her stomach became queasy.

"Okay, Rob. Let me give you a call back in about 30 minutes."

"Talk to you then, sir," the attorney general replied.

"So, Nia, I brought you in here because I've been hearing a few things. I'm hearing that maybe you were considering leaving us."

I knew he was going to find out. But he's still not completely letting on that he knows. Kimberly may have told him. Or maybe someone else tipped him off. After all, there is an investigation going. But how do I answer? In just seconds several different scenarios quickly ran through Nia's mind, as she tried to process the situation. Then she decided to just explain the whole story. President Davis sat expressionless as he listened carefully.

"And so, did you accept the offer?"

"No, sir. I turned them down several different times."

"I see. So now what was Jimmy getting out of the deal? Do you know?"

"He was promised a Senate seat."

"Oh, really? Did you ever contemplate telling me all about this?"

"I did, sir. But…well, let's just say I was told not to say anything to you."

"By who?"

"Well, although I hate to say it, it's important that you know. Sir…it was Tanner."

"It was?"

"Yes, he said that he would handle it. I was going to tell you about the situation anyway, but I spoke with Kimberly and she kind of alluded to the fact that you knew what was going on anyway and not to worry about it."

"Well, Ms. Taylor, I think that you did an excellent job of fending off the lobbyist and Rothschild and Smith Financial. I just wanted to hear more of the details directly from you. That's all I had. Keep up the good work," President Davis said, excusing Nia.

She sat speechless for a moment. "Okay…that's it, sir?"

"Yes, that's it for now. Thanks."

"Oookay, sir," Nia replied, completely confounded by what had just transpired. The president had left her more confused than she was prior to their impromptu meeting. She knew that by turning down the offer she had done nothing wrong, but worried that visiting Rothschild and Smith Financial may have rubbed President Davis the wrong way.

Chapter 33

THE UPCOMING MID-TERM ELECTIONS WERE RAPIDLY APPROACHING and were going to have a monumental effect on President Davis's administration. The Democrats currently had control of Congress, but early forecasts predicted that the Republicans were sure to take majority control in the House of Representatives and could also possibly take over the Senate. Congress had already been shooting down virtually everything President Davis tried to put through, but losing majority status would be disastrous.

Just two and a half short years after the American public voted Michael Davis into office those same Americans where trying to help run him out. President Davis had inherited one of the worst economic crises in American history and the Republicans had successfully duped the American people into believing that the present state of the country was his fault. They also fought every initiative the president put forth to ensure that he wouldn't be able to revive the country. Never before in history had a president been so maligned and disrespected. The Republicans *pure* hatred for the president was clearly evident. Many believed this hatred was rooted in racism, while others thought it lie in a difference in fundamental beliefs, but either way, the Republicans appeared to be succeeding. The president was at his lowest approval rating since taking office. Every major news show across the country was predicting that the Democrats would lose majority control of the House of Representatives.

Just when Nia thought the political chaos couldn't get any crazier, three days before the mid-term elections she received an email that virtually knocked her out of her chair. It was a memo announcing that Tanner Long was no longer a part of the staff. Due to the fact that the memo didn't disclose why Tanner was leaving or where he was going, everyone knew he had to have been fired. Nia sat with her mouth gaping open in complete shock. Although Tanner was a complete jerk, he was also one of the most prominent figures in the West Wing. In her mind, Nia immediately tied the termination to the Klein Schultz investigation.

He had to have been tied up in that nonsense.

She wondered just how he was caught up in the situation. The timing of the firing also had her puzzled. *Did he take money from them? Was he trying to set President Davis up?*

The firing also made her nervous for her own well-being. *I really hope I didn't piss POTUS off by going to visit Rothschild and Smith Financial.*

Nia wanted to call around to see if anyone knew why Tanner was let go, but it was such a touchy subject that she knew no one would discuss it at work anyway. With just three days left before the mid-term elections, she was buried in work which helped her keep her mind off of the situation and forge ahead.

Chapter 34

THE FIRING OF TANNER CAUSED A MEDIA FRENZY. THE STORY WAS featured as the headline for every news outlet across the country. With just 48 hours left before the mid-term election, President Davis fired his chief of staff. It was appearing more and more like the helm of the ship had spun completely out of the president's control. Meanwhile, no one knew the real reason why Tanner was fired. The rumors swirled. Some pointed to the federal investigation into Washington lobbyists, while others claimed President Davis and Tanner didn't see eye to eye. Either way, the pressure was mounting on Nia. She couldn't help but wonder if she'd be next. Later that afternoon, President Davis's secretary called her to the Oval Office.

Oh God! Here we go. Nia grabbed a pen and pad and scampered down to his office. Although she knew President Davis would likely be dealing with her one-on-one more frequently until he found a replacement for Tanner, every call from him made her nervous. The anxiety was overwhelming and caused her equilibrium to be slightly off. As she walked down the West Wing corridor, she struggled not to stumble. As she arrived at the Oval Office, she inhaled deeply before entering.

"Come on in, Nia. How are you this morning?"

"I'm fine, sir. How are you?"

"I'm hanging in there. It's been quite a week," he said and then sighed. "Well, I'm sure you've heard about Tanner by now."

"Yes, I have. Hated to see him leave." As much as Nia hated Tanner, without knowing all of the details surrounding his unexpected termination, she had mixed emotions.

"Unfortunate, but chief of staff isn't for everyone. Being a member of the White House staff in general isn't for everyone. Wouldn't you agree?"

"Yes, absolutely, sir."

"And that's why I called you in here today, Nia. We're experiencing some difficult times right now, and as difficult as it may be, I have to make some tough decisions."

This is it. It's my turn. Just say it already, POTUS!

"Nia, I really hate to tell you this under these circumstances, but I'm going to have to—" Just then, his phone rang, interrupting him mid-sentence.

"Yes," President Davis answered, noticeably irritated.

"Sir, I'm sorry to interrupt you, but I've got an important call on the line," his secretary explained.

"Who is it? I specifically told you not to interrupt me unless it was an emergency."

"Sir, it's your son."

"Oh, I'm sorry, Jessica, put him through."

As President Davis assured his 10-year-old son that he'd be at his upcoming basketball game, Nia sat fearing the worst.

I love that little boy, but I sure wish he'd stop whining so we can get this over with.

"Alright, Nia, sorry about that. You know family always comes first. Now, where was I? Like I was saying, I really would have rather done this under different circumstances, but I have to tell you now," President Davis said sternly, as he momentarily glared deep into Nia's eyes like a concerned parent to their child. "I'm going to need a lot more from you now, Nia. Losing Tanner is going to put a lot more pressure on you. Are you up for the challenge?"

That's it? Oh my God, he scared me half to death. "Of course, sir, that's not bad news. Whatever you need," Nia replied, and then exhaled in relief.

"I'm glad to hear you say that, but it's going to require much more from you than just pulling a little additional weight…being the *chief of staff* also takes a certain kind of *moxie,* but that's an intangible that I'm very confident you possess," he said with a coy smile.

"Sir, I'm sorry, but it sounded like you just referred to me as your *chief of staff*?" Nia replied with a look of sheer bewilderment.

"I know exactly what I just said, Nia. Have you had your coffee yet? You seem to be a step or two behind today," the president said with a boyish grin.

"If you're saying what I think you're saying…"

"That's what I'm saying."

"I'm speechless. Mr. President, I'm honored that you would even consider me as Tanner's replacement," Nia said in shock.

"You wouldn't be a replacement though, Nia. You'd be my *new* chief of staff. Now take your time and think about it. Go home and talk it over with your fiancé and let me know what you think. But I must admit I'd be pretty disappointed if you said no."

"Sir, I'll definitely talk it over with him, but I've already made my decision. There's no way that I could turn down an opportunity to serve you in this capacity. I'd be honored. I can tell you right now, the answer is yes," Nia said, beaming, as she reached out to shake President Davis's hand.

"I'm so happy that you're interested in taking on the challenge. I couldn't think of anyone that I'd rather have as my right-hand person," he said, as he firmly grasped Nia's hand and stared deeply into her eyes. "Now let's keep this quiet until we do an official press release."

"Of course, sir, will do."

Nia left the Oval Office in a daze. She was so excited that she took an early lunch so she could leave the White House grounds to give Terrence a call from her cell phone to tell him the good news.

"Hey, sweetie, guess what?"

"Hey, I have to tell you something too, but you go first."

"You're not going to believe this."

"What? Is everything okay?"

"Yes...I just got promoted to chief of staff!" Nia said in excitement.

"Are you serious?" Terrence said with a note of pride in his voice.

"Yes! Tanner got let go today and POTUS offered me the position."

"Yes! Hell yes! Congratulations, sweetie!"

"Thanks, sweetie!" Nia responded.

"We have to celebrate."

"Yes, we do. I'm so excited."

"And it's perfect timing. You know the firm's anniversary party is this weekend."

"Yeah, but I can't tell anyone until it's been officially announced. So make sure you don't repeat this, but isn't it exciting?"

"When are they going to announce it?"

"I don't know, probably not for a few weeks."

"Damn! Is there any way we can speed the process up? It'd be perfect if you had that promotion before the party Friday night."

"No, Terrence, we can't speed it up! McLoughlin and McLoughlin will just have to wait, and who cares...I thought you'd be excited for me. And all you can think about is this helping you make partner? Wow!"

"No, sweetie, you know I'm happy for you. I'm sorry if it seemed that way. It's just such a coincidence that my event was coming up."

"You're going to make partner on your own merit. You just have to be patient."

"Exactly. Anyway, forget that. Let's talk about celebrating tonight. What time are you getting off?"

"I'm definitely leaving on time," Nia said.

"Let's go have a celebration dinner."

Chapter 35

TO TERRENCE'S DELIGHT, NIA LEFT WORK EARLY THE DAY OF McLoughlin and McLoughlin's anniversary party and the two arrived at the event on time. As soon as they entered the party, Terrence began to turn on his charm. He was the sole black attorney in the firm, but thanks to this gift of charm that he possessed, he had quickly built a strong rapport with virtually everyone at the firm.

"Hey, Brian! How's it going, Aaron! Have you guys met my beautiful fiancée Nia?" Terrence worked the room. He left no stone unturned, mingling with any and everyone, but his eye was on the prize. All that he could think about was getting in front of Blair.

"Hi, Jerry. Have you seen Blair?"

"No, but we're sure glad that the big boss let you come," Jerry said with slurred speech.

"Come on, Jerr. What, you don't think Blair wanted me here?"

"No, I mean your fiancée!" Jerry replied and then roared in laughter.

"No more drinks for you, Jerr. Seriously, have you seen Blair? I've been looking all over for him." Terrence glanced around the room. "Oh, there he is," he whispered in Nia's ear. "Come on, Nia, hurry up." He grabbed Nia's hand, virtually yanking her from her feet as he swiftly shuffled through the crowd towards the head of the firm.

"Blair, congratulations!" Terrence said, with his hand extended.

"Thank you, Terrence. Nia, I'm so glad you could make it! Thank you for coming," Blair said as he greeted Nia with a warm hug and then shook Terrence's hand.

"Congratulations, Blair. Fifty years is a tremendous accomplishment," Nia said.

"Thank you. We're very fortunate and proud," he responded.

"You should be, Blair. You've done a marvelous job," Terrence interjected and Blair responded with a nod and a half-hearted smile.

"So, how are you, young lady? How are things going over at the White House?" Blair asked.

"Busy, but well."

"That's an understatement," Terrence said. "Blair, between you and me, you're looking at the *new* White House chief of staff!"

Nia's jaw dropped.

"That's right, you're now looking at the second most powerful person in Washington," Terrence said, as he boastfully tugged at his belt and expanded his chest out proudly.

Uhhh, I can't believe he just did that!

"Wow! What an incredible accomplishment, Nia. Congratulations!" Blair blurted in excitement, yanking his signature unlit cigar from his mouth. "Nia, don't move, there're some people I'd like for you to meet." Blair dashed away.

"Have you lost your mind, Terrence?" Nia snarled.

Terrence stood dumbfounded. "Nia, it's no big deal. I made sure to tell him not to tell anyone."

"Stanley, I want you to meet Nia Taylor, the new White House chief of staff." Blair introduced Nia, beaming.

"Hello, Stanley. It's a pleasure to meet you," Nia greeted the businessman blandly, struggling to maintain her composure as she fumed in anger.

"No, the pleasure is all mine," Stanley responded eagerly.

"Gentlemen, please excuse my fiancé. He tends to get a little overly excited at times. I am *not* the new chief of staff. I'm the deputy chief of staff." She grabbed Terrence's hand, pulling it down to her side while sinking her nails into his skin.

"Still a very interesting position," Stanley commented.

"Oh, I'm sure you'll probably be replacing Tanner Long," Blair said with a twinkle in his eyes. "She probably just can't talk about it yet."

Nia smiled and then cut Terrence the look of death.

"And, Nia, Stanley is the CEO of Quantum Aerospace," Blair added.

"Ms. Taylor, most of our work is government contracted," Stanley said.

"I'm actually very familiar with your work," Nia responded confidently, to the CEO's dismay. Although she was one of the few White House staffers who had a solid understanding of almost every aspect of the interworkings of the government, she found the military especially captivating and followed it closely around the West Wing.

"So, from my understanding President Davis is considering beefing up and ordering more Apaches since tensions are rising in the Middle East," Stanley said. "Oh, I'm sorry...the Apache is a military helicopter. We build the transmissions, as well as the landing gear for it."

Nia gave an inward sigh at his tone of condescension. Even though she held one of the most prestigious positions in the country and obviously was highly educated, she still had to deal with the same stereotypes that women all over the nation experienced when dealing with egotistical male executives.

"I'm familiar with the Apache, as well as your company's work," Nia said modestly, with a coy smile.

"Yes, but you may not be aware of its *significance to our military*. The Apache has been instrumental in the military's missions for years." He continued to boast, as Nia patiently listened with a smile.

"Well, like I said, I know a *little* something about the Apache and your company. Quantum's done a fine job helping to build it, and you're absolutely right; the Apache has been a tremendous asset over the years. *However,* the Chinook CH-47 may be our MVP. In particular, we've been extremely impressed with the MH-47G. It's had an immeasurable benefit," Nia explained in a nonchalant manner. "In Afghanistan alone, it's been our single most valuable aircraft. We utilize it to insert our troops, nutrition, *and* ammunition into the region. We're particularly impressed with the avionics and transmission of that aircraft. Now, does your organization build the transmission for that as well?" Nia asked condescendingly, knowing good and well that Quantum Aerospace didn't do any work on the Chinook helicopter.

The Quantum Aerospace CEO paused for a moment, clearly stunned and embarrassed. "Well, no, we don't do any work on the Chinook."

"Well, how about the new Z-14 Tornado prototype? Just the other day the president and the army's foremost expert in this area, General McDonald, mentioned how interested they were in that aircraft. Is your organization involved with manufacturing that?" Nia asked with a slight grin.

"No, unfortunately we don't have that contract either." The CEO was dumbfounded at that point. "But we do have some interesting prototypes we've been working with that I'd love to introduce to you sometime…maybe show you around our facility when you have time?" he asked humbly.

"Sure. Do you have a card, Stanley?" Nia asked apathetically, as Blair stood by anxiously.

"How does next week sound?" the Quantum Aerospace CEO asked with eagerness in his voice.

Before Nia was able to decline his offer Terrence abruptly interjected. "Yes, the *four* of us should get together soon. I'd love to see your facility," he said, as he whipped out his business card. "Here's my card, Stanley."

"Stan, I'm glad you came and hopefully we can get together soon. I'd like to talk more about how our firm can benefit your company," Blair added, also seeking to seize the opportunity.

Nia had known that she'd likely be used as a pawn by Blair that evening, but what Terrence had pulled was inexcusable. "Blair, can you excuse us for a moment. I'd like to freshen up a bit. We'll be right back."

"Sure, I'm sorry. I guess I'm being a little possessive of your beautiful fiancée tonight, Terrence," Blair said with a smile. "Please, by all means. I'll catch up with you guys later. But, Nia, don't you leave just yet. I've got a few more people that I'd really love for you to meet."

"Sure, Blair. Don't worry, we'll be right back," Terrence said grinning, as Nia clutched his arm and headed to the lobby.

"Let's go."

"Sweetie, you've got to be kidding. The party's not over."

"Terrence, have you lost your mind? I'm not supposed to tell *anyone* about the promotion yet!" she whispered in frustration.

"I know, Nia, but these people won't take that to the media," Terrence said, deploying a convincing tone.

"It's confidential and I told you specifically not to say anything to *anyone*."

"You're right. I'm sorry. I shouldn't have done that. I just got lost in the moment. I'm just working so hard to convince Blair I deserve to make partner, sweetie. I promise I won't tell anyone else."

"If you bring it up one more time…even allude to it, *I'm leaving*."

"Alright, alright. Come on, sweetie. I promise I won't bring it up any more. Come on, let's get back in there. I want to find Blair."

As they re-entered the party, an attractive, young, curvaceous Latina woman in a tightly fitted dress tapped Terrence on his shoulder.

"Hey, Terrence," the young woman said in a sultry tone with a thick Spanish accent.

"Tina!" Terrence responded and then gave the woman a big hug. "Nia, this is Tina. She's our new secretary," Terrence said, as he turned to Nia holding on to the young woman's hand.

And why is he holding her hand like that? "Nice to meet you," Nia said in an annoyed tone, as she gave the girl a quick once over.

"It's nice to meet you, Nia. I've heard so many wonderful things about you."

"Is that right?" *Funny, I haven't heard anything about you,* Nia thought, as she cut Terrence a wicked glare.

"Yes, and I really admire you and your career," the woman went on. "From one woman of color to another, I am so proud of what you've accomplished. I really look up to you."

"Well, thank you, Tina."

"Tina is the brightest young person in the firm," Terrence added.

"Look at you, workin' it as usual, Terrence. He always knows the right thing to say. He's so cute. You're such a *lucky* woman, Nia," the young Latina woman said, winking at Nia while Terrence grinned from ear to ear.

I know she didn't just flirt with my man right in front of my face and then wink at me. "Yeah, he's quite the charmer…isn't he?" Nia replied with a faux smile. "Well, Terrence, I think we shouldn't hold this young lady up any longer. I'm sure her *date* is probably somewhere looking for her," Nia suggested.

"Oh, I didn't bring a date. Believe it or not, I don't even have a man. It's so hard for a single lady to meet a nice man in this country. They all want you to share them. In Peru, a woman won't date a man that is spoken for, but here it happens all the time. But I just won't settle, Nia," the young woman explained, accentuating every R that rolled off of her tongue.

Yeah, sure you won't. "Good for you. Okay, come on Terrence, I'm sure she'd like to do some mingling."

"Oh, that's okay, it's just an honor to meet you, Nia, and I talk to Terrence all day anyway," she added with a giggle.

I bet you do.

"Oh, this girl can talk. She's definitely going to be a trial lawyer someday," Terrence joked.

"I have to finish law school first, Terrence. You're so silly. Nia, he is soooo funny. Every day your husband has all of the secretaries in stitches. Oh, I'm sorry, I mean your fiancé."

Oh, she's trying to be funny. Alright, that's enough of this heffa. "No, he's not my husband, *yet*," Nia snapped. "Anyway, it was a pleasure meeting you… Trina, was it?"

"No, Nia. It's Tina," Terrence corrected Nia, and she rolled her eyes back at him in return.

"Oh, yeah…Tina. I'm sorry about that. Anyway, come on, Terrence," Nia said and then yanked on his arm and walked away from the young Latina woman.

"You're batting a thousand tonight, aren't you, Terrence?"

"What do you mean, sweetie?" Terrence asked with a look of innocence.

"You know what I mean."

"Are you jealous? I can't believe it. I've never seen you jealous before."

"I'm not jealous and you're not funny."

For the rest of the evening Nia gave Terrence the cold shoulder and barely said two more words to him.

Chapter 36

DURING THE RIDE HOME FROM MCLOUGHLIN AND MCLOUGHLIN'S AN-niversary party, Nia and Terrence rode in complete silence. On the surface, she usually ignored him always parading her around, using her success as a ploy to gain business and attention, but deep inside those repressed feelings festered. Nia sat in the passenger seat of Terrence's large SUV sweltering in anger.

"So you're just going to keep giving me the silent treatment?"

"I'm not giving you any silent treatment. Trust me, I just have a lot to say and I'm gathering my words so I won't explode on you and find myself screaming."

"I'm sorry, Nia. I know I shouldn't have mentioned your promotion, but I'm just so proud of you."

"Do I look stupid?"

"No, what are you talking about?"

"You know what I'm talking about, Terrence! You were using me. You were using my promotion to make you look good."

"I can't believe you'd say that."

"Why can't you? You know it's true. Just admit it. Then I might not be so pissed at you."

"Okay, fine. I can admit to throwing it out there to make Blair realize our value, but it wasn't to use you."

"Our value? Terrence, you work for McLoughlin and McLoughlin, not me."

"Yeah, but we're a team. We complement each other."

"We didn't seem like such a good team when you and that little tramp were flirting with each other earlier."

"What are you talking about, Nia? I wasn't flirting with her. I was just joking around. You know how I am."

"Do I look stupid? The one thing I am *not* is stupid. If you want to flirt while I'm not around, that's up to you, but don't do it in front of me. That's flat-out disrespectful and unacceptable!"

"But how was I being disrespectful? Give me one example."

"Holding hands, Terrence. Tell me that wasn't disrespectful."

"Okay, I could see how you could think that, but after we hugged she just held on to my hand. Sweetie, you know I'm not interested in her…"

"I don't care if you were, or weren't. It was disrespectful and you'd be pissed if I ever pulled something like that."

"You're right. I guess I got a little carried away, but I'm not interested in Tina and I wasn't using you with Blair. I'm just playing the game, trying to make partner."

"There is no game, Terrence. You just have to keep working hard and it'll come in due time."

"But you don't understand. I'm just trying to contribute. I don't think you get how hard it is to be in the shadow of your woman's career. And it's not like you're just some successful businesswoman or corporate executive, your boss is the damn President of the United States, Nia! You're one of the most successful and powerful women in the entire country. So, what the hell, how do I compete with that? I'd have to *BE* the damn president to compete with your career! And you can roll your eyes if you want to, Nia, but that's just hard for a man to accept. The roles in this relationship are all fucked up," Terrence said in disgust. "I moved here for your career. That's a big sacrifice. Knowing my career will never be able to compete with my woman's is a big blow to my ego and I don't have a problem admitting it. I'm sorry."

"Terrence, I know it's been tough on you, and I appreciate the sacrifices that you've made for me. But I don't feel like you're inferior to me, or you're any less of a man because in some ways I've been more successful. Like you said, we're supposed to be a team. You can't let society dictate your role in a relationship. And at the end of the day, you contribute with a paycheck, moral support, and by just being my partner," Nia explained in a sympathetic tone.

"I know, but it's hard, Nia. I have a lot of pride, and I want to be successful too. I have dreams, just like you do, and I want to provide for my woman and be the man of my household."

"I know you do and you're working to accomplish those dreams, but you can't use me to achieve them either. That's contrary to everything you just said you were trying to achieve."

"Now, you know I would never use you. I just know how these clowns think, and your title impresses them. I'm sorry if you think I was trying to use you. I would never do that."

"I know you may not mean to, but that's what it equates to."

"Well, it won't happen again," Terrence said, gazing over at Nia momentarily as he drove down the winding highway. "But you know I love you and I'm just so proud of you." Terrence knew that just uttering those three simple words, "I love you," aroused an emotion in Nia that nothing else could. When she was a child her mom had told her she loved her every chance she got, but after she passed away, Nia didn't hear the words "I love you" again until she began to date. Although her grandmother *treated* her with love, she rarely said it. While this seemed like an insignificant aspect of her past, the power of those three words was immeasurable and always managed to get Terrence off of the hook when he was in her doghouse.

"Although it's difficult for me to walk in your HUGE shadow, I'm still proud of my baby." Terrence paused for a moment, then grinned, flashing his infectious dimples.

"It's not that simple, Terrence. You can't just apologize and flash your little dimples, thinking you're off of the hook," Nia scolded, as Terrence grabbed her hand and kissed it again and again. Then he began to sing playfully.

"There goes my baby. You don't know *how* much *you* mean to me. There goes my baaaabyyyyy!" He laughed each time his voice cracked with every high note of Usher's classic hit song, "There Goes My Baby." Nia tried to fight back a smile, but it still managed to peek through.

"You are so corny, but you're not getting off so easy. You better not tell *anyone* something I tell you is confidential again, Terrence. I'm serious."

"I know. I promise, sweetie, it will never happen again."

"And you're not off of the hook for flirting with that little tramp, either."

"I swear I wasn't flirting with her, sweetie," Terrence said with an innocent grin.

"And you better not be messing around with her, either. I don't have time for games, Terrence."

"You know I'm not, sweetie. You know me; I'm always trying to make everyone laugh and like me. I just can't help it, but that'll never happen again. I got what I want. Sexy, intelligent, beautiful, successful, alluring, just a flat-out..."

"Alright already."

"Flat-out stunning. A dime-piece, as they say," he said, laughing.

"You are *so* ghetto. Alright, alright...I guess I'll give you a pass this *one* time."

Chapter 37

MONDAY MORNING PRESIDENT DAVIS MADE THE INTERNAL AN-
nouncement to the entire White House staff that Nia had been promoted to
White House chief of staff. Some were surprised, but most weren't. Nia was
well respected and many thought she should have been the president's pick for
chief of staff to begin with instead of Tanner Long. Nia had never put much
thought into it. She knew Tanner had his strengths, and he absolutely had
his share of weaknesses, but she'd always felt he definitely possessed the one
character trait that every chief of staff had to have to be successful: an incredibly thick backbone. Tanner's backbone had the kind of girth that legends are
made of and was perhaps the sole reason President Davis had selected him for
the job.

In the days following the announcement, Nia sensed that she was being
treated differently. When she arrived at the ground-floor entrance to the
White House, the ordinarily stoic guards who had barely spoken to her in the
past now greeted her with enthusiasm.

"Good morning, Ms. Taylor. How are you this wonderful morning?"

All throughout the White House she received a similar energy from the
entire staff. And White House aides jumped at her every word. She also began
to exude a different sort of energy herself. She had a new air of confidence—a
confidence that bordered on cockiness and wasn't well received by her staff.

Later that morning, President Davis made the announcement to the rest of
the country during a White House press conference.

"Good morning. I am proud and excited to announce that we have selected
our new White House chief of staff. This position is extremely important
to us. The chief of staff has the unenviable responsibility of keeping me on
course..." President Davis said with a smile, as a chuckle could be heard from
the press secretary who was standing behind him, "as well as the entire White
House staff. The chief of staff is the backbone of our White House. They work
tirelessly to help us accomplish our goals each and every day. And their role
often goes unsung by the media. However, it certainly doesn't go unsung in
this office. We never take for granted the value of this position. This administration is amidst a difficult period. We have inherited a severely troubled
economy, wars, issues with education, energy, and challenges that, perhaps,
no other administration has ever faced. And it's imperative that we face these
challenges with our best leaders. In particular, in the role of White House chief
of staff, I need someone that is exceptionally bright; someone that has a broad
grasp of the challenges that lie ahead. Someone that is not afraid to be candid

with their opinions. Someone that doesn't mind beginning each day with me and seeing this mug late into the evening." He smiled and paused momentarily while the members of the press laughed. Comedic timing was a natural gift of his.

"Someone that I can count on. Someone that I have unequivocal faith in, and quite frankly, someone that can flat-out deliver." President Davis once again paused and slowly scanned the audience of journalists with his typical charisma building the anticipation.

"Although this position had a long list of requirements, it was a simple choice. I am proud to appoint Nia Taylor to the position of White House chief of staff, effective immediately." He then turned to Nia as she arrived at his side at the podium. He began to clap vigorously along with the press.

"I'm sure many of you are quite familiar with Nia. She has served as my deputy chief of staff over the past two years. She has worked in the private sector as an executive for a Fortune 500 company. She was my campaign manager when I ran for Senate. She was my chief of staff in the Senate and my co-campaign manager while I ran for president. She has an incredible mind, which I might add was honed at my alma mater, Harvard. She is tenacious. She won't back down from anyone and she always gets the job done. Around the White House, if we have a problem that no one else can solve, we put Nia on it. She has the uncanny ability to stand on your throat, while at the same time smiling down with her hand extended, offering to help you up." The press snickered.

"Around the White House, we affectionately refer to her as 'The Terminator...'" The press chuckled. "Not because she's Arnold **Schwarzenegger's** biggest fan..." The press chuckled again. "But because Nia will terminate anything that stands in the way of her solving a problem." A huge grin surfaced on President Davis's face as he delivered the punch line.

"Seriously, Nia is known as one of our most adept problem solvers. I have full confidence that she will solve any problem that I put in front of her and I am thoroughly excited about working with Nia in this new role. So, without further ado, I'd like to introduce you to the *new* White House chief of staff, Nia Taylor."

President Davis then turned and gave Nia a warm hug, said congratulations, and began to once again applaud along with the press. She could feel the force of butterflies whirling in her gut, as she fought to contain the adrenaline that raced through her veins. As the applause died down, she managed to gather herself and then stepped to the podium.

"Thank you, Mr. President. It is truly an honor to be chosen as your chief of staff, and have the opportunity to serve the people of this country in this new capacity," Nia said, peering over at President Davis as the troublesome butterflies completely fled. "I can't express how much admiration I have for President Davis. It has truly been a privilege to work for this man, and I am extremely excited about having the opportunity to now work more closely with him. I understand that this is a tremendous responsibility, and I want to assure the American people that I am committed to working tirelessly for them, and for President Davis. I have set lofty goals for myself in this new role, and I intend to work around the clock to achieve those goals. More importantly, I intend to work around the clock to achieve the president's goals. Now I'd like to take a moment to address your questions."

"Nia, William Summers, *New York Post*. Why do you think that you're the most qualified person for this position when there are so many other candidates that are even more qualified than you are?"

"That's not for me to answer. My job is simply to answer the call and utilize the many years of experience that I *do* possess to deliver. Next question please," Nia said.

"Nia, Steve Blake from the *Chicago Tribune*. Will you get tired at the end of the day of looking at President Davis's, as he called it, mug?" the journalist said, laughing.

Nia laughed for a moment along with the press and then responded, "I've known President Davis and his beautiful wife for a long time now…and I think how I answer this question may be my first critical decision in this new role." She smiled. "And I think I'd be wise to side step it and defer that question to the First Lady. She would be better able to address that since she literally goes to sleep each night and wakes up each morning to his *mug*, as President Davis so eloquently put it." Nia grinned, as the press rumbled with laughter.

"Nia! Everett Bailey, *Seattle Press*. How does it feel to be the first African American White House chief of staff?"

"It's wonderful, and it feels equally wonderful to be the first female White House chief of staff. I feel very fortunate to be able to lay that sort of foundation for young women and people of color all over this country."

"Nia, who's going to fill your role as deputy chief of staff?"

"Well, as you know, Gregory Connors has been doing a fine job as our other deputy chief of staff, so the position isn't completely empty. However, Greg taking on my responsibilities and trying to keep up with his present responsibilities would be a lot for one person to handle, even Greg. I'm sure in the coming days the president and I will sit down and discuss that issue."

Another reporter stood up. "Nia, the federal investigation into Klein Schultz was said to have included you." Nia's heart rate surged. "You're said to have been offered a large sum of money and a future CEO position with one of their crony companies. Is this true?" the journalist asked, sneering. "And if so, how much money did they offer you? And furthermore, did you take the offer?

And will it land you in trouble?" The reporter rapidly spouted question after question.

Damn it! I was hoping no one would bring this up, she thought, as her internal thermometer, again, began to rise. "I'm sorry, what was your name?"

"Joe Stevens, *Wolf News Network.*"

"Well, Joe, as I'm sure you are well aware, that investigation is ongoing, so I can't say too much about it. And quite frankly, there really isn't much to say about it anyway."

"That's not what I've been hearing, Ms. Taylor," the journalist immediately rebutted. "There are reports that you were offered a multi-million dollar a year salary in return for a favor. Is this true?"

"Well, Joe, I have nothing to hide and really nothing of any substance to share with you about that investigation. If you have something newsworthy to cover on the issue, you wouldn't be doing your job not to. But I have every confidence in our Federal Bureau of Investigation. They'll find out if there were any wrong doings. Okay, I think that's it. I'm sure my boss has lots of work for me to do," Nia said with a warm smile.

"White House Press Secretary Kevin James will be coming up next. Thanks a lot, guys. Have a great rest of your day!" Nia closed her interview to applause, as the *Wolf News Network* journalist Joe Stevens sat with a menacing grimace on his face.

Chapter 38

THE MORNING AFTER THE BIG ANNOUNCEMENT, AFTER A DOCTORS visit for a routine physical, Nia headed in to the West Wing several hours later than her typical 6:30 AM starting time. As she zipped down Pennsylvania Avenue with her peppy little two-door BMW Coupe hugging the concrete, she and Terrence's favorite song, Usher's "There Goes My Baby," began to play on the radio. A smile emerged on her face and she began to hum the hit R&B single and reminisce about her relationship with Terrence. She also began to reflect on the long, difficult journey she had taken to arrive at her new role as chief of staff. Although her journey hadn't been anywhere near as smooth as the freshly paved Pennsylvania Avenue asphalt she was traveling on, her promotion had provided her with a rejuvenation of sorts. Her mood hadn't been this upbeat in months. Then her cell phone began to ring.

"Nia! Congratulations! Girl, you didn't say a word. How long did you know?" Carla said excitedly.

"Hey, girl, thanks! I found out a few days ago, but you know I couldn't say anything."

"So how do you feel? Are you excited? Nervous? What?"

"Of course I'm excited, but not really nervous. Other than yesterday's press conference, I haven't felt nervous at all."

"Well, you know we need to celebrate. I have to come up there to cover a story in a couple of weeks and we should all get together for lunch."

"Yes, we should. I had so much fun when we were down there," Nia said with a smile, as she pictured their last get-together in her mind.

"Girl, I am so proud of you. You have accomplished so much. Ugh…making me tear up. Gonna ruin my make-up and I have to start my segment in a few," Carla said.

"Don't make me mess up my make-up either, Carla. So when are you coming? So I can make sure to clear my schedule."

"Like I said, I'm coming up there to do a story in a couple of weeks. I'll check with Val and Bev to see if they're available for lunch and get back to you."

When Nia had arrived at the White House and entered for the first time officially as the new chief of staff, she had immediately noticed a pronounced difference in the way she was treated by the staff. Although they had been overly nice, it was almost irritating to Nia—she despised phoniness and hated being patronized even more—but she'd had no time to think about it. Not only was it her first day in her new role, it was also the morning of the mid-term elections.

Nia forged ahead, anxiously trying to wrap her arms around her new role.

Psychologically, she had to fight the urge to want immediate organization and control. Nia was the kind of person who lived for organization. Not only did she have photos of all of her shoes attached to each and every shoebox (an idea she had gotten compliments of "The Oprah Winfrey Show"), she also had them organized by usage category (casual, dress, etc.) *and* in alphabetical order. Likewise, she took this same approach to her job and she had worked all night in preparation for her first day as the chief of staff.

Although she had headed up the ever-so-important morning staff meeting numerous times in the past, she felt she had to approach it differently this time—from a perspective that would set the tone for the staff going forward. Furthermore, Nia expected tensions to be high since it was the morning of the mid-term elections, and tension among the staff would likely be the case all throughout the West Wing.

That morning, Nia manned the staff meeting with the authority of a captain on his ship. She gripped the sides of the podium firmly, delivering commands to the staff with expert precision, setting new, much higher expectations for everyone. The looks on the staff members' faces told a story—looks of shock and dismay were seen all throughout the room.

At the close of the staff meeting, Nia dashed over to the Oval Office for her morning meeting with President Davis. She entered the Oval Office exuding the same level of confidence she had displayed at her staff meeting.

"Good morning, sir."

"Good morning. Well, we know it's not looking good, but we have to dig deep today. What's our schedule like?" President Davis asked.

"Well, sir, to start, you have 24 radio interviews this morning."

"How much time are we talking for each one?"

"We're talking about five-minute blocks of time for each interview and they have to be exactly five minutes, which I have stressed to the shows' producers."

"I'd like to spend a bit more time with certain stations," he instructed, as he scanned the list of stations which contained formats as broad and colorful as a rainbow.

"Definitely would like to spend more time with my man Steve Harvey. He has provided an unbelievable amount of support and I think has an exceptional influence on his listeners. Same goes for the 'Tom Joyner Show.' And of course, I have to spend some time with Ryan Cameron in my adopted hometown."

"But, sir, Ryan Cameron is on in the afternoon and we don't have you scheduled to do any afternoon shows…we have to do CNN and a few other network call-in interviews in the late afternoon."

"Yeah, well, we'll just have to fit it in. And make sure to add the 'Rickey Smiley Show' to this list too. We need the young people to get out and vote and he's been a huge supporter of us."

"Okay, sir, no problem. Next on our agenda is your trip to Africa in two weeks," Nia said, as her Blackberry buzzed with a new text message. As President Davis discussed the hunger crisis going on throughout Africa, Nia inconspicuously glanced down at her cell phone to read the text, which read, *Hey girl! talked 2 Valerie and Beverly...they can meet when I come to town!*

"...and Nia, before we leave, it'd be good for you to go over our agenda with General McDonald," the president suggested as Nia was slightly distracted by her cell phone.

"Sir, did you say *we*?" Nia asked in surprise.

"Well, Tanner was scheduled to go, so I just assumed that you'd be going now."

"Oh," Nia responded in shock. *Oh shoot, I forgot about that*, she thought. "Sounds good, sir."

At the conclusion of her meeting with President Davis, Nia went back to her new corner office, where the sun was blazing through the windows. The new surroundings seemed to have given her a new energy.

Uhhh, I am so glad to finally have a spacious office again and actually have some sunlight! Nia thought as she stretched her arms out wide. Then she grabbed the phone and called one of her aides.

"Cindy, I need you to jump on something right away. POTUS has decided that he wants to do a call-in interview with the 'Ryan Cameron Show' on V103 in Atlanta. I need you to set that up immediately," Nia instructed Cindy firmly.

"Sure, Nia, but I was finishing up those phone calls to the congressmen. As soon as I finish, I'll call V103," the aide responded.

"Cindy, I didn't *ask* you to call after you were done with what you're doing, I said I *need* you to call right away!" Nia snapped.

"I'm sorry, Nia. I'll call V103 right this moment," the aide responded sheepishly.

"I don't have time to explain everything I ask you to do. I just need you to do it!" Nia said and then slammed the phone down on the hook.

By then, it was time for the first of President Davis's call-in radio interviews. She zipped back down the hall to the Oval Office. The first call was the "Steve Harvey Morning Show."

"...Steve, I know you're a man that follows politics closely and you do a great job rallying your listeners around a cause. Well, as you know, today is the mid-term elections and some important things are at stake with this particular election. But, I'd like to first talk about something that's even more important," President Davis explained to the popular radio host and comedic icon. He leaned back in his seat with Nia sitting across from him with her chair firmly planted in the center of the Oval Office carpet's Presidential Seal.

Where is he going with this? The only talking points for this call-in are on the mid-term election, Nia thought as she subtly indicated a sheet of paper that contained a meticulously thought-out list of predetermined mid-term election talking points. But President Davis ignored her gestures and went on talking.

"Steve, Nephew Tommy, Shirley, Carla...*humanity* supersedes any and everything. Although this mid-term election is extremely important, there is something going on that absolutely dwarfs it in terms of importance," he explained passionately.

Oh my goodness, what is he doing? I've got to say something! Come on POTUS, not on my first day on the job, Nia thought. Her palms moistened from anxiety, as she felt like President Davis was straying from the talking points. One of the most important jobs of the chief of staff was to act as the needle to the president's compass. A president is constantly overwhelmed with so much information that human cognition of all of it is virtually impossible. Consequently, even the sharpest and most well-disciplined Presidential mind can get off track from time to time.

That's it; I have to do my job!

Nia began to *vehemently* point to the list of talking points which lay perpendicular to President Davis in the middle of his desk. But he, once again, went on completely ignoring her gestures.

"There are some people that desperately need our support right now. Africa is presently experiencing an unimaginable crisis. Somalia, specifically, is facing one of the worst bouts of famine that the world has witnessed in generations. It's estimated that a quarter, or one point five million, of the population of Somalia is currently displaced, and better than 10 million are in dire need of food. They need our help."

"Sir, I couldn't agree with you more. So how can we help?" Steve Harvey asked.

Steve, every moment counts. I implore your listeners to take action...*right... this...moment...*and go to www.icrc.org for more information on how they can help. Okay, thanks for letting me get that off of my chest. Now, let's shift gears and get back to this mid-term," President Davis said, as Nia gave a sigh of relief.

Phew, I didn't know where he was going with that...thank goodness it was down the right path, Nia thought to herself, as President Davis began to explain the importance of voting in this mid-term to the "Steve Harvey Show" listeners.

The day's interviews were important because the mid-term election races were tight, and maintaining the majority in the House of Representatives was on the line. Nonetheless, the months of preparation and the president's last-minute efforts to rally voters were futile. The Republicans won the majority of seats in the House. The Democrats did manage to hold on to the Senate, but losing the House was devastating to the administration.

Chapter 39

NIA'S DAYS SEEMED TO BE GROWING LONGER AND LONGER IN HER NEW role, but she just worked even harder. She routinely left the West Wing after midnight. The Friday before Nia's weekend with the girls, she decided to leave the office early for a change. Things had finally begun to simmer down since the Democrats had gotten their butts whipped in the mid-terms, and Nia thought she'd give herself a treat by leaving work at the time most Americans headed home, in preparation for her big weekend with the girls. The only thing left on her agenda was checking in with deputy chief of staff Gregory Connors before she left for the day. She decided to stretch her legs a bit and walked across the hallway to his office.

"Hey, Greg. Are you busy? Is that an important call?" Nia asked in a whispered tone after noticing he was on the telephone.

"No, just give me a minute. This is just Randy," Greg responded. Then he leaned forward in his seat and finished his conversation while Nia stood in his office doorway.

"No, Randy, you guys are just mad because you got a shellacking!" Greg laughed. "Yeah, sure, don't blame POTUS. You guys were up by five when he missed those free throws. Yeah, okay, Randy. I'll catch ya later, bud." Then Greg hung up and turned around to Nia.

"I'm sorry about that, Nia. What's going on?" Nia stepped into Greg's compact, little office with a look of confusion.

"Greg, didn't you see me standing here?"

"Yes, I'm sorry about that, Nia," Greg apologized, as Nia quickly closed his office door and remained standing with her arms folded, peering down on Greg.

"I really think that was disrespectful. What if I needed something important? We don't have time to chit chat with our friends on the phone…especially not when your boss is waiting to speak with you."

"Yeah, but, Nia, that was Randy, POTUS's personal aide. We were just talking about last night's pick-up basketball game with POTUS and the fellas. When you asked what I was doing, it didn't seem like it was anything important. Come on, Nia, you know me. If it was important, I would have hung up as soon as you came in. Plus, I didn't want to be rude to POTUS's guy."

"Unless it's an emergency, work related, or it's *POTUS himself*, Greg, you should always show me the respect of getting off of the phone when I enter your office," Nia responded sharply with a frown.

"I apologize. It won't happen again," Greg replied with a look of frustration.

"It better not, Greg. We shouldn't even be having this conversation!"

"You're right, Nia. Again, I apologize."

"I forgot what I even came in here for...I'm leaving. I'll email my question later. Have a good weekend," Nia said curtly.

"Yeah, you too," Greg responded blandly, trying to hide his anger. When Greg and Nia had initially entered the White House, dealing with Tanner as their boss had caused them to quickly bond and their relationship had only gotten stronger as time passed. But Greg sensed that Nia was beginning to change with her new role and he was not at all happy with her new attitude.

Chapter 40

THE FOLLOWING MORNING, NIA MET UP WITH HER GIRLS FOR BRUNCH at Puro Café in Georgetown. When Nia arrived she found Carla already seated chatting on her iPhone.

"Hey, girl!" Carla exclaimed as she stood and gave Nia a warm hug. "Jeff, I have to go. I miss you too, punkin. I'll call you later." She punched the End button on the phone. "Girl, you look great. I thought you'd look all hagged out by now…especially with this new gig," Carla said, sipping on a latte.

"Thanks, I guess. Anyway, you look good, too," Nia replied.

"Val and Bev went to the bathroom," Carla informed Nia just as the two ladies arrived back to the table.

"Congratulations!" Valerie and Beverly said in virtual unison. Nia rose and the ladies exchanged warm hugs.

"Okay, so tell me all about the big promotion!" Val said, bright eyed.

"There's nothing really to tell," Nia answered nonchalantly.

"Whatever, girl. You're the second most powerful person in Washington now and you don't have anything to tell?" Beverly said. "Trust me, she's got a lot to tell."

"I'm serious and why does everybody always say that nonsense about the chief of staff being the second most powerful person in Washington?" Nia said shaking her head.

"You know you're the *woMAN* now. Everybody has to come through you to see POTUS. 'Cause they have to kiss your big black butt for the rest of his term," Beverly said in her typical laid-back *oh by the way* tone.

"First of all, my butt isn't *that* big and it's not black…its dark brown." Nia laughed. "And second, nobody has to kiss anything."

"Yeah, well you'll change that tune soon because you're about to create a lot of enemies, and if you don't have that 'kiss my butt' edge, they'll run all over you," Beverly explained.

"But look on the bright side, corporate America will be drooling all over you now. If you can handle this, you can handle anything in the corporate world, that's for sure," Valerie interjected.

"So wait a minute, let's go back to the, 'everybody comes through you now to get to President Davis' thing. That is some powerful stuff," Carla added with eyebrows arched. She was always captivated with power.

"Yup, even the most established congressmen have to go through Nia now to get to POTUS. And you better make sure their uppity asses kiss your butt too, Nia, especially that old crusty Senator Burk. I can't stand him," Beverly said, rolling her eyes and slurping on a latte.

"I'm not thinking about him and you know I don't care about making ene-mies. The nonsense has already started though. The other day POTUS had me take an *established* congressman, and I'm not going to mention his name, off of the invite list for an upcoming White House dinner. That congressman called me throwing a fit, cursing and screaming at me."

"Did you tell him POTUS took him off the list?" Carla asked.

"Nooo, I can't do that. I can't throw POTUS under the bus. It's my job to take the heat for that kind of decision. I just had to tell him that he wasn't invited. If he thought it was my decision to take him off of the list, oh well," Nia said.

"What? That's kind of crazy, girl!" Carla said. "You are going to have a lot of enemies soon."

"Wait, then he tried to sneak behind my back and call POTUS's secretary to get an appointment, but she directed him right back to me. Then he was twice as mad." Nia chuckled.

"What did you say, girl?" Carla asked.

"I just explained that if he wants to get to POTUS he has to go through me, and yelling, screaming, and cursing won't get him anywhere."

"How'd he react?"

"Girl, he's my new BFF," Nia laughed. "Ever since then he's treated me better than any other congressman."

"Damn, girl, you really are the second most powerful person in Washington," Carla said, grinning and sipping.

"Nah, I just had to step into this new role aggressively to let everybody know that I wasn't a pushover and set the tone," Nia explained, as her phone began to ring.

"Is that Terrence's damn phone calling you again? You better watch him," Beverly blurted out.

"Hmmm...no, it's Greg. Excuse me, I better get this. Hi Greg," Nia answered. There was a pause as she listened. "Oh you have got to be kidding. That son of a gun! Damn it! Just what I need right now. Thanks, Greg." Nia ended the call, dropped her forehead into the palm of her hand, and shook her head.

"What's going on, Nia? Is everything okay?" Val asked.

"That was my deputy chief Greg Connors calling to tell me this jerk reporter named Joe Stevens, who tried to front me at the press conference announcing my promotion the other day, has people buzzing on Twitter about me and the The Social Hub/Klein Schultz investigation," Nia explained.

"How did I miss that..." Carla said. "Yup, I see it now. It was one of the top trending topics on Twitter. Let me see what he's been saying." She quickly slid her index finger across her iPhone's screen. "Oh, listen to this tweet he sent out a few hours ago…'President made ANOTHER big mistake with his new pick for chief of staff, Nia Taylor. Can you say white-collar criminal?! http://ReporterJStevens.blogspot.com/!' Damn, what is his problem?"

"You know his problem…" Beverly added. "First, he has to write about the first black president and now he has to deal with this—the first black White House chief of staff, and even worse, the first female chief of staff. I wouldn't even worry about his silly nonsense."

"I don't know what his problem is. Like I said, out of nowhere he tried to front me at the press conference."

"Yeah, he's crazy. What do you have to do with The Social Hub and Klein Schultz anyway?" Carla asked.

Here we go. This offer just doesn't want to go away! Now they want to know… I shouldn't even tell them. Hell, I didn't even do anything wrong. I didn't even take the damn offer, Nia thought.

"Yeah, why is he associating you with them?" Beverly asked.

And, Beverly, you're the last person I need to know about this, with your big mouth. Oh, forget it. "It's a long story, guys. Klein Schultz tried to get me to get in POTUS's ear about some proposed legislation and tried to get Rothschild and Smith Financial to give me their CEO position in return. You know they're all in bed together."

"What? You never told me that. Why would you get involved with that kind of nonsense?" Beverly interrupted.

"That's exactly why I didn't say anything, Beverly. I knew you would jump to conclusions…you didn't even let me finish," Nia snapped.

"Listen to this. 'Want to see a NEWS WORTHY article Ms. Taylor? Read about yourself at http://ReporterJStevens.blogspot.com/!' WTF! Why is he going so hard at you?" Carla asked.

"That's what I don't get. I didn't even snap at him when he fronted me at the press conference."

"Uh-oh, here he goes again," Carla began to read another tweet by the reporter. "'Make sure justice is served & put Taylor where she belongs…behind bars! This is who Prez wants running staff. Just another bad decision!'"

"Girl, all I can say is you better get a good attorney."

"Really, Bev?"

Chapter 41

THE REPUBLICANS IN THE PREVIOUS PRESIDENTIAL REGIME HAD AN-
nihilated the U.S. economy, as well as heavily contributed to the demise of the
entire world's economy. The new administration had inherited a slew of problems: multiple wars, poor foreign relations, the highest unemployment rate in
decades, and a nation full of confused and very vulnerable citizens.

The Republicans desperately wanted to regain the White House. They pres-
sured the current president from every angle, fighting any initiative that he
brought forth. To make matters worse, many of President Davis's so-called
Democratic comrades withered under the peer pressure. This, coupled with
the Democrats losing the House of Representatives, seemed like it was the
final knockout blow, but fortunately the economy showed signs of recovery
and President Davis's approval ratings were rising. This gave the president and
his administration a moment of relief, but just a moment.

Jim Curry, the new Speaker of the House, was slowly emerging as the
Republican Party's superstar and future presidential candidate. No one in the
current administration was surprised about his popularity because of his affil-
iation with the powerful super PAC "Recapture Our Excellence."

The day of Curry's appointment to Speaker of the House, Nia met with
President Davis to go over their typical agenda. The changing of the guard in
the House of Representatives and a lingering issue with the ever-so-controver-
sial Guantanamo Bay Detention Center appeared to have President Davis a bit
on edge. During his election campaign, he had vowed to shut down the notoriously well-known U.S. detention center, which housed many suspected ter-
rorists who were considered extremely threatening to United States national
security. The issue of the center was controversial on a variety of levels. Many
U.S. citizens didn't want it closed and the terrorist suspects moved to U.S. soil;
meanwhile, it had disgraced the country because of the extreme intelligence
tactics which had been previously employed at the center.

"What are your thoughts on the situation, Nia?" President Davis inquired.

"Mr. President, I respectfully disagree with you," Nia replied firmly.

"Oh, you do?" he responded. "It's too controversial; we have to back out at
this point. I know we made campaign promises, but it's not worth the head-
ache. You have to know when to fold 'em, Nia."

"But we have to keep our campaign promises. Sir, you're a man of your word,
and you know when it comes time for re-election they'll bring this back up."

"Nia, it's noble to uphold campaign promises, but what good is that if
Congress is going to fight us tooth and nail? All the legislation they've thrown

together to fight this is just another way to undermine us and prevent us from winning anything. And the main pushback is coming from Democrats," President Davis replied, leaning back in his chair with his fingers laced together and tucked neatly under his chin.

"Yes, but we both know that this country's needs are always shifting. That's what makes this job so difficult. That's what makes the decisions so difficult, but we have to stick to our promises. Sir, I promise you, if you don't close the Guantanamo Bay Detention Center, like you promised in your campaign for office, they'll use this against you when it comes time to campaign again in 2012."

"Decisions…you don't make any decisions, Nia! That's not what you do as chief of staff!" the president said, raising his voice and springing forward out of his chair.

"I understand that, sir," Nia replied with a hint of irritation in her voice, "but the point that I was trying to make was that the ever-changing needs of this country are what make *your* job so difficult. But just because the political climate shifts, it doesn't mean we have to be as wishy-washy and back down from our promises…especially if we still believe them. Either way, I feel confident that whatever decision you make will come out fine. Sir, I was just responding to your request to give you my opinion."

"Wishy-washy…? So are you saying that I'm a wishy-washy President?" He stood over Nia, glaring down at her.

"No," she replied, as she eased her chair back and began to stand up.

"Well just what the hell *ARE* you trying to say then? It's not me, it's the media!" President Davis yelled. Nia stood, a bit dazed and in shock. This was totally out of the president's character. Nia had never heard him so much as raise his voice, let alone yell. She took a deep breath and paused momentarily, seeking to compose herself and not give heed to the adrenaline surge. Although her anxiety caused her to stand there practically trembling, Nia's competitive nature and innate diva-like moxie kicked in, virtually taking control of every word that spilled out of her mouth.

"Sir, with all due respect," Nia began to speak in a snappier tone, "regardless of what the media is saying, it's your responsibility to not succumb to their pressure and stick to your guns…no matter what. That will pay off in the campaign when your integrity is at question. And even if it doesn't, sir, you are the most forthright person I have ever met."

"What's your point? Are you now questioning my integrity?" President Davis asked loudly.

"I don't know if you are just exhausted and need a break, or just need…"

"Or just need what, Nia? Go ahead…in your first month on the job…go ahead and finish telling the *President of the United States of America* what the hell he needs!" he barked as he slowly moved forward, stopping directly in front of her, virtually brushing noses. "Go ahead, Nia...tell me!" he yelled once more, as he stared deep into her eyes.

Nia swallowed with a gulp that resonated throughout her entire body, causing her to slightly tremble. *I can't believe him. I can't believe he's this pissed. He's letting this pressure get to him. He's the one that asked me what I thought. I've never seen him act like this...is he losing it?* She stood perplexed and then took a step backwards to regain her personal space.

"Mr. President, with all due respect, I really don't like to argue with you. And perhaps this *may* be our first argument, but what I want to make clear to you, sir...and again, I say this with all due respect...I can agree to disagree with you and absolutely concede to your decision, but what I CANNOT do, is lie to you. I have to give you my honest opinion when you ask me. If I didn't, I wouldn't be doing my job and I would be doing an injustice to you to just agree with everything you say. I didn't accept this position to be your 'yes woman,' so to speak. And correct me if I'm wrong, but the job of a chief of staff is to always put the president's best interest first, even if that means telling him something that he doesn't want to hear. Sir, and completely aside from our initial discussion, perhaps what is more important to me is that you are acting completely out of character. Are you okay, sir?"

"Okay? I'm still waiting for you to tell me what I *need*," President Davis continued to press.

"Well, sir, I'll be honest with you—" Nia began to respond.

"*Well*, I wish you would," he interrupted.

"Sir, please forgive me for utilizing this colloquialism with you, but I'm just going to 'keep it real' with you...what you may *need* to do is have a talk with the First Lady. I think she'd be as concerned as I am with your present state," Nia said with an ever-so-slight roll of her neck, and then she realized what she had just done. Silence momentarily entered the Oval Office for what seemed to Nia like an eternity.

Oh my God! What did I just do? I can't believe I just snapped at the president like that. I guess I better go clean out my office, Nia thought, as the anxiety left her skin tingling. Then out of nowhere President Davis burst into laughter.

"I can't take it any longer!" he said, laughing hysterically, as Nia stood by with her mouth gaping open and her eyes nervously scanning the room back and forth.

"Nia, I was just trying to make sure you could handle this job. I'm sorry I may have taken it too far, but I just wanted to see if you would stand up to me if you had to, and you passed the test with flying colors. You almost did *too* well...ya know, the whole *need* to have a talk with your wife line was a bit much. We may have to talk about that line later, but you handled yourself well," President Davis said grinning. "Like I said, I'm sorry to put you through all of that, but you have no idea how it drives me crazy that I have all of these 'yes men and women' around me," he explained.

"Sir, would the Secret Service rush in here if I said I was going to kill you? Because I could strangle you right now," Nia said laughing. "I can't believe you had me that worked up. I just wanted to be honest with you, but when you started acting so outrageously out of character, I began to get really worried about you. I was like, I can't believe he's getting so angry just because I disagree with him...totally out of character. But only you—no other president would have pulled a stunt like that," Nia said, grinning profusely and shaking her head.

"You really are 'The Terminator' aren't you? You know, seriously Nia, you've adjusted well to this position, but I had noticed you seemed a bit nervous a few times when you had to push the envelope with me. The president and chief of staff have a tricky relationship. I know I'm your boss and the president, but don't be hesitant about voicing your opinion, especially when I ask, and sometimes it's okay if you even have to give me a reality check every now and then. I listen to an onslaught of issues each and every day, and I'm human. I may fall asleep on an issue and potentially make a bad decision. Or even worse, just flat-out get out of whack. And that's when I'll need you to step in and be my voice of reason. Whatever you do, just don't be a 'yes woman.' I know you'll be respectful," President Davis said with a look of sincerity. "And remember, I didn't just choose you because you're one of the most intelligent people around here, although it did help that you graduated from my alma mater," he said with a chuckle. "I also chose you because you've got moxie and courage. I also knew you'd go to battle for me and have my back. And *that's* what makes a good chief of staff."

"I am so relieved, sir. I definitely understand what you're saying, and the last thing I want to do is patronize you by telling you what I think you want to hear. I just prefer to be a straight shooter anyway. But I was kind of apprehensive about speaking up and giving you my opinion in certain situations... after all, you are the president. So, thank you for clearing that up for me. I feel so much better now that we've gotten that out of the way. But I should have known you were up to something...you were acting so strange. I don't think I've ever heard you raise your voice," Nia said with a smile.

"I just missed my calling, that's all. 'King Kong...ain't got nothin'...on me!'" he said, laughing, in his best Denzel Washington voice, barely able to finish the famous line from the award-winning movie "Training Day."

"Oh my goodness, now *that* was a YouTube moment. That was like a billion hits waiting to happen, sir. But please don't quit your day job," Nia said as the two made eye contact and began laughing hysterically until tears filled their eyes.

Chapter 42

NIA HAD NOT ONLY BECOME RESPONSIBLE FOR ASSISTING THE MOST important man in the world, she was also responsible for leading the most important staff in the world. Although she was innately a confident person, just as in the case of most leaders in positions of extreme power, she needed to exude an even *higher* level of confidence. But this confidence had to be greater than that of a typical manager or leader because she was managing some of the brightest minds in politics, who she knew would constantly challenge her. Yet, also just as in the case of most leaders in powerful positions, Nia now had to effectively walk the fine line between confidence and arrogance.

Many leaders who have tried to successfully navigate this perilous tightrope have carelessly faltered to either side. Respect seems to be an essential correlating factor. The *meek* often never gain, or are able to maintain, the respect of unsavory subordinates, who in many cases are gunning for their position. Meanwhile, the *arrogant* simply lose the respect, and consequently, the loyalty of their followers. Additionally, Nia was now charged with leading former co-workers with whom she had built strong relationships over their time together. Either way, the delicate undertaking was already underway. Nia had fearlessly strutted far out onto the shaky, narrow tight-wire of leadership, and in response to the natural pressure to "step her game up," chose to lead her staff more authoritatively. And this new, more authoritative style of leadership didn't sit well with everyone.

Many staff members were unhappy with their new chief of staff. Ironically, they had dealt with Tanner's arrogance for his entire time at the helm, but they had known his arrogance was as much a part of him as his designer suits and corny one-liners. But they expected more from Nia. Everyone knew she was tough and aggressive, but also fair and level-headed. Many of Nia's old friends felt like she had changed, while numerous staff members felt disrespected and in turn she lost their respect. As a result, several staff members decided to get together for lunch to discuss just how to deal with their new boss.

"That is the most arrogant bitch in the West Wing!" staff member Ted Thompson barked.

"The promotion has clearly gone to her head! What did she say when you went to talk to her?" another staff member chimed in.

"I told her that you can't manage this kind of talent that way and she started going on and on about accountability and her achievements. She's crazy!" Ted explained furiously.

"When Tanner was the chief of staff he never acted this crazy. I mean, he was tough and his confidence showed, but he was fair."

"Who the hell does she think she's dealing with? I'm going to go to POTUS," another staffer interjected.

"No, that's not the answer. We have to teach her a lesson."

"What do you think we should do, Ted?"

"I already called Tanner and he gave me a few good suggestions. We'll just let her handle the aid to Somalia project alone, since she treats us like we're incompetent. Let's just see how POTUS responds to her dropping the ball with something like that," Ted said with his nostrils flared and nose turned up.

"Oh, that's dear to POTUS's heart. He's going to be pissed off."

"Exactly!"

Chapter 43

NIA ARRIVED HOME LATE THAT EVENING, EXHAUSTED. TERRENCE was working late at the firm. She entered her apartment, and as she routinely did, kicked off her pumps as soon as she entered the front door and then flopped down on the living room couch. As she lay back and tapped the remote control to turn on their 50-inch Sony flat screen television, her cell phone rang. She rolled her eyes, stared at the ceiling for a moment, and then took a deep breath. She knew it was Carla because she had a special ring tone set for all of her close friends.

"Hey, Carla." She answered the phone in a lackluster tone.

"Hey, girl, you'll never guess what happened," Carla immediately replied with her voice cracking.

"Are you okay? You sound like you've been crying. What's going on?" Nia sat up.

"You haven't seen it?"

"Seen what?"

"Girl, it's all over the Internet," Carla replied and then burst into tears.

"What?"

"Those damn paparazzi got pictures of me and Jeff on the beach…" Carla stammered. "On the beach, kissing!"

"Are you serious?"

"Yes, I'm serious. You can't have any fucking privacy!"

"Where were you guys at?"

"We were in Bora Bora."

"Why the hell were you kissing outside?"

"Nia, if you can't have privacy in Bora Bora, where can you have it?"

"Yeah, but you know better, girl. You know those paparazzi are desperate. You have to be careful wherever you are, especially with him."

"It just happened. It was supposed to be a romantic getaway and those damn paparazzi found us. It was those leaches from ZMZ dot com. It's crazy! Then before we could get back home it was all over the 'net. Hell, I started seeing stuff about it on my iPhone a few hours after we got back to our room."

"So what, though. You're divorced now and he's…please tell me he finally got divorced, Carla?"

"No."

"I told you should have waited 'til he got divorced. Was he even really separated?"

"He said he was—"

"But he wasn't?" Nia cut her off.

"I don't know."

"Oh, lord." Nia sighed loudly. "So what does he have to say about it?"

"He won't talk to me," Carla replied sheepishly.

"What? What do you mean?"

"We talked about it when the story first broke, but then when we got back to the U.S. he said we needed to stop communicating because it could affect the divorce now that it's out that we were messing around."

"Come on Carla, now was he really separated?"

"I don't know…" Carla said sounding confused and continuously sniffling.

"So he was lying about the whole thing?"

"I think he was. He already came out with a statement saying that he made a mistake and it only happened one time. Saying he loved his wife and hoped that she and his fans would forgive him," Carla rambled.

"So was he still living with her while you were together?"

"Oh, I don't know. It's so hard to tell…he's got so many houses…more than one in Atlanta alone," Carla said sounding bewildered.

"But, Carla, you had to know," Nia immediately snapped back.

"I'm telling you I didn't. It's not like you and Terrence—we both travel a lot, so half the time I don't know where the hell he is."

"So what kind of stuff were they saying on the 'net?"

"A bunch of lies…they started making up all this stuff about us messing around for years and even while his wife was pregnant. And I barely knew Jeff when she was pregnant. Saying that I ruined his marriage. Now *my* name is ruined. I look like a home-wrecker." Carla began to cry harder. Nia pulled the phone away from her ear and shook her head.

"Carla, I'm sorry, but you brought this on yourself. We told you not to do it, but all you could think about was how it would help your career and how exciting it was. Ridiculous. I really don't know what to tell you," Nia said coldly.

"What? My whole damn life is falling apart and that's all you can say is I told you so?"

"Well, just what do you want me to say, Carla? You knew this wasn't going to end pretty. You set yourself up for failure."

"I thought you would at least try to console your friend, Nia. I thought you would *say* I understand what you're going through. That's what I *thought* you would *say*!"

"But I don't understand what you're going through because the whole thing makes no sense. How can you get upset when you knew the man was married?"

"I can't believe you! I can't believe my best friend pretty much just doesn't give a damn that I just lost my man *and* my whole career is falling apart right in front of my eyes," Carla said in disgust.

"Carla, I do care, but he was a married man. What did you expect? I just don't have time—"

Carla cut her off. "You what? You don't have time? You selfish bitch!" Carla yelled and then hung up the phone.

"Hello? Hello?" Nia said and then hit the End button on her Blackberry. She shook her head and looked around in disbelief.

"I can't believe she's mad at me because she wanted to go run around with a married man. As tired as I am, I have to deal with this...as much stress as I'm under...they need to realize that I work for the *President of the United States* and I don't have time to deal with this type of nonsense," Nia fussed.

Chapter 44

CARLA SAT LIFELESS IN THE CENTER OF HER KING-SIZED BED, COM-pletely befuddled by what had just happened. She couldn't believe one of her best friends on the planet had virtually blown her off in her moment of distress. Although Nia was extremely private and rarely shared the challenges she had experienced with Terrence over the years, Carla had been there for her for a variety of other issues—her family, career, and life's general stresses.

I can't believe that bitch just treated me like that. And I can't count how many times I was there for her in the past.

Carla was devastated. Not only was she heartbroken and humiliated by what had just occurred with Jeff Conley, now she felt betrayed by one of her closest friends.

I gotta get Bev and Val on the phone. She quickly scrambled for her iPhone. "Hey, girl," Carla's voiced cracked as she greeted Valerie.

"Hey, Carla, I was just about to call you. I saw what happened on TV. Are you all right, girl?"

"I can't believe all this happened," Carla said, sniffling.

"I know. It's terrible, but you'll get through it."

"But my career is ruined." Just then Carla received another call. "Hold on, Val, this is Bev." She clicked over to the other line. "Hey, Beverly, hold on, I'm going to conference you in, I've got Valerie on the other line." Carla fumbled with her phone, as she struggled to see the conference icon through the swelling that surrounded her eyes.

"I heard what happened," Beverly said. "Are you alright, girl?"

"I am just *so* angry right now. I can't believe that this happened. And let me tell you how your girl just treated me. I called Nia to tell her what happened and she acted like she could care less. Just gave me a lecture and then asked me, 'What do you want me to say?' So I hung up on her. I don't know what the hell is going on with her."

"I'm not sure. I haven't talked to her much since she was promoted. Maybe she's just stressed out," Valerie said in Nia's defense.

"Nah, I talked to her," Beverly said. "She just done let that new position go to her head. She thank she done arrived."

Valerie huffed and responded, "I don't know, but anyway, it's not as bad as you think, Carla. You really don't look bad. Celebrities are different than politicians. People don't care about your private life."

"You don't understand. My career was just taking off. I was about to get my own show," Carla moaned.

"Val's right, Carla, look at old crazy Charlie Sheen and his tiger's blood." Beverly chuckled, managing to get a laugh out of Carla. "Look at all the crazy stuff he did and now this nut has a new show. People don't care. I'm not tryin' to be funny, but the truth of the matter *is*, sometimes this type of stuff makes celebrities even *more* popular."

"Bev's right. It happens all the time. It's really just publicity."

"That works for men, especially white men. Not a black woman," Carla replied.

"Girl, that's not true. Look at Kim Kardashian. Hell, they got her on tape having sex and helped her career. And she was having sex with a little boy. You know, Moesha's little brother," Beverly joked, once again prying a chuckle out of Carla.

"You are *so* silly." Carla chuckled. "Leave Kim Kardashian alone. That's my girl."

"Don't get me wrong, I'm not hatin' on Kim Kardashian. Black men love her."

"And ain't nothing wrong with that," Carla replied.

"I don't know about that. That's an entirely different story," Valerie interjected.

"Nothing wrong with it at all," Bev snickered. "She can't help it that they love that big ole donkey booty she got."

Valerie said, "Oh my goodness, how did we get started talking about Kim Kardashian's butt anyway?"

"Type a booty you can set a drink on. So big it looks awkward," Bev continued on with her typical dry wit. "Disproportionate. If you look at it good, it looks kinda lopsided." The three ladies laughed.

"Well, I've never looked at it *that* closely and really have no desire to either," said Val.

"Hell, what about Halle Berry. She be runnin' people over and she's as popular as ever."

"No, seriously, Carla, times have changed. Val is right, people only hold politicians to those standards. I think they just see celebrities as humans that make mistakes and as more of a reflection of themselves and the mistakes they make in their private lives...and just as a reflection of society, in general," Beverly explained with a serious tone. "So, don't worry, trust me, no one is going to judge you for this. And it was just a kiss. If you make a big deal about it, everyone else will. Just face it, you're a bona fide celebrity now, that's all."

"Bev's right," Valerie added. "People don't half pay attention to those tabloids anymore because most of the stuff isn't true. So don't worry about it, things will work out. Just keep doing what you've been doing and chalk it up to experience. Now you know how scrutinized you will be from here on out. And it wasn't a healthy situation for you anyway."

"I'll be honest; I was starting to fall in love with Jeff, too. We were becoming really close."

"Carla, it was a blessing. God didn't want you with that man. He knows what's best for you. You just have to be prayerful and what God has in store for you will emerge when you least expect it," Valerie explained in a comforting tone.

"You're better off without him. He was no good. He knew he wasn't leaving his wife and he wasn't going to do anything but bring you problems. Val's right; you just have to be prayerful."

"You guys are right. If he did it to her, he'd do it to me. And fans don't care anymore. It's just a lot to deal with all at once."

"You know we've both been there before, but that's when you just pray and lean on your friends," Valerie replied.

"At least some of them. The ones that care," Carla responded.

"What goes up must come down. That little bubble on her shoulders'll bust sooner or later. Girl, you know God has a way of bringing people back down to earth. God bless her," Beverly commented.

"She just has a lot of pressure on her shoulders right now. We just have to be supportive," Valerie rationalized in support of Nia. "Anyway, things are going to work out for the best. You'll be fine."

Chapter 45

NIA HAD ARRIVED TO WORK EARLY IN AN ATTEMPT TO GET A JUMP ON her day, but had been pulled into an impromptu meeting with the head of the Department of Commerce. After the meeting, she zipped back into her office and quickly clicked the power button on her computer. As she anxiously waited for her PC to fire up, she thumbed through a stack of paperwork that rested neatly in the center of her desk. Then she was suddenly startled by a voice.

"Hi, Nia. Do you have a moment?"

Nia's head popped up. "Oh, Mark, you scared me. I didn't see you standing there."

"I really need to talk to you for a moment, if you have time."

"Sure, have a seat. What's on your mind?"

The staff member nervously entered Nia's office. "Well, Nia…" Before the staffer was able to complete his sentence Nia's phone rang. She tapped the Conference button on her phone.

"Nia, POTUS needs an update on the Somalia Relief Package," the president's secretary said.

"We're good. We have all of the necessary paperwork lined up for the relief package."

"Okay, he just wanted me to check to be sure because you know he's doing his weekly YouTube address in about 30 minutes."

"Yes, I know, and he knows I can't make it to the taping, correct?"

"Yes, he mentioned that to me."

"Okay, thanks, Jessica." Nia ended the call and sat back in her seat bearing a big grin on her face.

"You just gotta love POTUS don't ya, Mark? He is so sincere with his efforts in Africa. Anyway, what's up? I only have a few minutes."

"Well, I really don't know how to say this…"

"Say what?"

"The relief package isn't ready, Nia," the staffer responded quietly. Nia's face crumpled in disbelief. As she processed what she had just heard, she became furious.

"What? Why not?"

The staffer quickly stood, closed Nia's office door, and then returned to his seat. "Nia, between you and me, Ted and a few others are trying to sabotage the project to make you look bad."

"I can't believe this!" Nia said in complete shock. "Why would they do something like this?"

"Well, they're pretty upset with you."

"Why?"

"They feel like you've changed. Like you've become arrogant and disrespectful to the staff," Mark explained apprehensively.

"So you're saying the relief package isn't ready?"

"No."

"Well, where are they with it?"

"I'm not sure, Nia."

"Mark, I appreciate you stepping forward to let me know. I'd like to talk with you a bit more later."

"Sure, Nia," the staffer responded and then exited her office. Nia flopped back in her chair and sat momentarily with her mouth gaping open. Then she quickly surged forward and grabbed her phone.

"Ted, I need you in my office *right this moment*," she demanded loudly. Moments later, Ted stumbled into Nia's office with a look of guilt. As he stood before her, his eyes danced in every direction but hers.

"What's up, Nia?"

"Ted, has the Somalia relief package been completed?"

"Well, not really."

"What do you mean, *not really*?" Nia snapped.

"Well, we ran into some issues with the paperwork."

"And why wasn't I notified?" Nia asked firmly, as she stood up with her arms crossed, staring squarely into Ted's eyes.

"We just ran into some issues and telling you about them wasn't going to fix anything," the staffer responded smugly.

"That is the most irresponsible and disrespectful response I've heard since I've been in the West Wing!"

"We still have two more days left before it's actually supposed to be processed, Nia. I didn't say it wasn't going to be ready then. It's just not complete as of today," the staffer snapped back.

"But what deadline did I give you, Ted?"

"Today, Nia, but…"

"Then there's nothing else to discuss. WILL YOU HAVE IT READY IN TWO DAYS?" Nia yelled with the veins in her neck bulging. It was the first time in Nia's career that she could recall actually yelling at someone in the workplace. But she knew that the Somalia relief efforts were dear to President Davis's heart and he would not be happy.

"Yes, it'll be ready," Ted responded with attitude in his voice.

"Well, that's unacceptable! I want it completed by noon tomorrow."

"Well…I…I…"

"I want this package completed and prepared to go out tomorrow. And I don't want to hear any excuses," Nia said, gritting her teeth with a look of sheer rage on her face.

"*Okay*, Nia. I'll jump right on it," Ted responded with his head down and shoulders slumped forward, as Nia followed him to the door.

"And, Ted, just so you know, I know what you were trying to pull and we *will* discuss that at a later date!" she said, gripping the side of her office door. As soon as he had cleared her doorway, Nia slammed her office door behind him.

"That son of a bitch!" she exclaimed loudly, as she turned and fell back lifelessly against the door.

POTUS! I've got to catch POTUS before he posts it to YouTube, she thought. Then she rushed back to her desk and grabbed her phone.

Chapter 46

THE DISGRUNTLED STAFFER CLOSED THE DOOR TO HIS OFFICE.

Let's just see how that makes that cocky black bitch look now, he thought, as he yanked his Blackberry from his belt clip.

"Tanner, it's me, Ted," he said quietly.

"Ted, how are ya, buddy?"

"I got her ass! I did just like you told me; I screwed up the paperwork."

"Great job, Ted! Just another thing to make him look bad."

"Yeah, and that bitch Nia, too!"

"Ah, don't worry about her; we have to focus on getting him out of there."

"Yeah, you're right. Now you know I'm going to catch hell for this one, Tanner. Are you sure you have something lined up for me on your side?"

"Of course, buddy. When we take office, you're a shoe-in for chief of staff. I'm headed to a series of satellite interviews right this moment which are going to set us up for the kill. Wish this thing would have broken before my interviews so I could have pounced on it on live national television. Doesn't matter though, I'm going to pounce all over him in the interview anyway," Tanner boasted.

"Well, make sure to tell Bill about it," Ted replied.

"Oh, I will. Trust me I will."

Chapter 47

"HI, JESSICA, CAN YOU CATCH POTUS FOR ME AND LET HIM KNOW NOT to mention the relief package because I found out the paperwork isn't complete after all?" Nia asked in embarrassment, as her stomach grumbled in distress.

"Oh, Nia, I just spoke with POTUS and he and the press secretary recorded their social media release early because we had to move up his satellite meeting with the president of the Soviet Union."

"Oh boy, Jessica, we have to get that post pulled from YouTube immediately," Nia said, and then hung up quickly to call Kevin James, the White House press secretary.

"Kevin, I need to get POTUS's last post pulled from YouTube immediately."

"Why, Nia?"

"The relief package to Somalia isn't ready to go out. Someone dropped the ball and I can't guarantee it'll be ready in two days."

"But he called to confirm and you said it was."

"I thought it was, but like I said, someone dropped the ball. Some last-minute complications arose."

"But, Nia, we can't yank it. It'll make POTUS look like an idiot! We just have to figure out a way to get it ready. Have you told POTUS?"

"Yes, I know. I'll take all of the blame for it. I'm going to call right now." Nia hung up the phone and then buried her face in her hands.

He's going to kill me. Oh well, I might as well face the music and call him.

Chapter 48

TANNER ARRIVED AT BILL ADLER'S AGENCY. HE WAS BUBBLING OVER in excitement. He couldn't wait to finally get his moment in the spotlight. Adler had orchestrated a series of live interviews. Tanner was also anxious to tell Adler what he had just heard from staffer Ted Thompson. This was one of the main reasons Adler had brought Tanner aboard—to be his *key* informant and aide in sabotaging President Davis from the inside out in an effort to make him appear incompetent. But the *foremost* reason Adler had recruited the ex-chief of staff was to assassinate the president's character.

As Tanner took the elevator up to Adler's fifteenth-floor office, he contemplated what he had just heard and daydreamed about what he thought was to come. *That's great news. That'll make President Davis look like a fool. I'm getting closer and closer. Tanner Long, vice president of the United States of America; and after that, president. My dad's finally going to be proud of me.*

The only way Adler had been able to lure Tanner into his cyclone of deception was by assuring him he would be a congressman and future presidential candidate Jim Curry's running mate. Although it wasn't the offer to run for president, which Tanner truly desired, it was the next best thing and a momentous step in the right direction.

"Hello, Bill."

"Tanner. Are you ready?"

"I was born ready, but I also have great news for you."

"Okay, but we've got to get you prepared. Your interview is in fifteen minutes and I'd like to go over our talking points."

"Well, I'll make it quick, but you just have to hear about President Davis's latest little gaffe." Tanner proudly explained the details of the president's impending stumble while Adler flipped through the interview notes. As Tanner got to the root of his story, he finally got Adler's full attention. Although this specific situation wasn't a part of Adler's overall plan to sabotage President Davis, it fed into it perfectly.

"Oh, great job, Tanner! Nice freebie. I'll make a few calls to give the media a heads-up as soon as we get done going over the notes. Now, Tanner, these interviews are going to be critical to the success of our overall plan. Are you good with the talking points we've laid out here?"

"Sure."

"Okay, remember, it's paramount that you stick to these talking points. You know they're going to try to get you off track and try to beat you up with questions."

"Bill, dealing with the press is my specialty. It's what I do. They'll be eating out of the palm of my hand when I'm done."

"Alright, but whatever you do, *stay focused*. I don't care what they ask you; just channel it back to this list of talking points," Adler stressed. "And it's okay to touch on Davis's questionable character, but don't say too much about that. Don't let the cat out of the bag. Not yet. We're going to go after his character in due time. We just want you to talk about his incompetence and what you saw on the inside…what you put in your book. The first interview is with NBN— the 'This Morning Show' with Jeff Conley."

Chapter 49

"HELLO, RANDY...," NIA GREETED PRESIDENT DAVIS'S PERSONAL AS-sistant hesitantly, "this is Nia. Is POTUS available?"

"He just ran upstairs to the bathroom, his son is in there. He's pretty sick. Keeps coming out of both ends...poor little fella."

"Thanks for that vivid description, Randy."

"I'm sorry. It *is* what it *is* though," Randy replied with a slight chuckle.

"Anyway, I really need to speak with him, and where's the White House physician?"

"He's up there. The little guy's going to be okay. They just gave him an anti-biotic and something to settle his stomach a few minutes ago. I'll have POTUS call you right back. He should be down in a minute."

"Okay, but have him call me *right back*, Randy. This is extremely important."

"Will do."

Nia paced back and forth on the plush blue carpet that covered her office floor as she awaited the president's call. Finally, after what seemed like hours, about 10 minutes later her cell phone rang. She immediately snatched her Blackberry from her desk and, without checking the caller id—which was something she rarely, if ever, did—answered the call.

"Hello."

"Hey, sweetie. Are you busy?"

"Oh, hi, Terrence," Nia responded in a disappointed tone.

"Well, it's great to talk to you, too," he joked.

"Oh, I'm sorry. It's already been a crazy day."

"What's wrong?"

"I am so pissed off right now!"

"Why?"

"One of my staff members is apparently trying to get me fired."

"What? That *is* crazy!"

"Yes, I'll tell you more about it later. Let me get off of this phone. I'm waiting on POTUS to call me back, so he can chew me out. Hopefully when I call you, I'll still be employed," she said, woefully shaking her head.

"Call me back and let me know how it turns out, sweetie. Try not to worry about it...it'll work out."

As soon as Nia ended her call with her fiancé, her office phone began to ring. She sighed heavily as she momentarily rested her hand on the handset before lifting it to her ear.

"Nia Taylor speaking."

"Nia, I just talked to Jessica. What the heck is going on?" President Davis asked with anger in his voice. It was perhaps the first time Nia could recall hearing that sort of rage in his voice.

"Sir, I'm very sorry about the mix-up. I take one hundred percent of the blame."

"Yeah, but how did it happen?"

"Well, sir, the person that I had managing that project didn't prioritize it appropriately and was off by one day with their completion projections."

"Nia, come on now. I'm surprised at you. Well, the YouTube post has been edited and reposted and Kevin has already sent out a press release on the mistake. You know…mistakes happen, but I am under too much scrutiny by the media for you to make *this* kind of mistake, and you know how I feel about the Somalia efforts. And you know this type of mix-up can't happen again, but what I'm more concerned with right now is your leadership."

"My leadership, sir?" Nia responded in puzzlement.

"Yes, Nia, I've heard about the staff's grumblings. I don't know if this mistake had anything to do with it, but you need to get the staff on the same page with you…'cause right now, it seems as if you have somewhat of a *mutiny on your hands*."

Chapter 50

ADLER PACED BACK AND FORTH IN THE CORNER OF HIS AGENCY'S ME-
dia room, feverishly making calls to deliver the news of President Davis's
erroneous YouTube post to his almost endless list of media sources. In the
meantime, Tanner sat in front of the camera just a few yards away tugging at
the flawlessly tied half-Windsor knot in his blue paisley necktie, as the NBN
camera crew worked diligently to set up for the live satellite interview.

Tanner had done an almost endless amount of interviews in the past, but
this one was different—it was his first live interview as a solo act. Additionally,
it was on the number one morning show in America. Tanner could hardly
sit still. After he was done fiddling with his necktie, he licked the tips of his
fingers and stroked his eye brows, trying to get them to sit perfectly for the
cameras. The lights that shown on his hair caused it to glisten perfectly too,
just as he had planned, thanks to the fat wad of mousse he had packed on it.

The cameras were all in place and the cameramen were ready for action.
Meanwhile, in the NBN studios, Jeff Conley quickly scanned his questions
in preparation for the interview. A make-up person sprinted over to the host,
dabbed his nose with powder, and quickly scurried away. Just before they went
live, Carla strolled onto the set. Her morning "around the town-like" segment
was up next. She was unaware that Tanner Long was scheduled to appear via
satellite on the show.

She approached an assistant producer. "What's this joker doing?"

"He's got a new tell-all book on President Davis coming out," the assistant
producer responded.

"Are you serious?"

"Yup, I sure am."

*I wonder if Nia knows about this. I'm not even going to call her after the way
she treated me, and she probably knows all about it anyway,* she thought and
then nonchalantly strutted away.

Chapter 51

NIA HUNG UP THE PHONE, SLUMPED BACK IN HER SEAT, AND SAT SI-
lently for a moment. Her energy was sapped. She was distraught over the slip-
up, but what hurt more was when President Davis questioned her leadership.

*I can't believe these cowards pulled this instead of coming to me. Now they
have the president questioning my leadership. Now I have to figure out how to
right this ship and how I'm going to deal with that damn Ted,* she thought, and
then her phone began to ring.

"Greg, your timing is perfect. I need your help with something extremely
important," Nia said sounding exhausted.

"Oh, I was actually calling to tell *you* something very important, but you go
first," her deputy chief of staff said.

"You know that Somalia relief package I had Ted working on?"

"Yes, what about it?"

"Well, that jerk dropped the ball on purpose with it. It's a long story, but
anyway, I need you to get with Ted ASAP and get it all straightened out."

"Sure thing. I'll take care of it right away. But now I have to tell you this.
You're not going to believe this, Nia, but Tanner Long is about to appear on the
'This Morning Show,'" Greg said.

"What? Are you serious?"

"Yeah, he's got some tell-all book coming out."

"Okay, thanks, Greg. I'll have to check it out, but let me get right back to you
because I have a call coming in on my cell." She hung up her office phone and
picked up her cell. "Hey, Terrence."

"I know you said you'd call me later, but I was too worried to wait. How did
everything work out?"

Nia sighed. "I just talked to POTUS, and of course he was pissed, and
rightfully so. I swear, this is like the worst day of my life," Nia said in disgust,
sounding completely drained.

"It's going to work itself out, sweetie. What exactly did he say?"

"I don't even want to talk about it right now. I'll just explain it to you when
I get home tonight. And I think I'll be home early for a change. I need to get
out of here."

"Awww, sweetie, I'm sorry. I hope you feel better. I'll be home late tonight.
We're meeting with a client for dinner, but I'll try to break if off early since
you're having such a bad day. Call me when you get home, sweetie."

*I guess I better turn the television on and check out what that nut Tanner is
up to.*

Chapter 52

THE RED LIGHT ON TOP OF NBN'S CAMERA, WHICH SPORTED THE NBN logo plastered on its side, began to glow as the "This Morning Show" started to broadcast Jeff Conley's one-on-one interview with Tanner. Conley was known for his interview skills and no-nonsense style of reporting.

"…so, Tanner, how do we know what's in this book hasn't been exaggerated just to sell copies and get publicity?" Conley asked briskly.

"Jeff, I have an impeccable record and am known for my integrity, so that alone assures the accuracy and validity of the information in my book," Tanner answered with a smirk, as Adler looked on stoically.

"But with all due respect, Mr. Long, it's my understanding that you were *dismissed* from the White House, so you'd have *every* reason to deface this administration in your new book. Not to mention, like I said earlier, tell-all books of this sort are *notoriously* exaggerated."

Tanner momentarily squirmed in his seat. The "dismissed" remark stung and had clearly disturbed him. "I'm glad you brought that up," he began to respond, but was distracted by Adler, who he could see out of the corner of his eye pointing to the paper in his hand—reminding Tanner to stick to the talking points.

"Uh, Jeff, you may need to get a new informant then, because I definitely wouldn't use the term *dismissed*. I chose to leave. That administration is a *mess*! They don't have a clue. What you need to do is ask your informant what they know about the federal investigation President Davis's current chief of staff Nia Taylor is involved in. Why don't you see what they know about Ms. Taylor's involvement in *that* investigation?"

Chapter 53

NIA SAT WITH HER MOUTH GAPING OPEN, STARING AT THE TELEVI-sion that hung on her office wall, as she watched Tanner not only try to smear the president's name, but also attempt to malign hers, as well. She couldn't believe he had written a tell-all book, but was completely blown away when he threw her under the bus by mentioning the investigation. The talk of the investigation had just blown over and she had thought it was behind her, but now it was back, front and center, on the highest-rated morning television show in the country.

I swear, when it rains, it pours.

Chapter 54

"TO OUR KNOWLEDGE SHE WAS CLEARED IN THAT INVESTIGATION. Are you saying you know something different?"

"No, Jeff, what I'm saying is she was involved in some shady dealings. Just like her boss, President Davis, she's got questionable character."

"And just what makes you question President Davis's character?"

"Look, I'm not going to go into detail on that subject," Tanner said, veering back to his talking points and adhering to Adler's and Straus's plan. "What I will tell you is that he doesn't know what he's doing. The West Wing is a madhouse."

"Can you give us some examples?"

"Sure. For one, he's indecisive. He'll tell you one thing and then do another. And the entire administration drops the ball routinely. You mark my words, they'll drop the ball on something in the coming days. You guys—the press, that is—just have to take heed of these errors. Like I said, I wouldn't be surprised if there isn't a blunder brewing as we speak," Tanner said confidently, as Adler looked on smiling.

"I don't know if you knew this, but it's funny that you mentioned, as you put it, that a blunder is probably brewing in the White House, because the White House did just make a slip-up this morning. According to sources, the relief funds that were promised to the people of Somalia, who have been plagued with incredible droughts and are dying at inconceivable rates, isn't going to make it. President Davis posted a message on YouTube this morning that the funds were on their way, but shortly thereafter had to pull the message because the funds, in fact, aren't even available yet. Meanwhile, the men, women, and children of Somalia will have to continue to starve for another day."

"That's exactly what I'm talking about, Jeff. Perfect example," Tanner said matter-of-factly, beaming, while Adler sat just yards away with his cell phone buzzing out of control.

Chapter 55

NIA'S PHONE ALSO BEGAN TO RING NON-STOP, AS SHE SAT WITH HER hand pressed against her forehead watching Tanner's interview, until she heard a tap on her door.

What now? she thought.

"Come on in." It was Nia's workout buddies, staff interns Heather and Maria.

"Nia, did you hear that Tanner was being interviewed on the 'This Morning Show?'" Maria asked.

"Watching it right now," Nia responded in a monotone.

"I would have never guessed that he'd do something like this. This isn't the Tanner I knew," Heather professed.

"Well, it's the Tanner I knew," Nia snapped back as the three ladies stared, mesmerized, at the screen.

Chapter 56

"YOU MAY HAVE A POINT, TANNER. EITHER WAY, SO EXACTLY WHAT can we expect from your new book?"

"Expect the truth. The truth about the White House and President Davis. The man's just not fit to run our country. Jeff, he just doesn't know what he's doing. And while everyone thinks he's such a nice, down to earth guy, after they read my book they'll realize that's just not true. He's got some serious character flaws, and who wants this kind of person running their country?"

"Well, it's obvious that you'd like to see someone else running the country. My next question is, who? Who do you think would be a better fit for the job?"

"Jeff, I don't have that answer for you right this moment. I do have someone in mind, but I don't know if they'd like for me to share that with the world, just yet."

"I see. Tanner, would that person happen to be you?" Conley fired.

Chapter 57

AS THE THREE LADIES STARED MESMERIZED AT THE SCREEN IN ANticipation of Tanner's response, Nia thought to herself, *So he was serious when he said he wanted to run for president someday.* Just then the ladies were startled by a deep voice.

"Ms. Taylor, someone sent you flowers," the White House mailroom attendant said.

"Oh, thanks, Derek. Set them right here on the end of my desk," Nia said, as she walked around to the front of her desk and Heather and Maria gushed in delight.

"Awww, who sent you flowers? Hmmm, they smell so fresh," Heather said, as Maria quickly grabbed the card from the corner of the long-stemmed red roses and began to read it.

"*Of course*, they're from Terrence," Maria said, as she began to read the card until Nia quickly snatched it away.

"Thank you, Maria," Nia snapped, as she pulled the card close. She then paused and turned back towards the television. "Darn it! We missed Tanner's response. Where's the control? We have to rewind that!"

Chapter 58

TANNER BLUSHED. HE WAS BUBBLING OVER IN DELIGHT FROM THE AT-tention. Meanwhile, Adler's eyes widened, as he thought Tanner was about to let the cat out of the bag.

"No, it's not me, Jeff. While I'm confident I could handle the job," Tanner began to explain grinning proudly, as Adler looked on intensely, "it's not my time." Adler looked relieved.

"Well, can you at least tell us if *this* person is a Democrat or a Republican?"

"That's a good question, Jeff." Tanner paused and peered over at Adler. Adler gave him a piercing stare. "But does it matter?"

"Well, quite frankly it does. You previously worked for President Davis as his chief of staff. If you now decide to align yourself with the other side, which you're obviously doing since you're being broadcast live right from well-known Republican strategist Bill Adler's office, that could be construed as becoming a turncoat," Conley aggressively persisted. "That could make many ponder the validity of your book since you were dismissed—excuse me, since you left the White House on uncertain terms."

Tanner was once again noticeably disturbed by Conley's reference to his dismissal from the White House. His smirk quickly disappeared and he wiggled uncomfortably in his seat, as Adler continued to stare at him piercingly.

"Like I said, it really doesn't matter at this point whether they're Republican or Democrat. The bottom line is President Davis is failing and I saw it first hand from inside of the White House."

"So do you *now* consider yourself a Republican?"

"Again, that's neither here nor there. Our country is in horrible shape, I'm concerned about the direction we're going, and I wanted to share what I saw with the country in my book. It's that simple."

"Interesting, Mr. Long. Very interesting. Well, we appreciate you coming on to speak with us this morning. Thank you for your time."

"Thank you, Jeff, and don't forget people can find my new book at TannerLong dot com," Tanner said, managing to squeeze in one last plug.

"Again, thank you, Mr. Long," Conley said sternly, ending the interview. The red light atop the NBN camera stopped glowing.

That son of a bitch tried to trip me up, Tanner thought, as he ripped the wireless mic from his lapel.

Chapter 59

NIA FOUND HER TELEVISION REMOTE, WHICH WAS BURIED UNDER the paperwork on her desk. She then quickly tapped the Rewind button. The ladies turned their attention back to Tanner's interview, anxiously awaiting his response to Jeff Conley's previous question of whether or not Tanner should be running the country. Their eyes were once again fixed on the high definition television screen, as the DVR began to replay Tanner's response.

"No, it's not me, Jeff. While I'm confident I could handle the job, it's not my time."

Nia was surprised. She had thought Tanner was surely setting the stage for his future candidacy. "I thought for sure he was looking to run," Nia blurted.

"You think?" Heather asked, but was met with a synchronized hushing sound from Nia and Maria. The ladies then listened to the rest of the interview replay in silence.

"Okay, guys, the interview is over. Tanner didn't disappoint. He lived up to his reputation. Now let's get back to work," Nia ordered with an undertone of aggravation.

"I still can't believe he wrote a book like that," Heather mumbled as she exited the office. Nia rolled her eyes and closed the door behind the young women. She then went back to her desk, flopped down into her seat, snatched Terrence's card from the desk and proceeded to read.

I'm sorry you're having such a rough day. Hope this brightens it a bit and reminds you how much I love you. Love Always, Terrence.

How sweet. He couldn't have sent this at a better time. I should give him a quick call to say thanks while I have a free moment, she thought, as she picked up her cell phone.

"Hey, sweetie, thank you for the roses. Trust me, I needed that."

"I'm glad it brightened your day some."

"It did. It's just what I needed. The day has been like one *big* nightmare and it's just getting started. Did you hear about Tanner's interview?"

"Yeah. I didn't see it, but somebody just told me about it."

"I can't believe him writing a tell-all book. I can't wait to hear what POTUS has to say."

"He's just trying to make some money," Terrence responded.

"Nah, he has money and plenty of it. He's up to something. Get this; they interviewed him via satellite from *Bill Adler's* office."

"Oh, so now he's in bed with that shady character?"

"Yes, he's up to something. I swear it's like one problem after another. I'm getting out of here on time today. I'm leaving at 5:30 PM on the dot."

"You should. You really need a break, sweetie. Just promise me that you won't turn that laptop on when you get home…you just need to go home and rest."

"I promise I won't. Not tonight. This has been an exhausting day and I still have to run over to Dr. Patel's office at noon for my follow-up appointment. I just can't wait to kick these heels off and curl up on the couch."

"Well, you know I'll be home late tonight. We're taking that new client out that I was telling you about last week. Anyway, call me when you get home to let me know you made it in safely. Love you, sweetie."

"Love you too."

Chapter 60

AFTER THE NBN CREW HAD PACKED UP AND EXITED ADLER'S AGENCY, Adler and Tanner headed back to his office. Tanner was unhappy with the interview. He felt like Conley's frequent mentions of his dismissal from the White House had turned the interview on its ear, and spun it into a maligning of his own character.

On the other hand, Adler was thrilled with the interview. He felt Tanner had hit all of his major talking points; in particular, he praised Tanner for raising questions about President Davis's and his new chief of staff's characters. Adler's and Straus's entire plan focused on attacking the president's character, and in Adler's mind, once Tanner had touched on that issue, everything else was icing on the cake.

Up to that point, Adler's and Straus's plan had been unfolding perfectly. They had successfully rallied some of the country's wealthiest and most influential billionaires around their cause. Their super PAC had raised twice as much money as any Democratic super PAC. Their Republican cohorts in Congress banded together and blocked the president's initiatives. One leading senator even went so far as to publically state that his *number one* priority was to help the Republicans defeat President Davis, clearly putting their own agenda before the welfare of the country. Never before in history had a president received such resistance and intense scrutiny.

Adler's next focus was to unleash a smear campaign that they believed would be the death of President Davis's character, and ultimately lead to his impeachment. And Tanner had just kicked off the campaign. But unbeknownst to Adler, he had a traitor aboard his political warship.

Chapter 61

NIA SAT PATIENTLY WAITING FOR DR. PATEL IN ONE OF HIS EXAMINA-tion offices, as she gazed at the office's sterile white walls in a trance. *I sure wish he would hurry up. I have so much to do when I get back to the West Wing,* she thought. Then she heard a tap on the door.

"Yes, come in," Nia responded, as Dr. Patel had already begun to slowly open the door.

"Nia, good to see you," Dr. Patel greeted.

"Good to see you, Doctor."

"Well, Nia, I just wanted to bring you in to go over the results from your examination—specifically, the mammogram. There is no need to be alarmed, but we discovered a small lump in your breast that, given your family history, needs further examination. I'd like to do a biopsy to examine the area further, just to be sure."

Nia's stomach sank. "I see. How soon do we need to do this?"

"As soon as you have time."

"Okay, thank you, Dr. Patel," Nia said as she exited the examination room in a daze. Despite her family history, the news was still jolting. *What next?* she thought wearily.

⤳

After Nia arrived back to the West Wing, the rest of her day seemed to last forever. And just as she had promised her fiancé, for the first time in months, when 5:30 PM hit, Nia packed it in and headed home at what most Americans call normal quitting time. She arrived home physically and mentally drained. She stumbled into her apartment clutching the bouquet of red roses that she had received from Terrence earlier in the day and set them alongside her cell phone on the end table which was adjacent to their wraparound leather sofa.

"Uhhh, what a day!" she said aloud with a sigh. She then kicked off her pumps and flopped down on the sofa releasing yet another large sigh. As she flicked on the television and sunk down into the sofa, she could hear a voice begin to speak as the picture slowly resolved into view.

"...and President Davis didn't have any answers for the White House's latest fowl-up. I guess thousands of Somalis will just have to continue to suffer while the White House tries to figure out how to simply write a check from the American people's checkbook," the reporter babbled. Nia immediately clicked the Off button on the remote and dropped her head into her hands.

"I can't even watch television!" she barked.

Then she grabbed a blanket from the closet, lay down, and snuggled under it. Shortly thereafter, Nia drifted off to sleep. She slept for several hours until she was startled by the buzzing of her Blackberry. She looked around anxiously for the phone.

"Hello," she answered groggily.

"Hey, sweetie, you forgot to call me. I was getting worried about you," Terrence said.

"Oh, I'm sorry. I came in and fell asleep on the couch. I'm *so* exhausted."

"Can you give me change for this fifty?"

"What?"

"I'm sorry, sweetie. I had to make a quick stop at a gas station."

"Oh."

"Yes, all ones please," Terrence directed the cashier.

"What are you doing? And why are you getting change in ones?" Nia asked.

"Oh, I just got this change to pay the parking valet at the restaurant. I don't like giving them my credit card."

"Okay. Be careful. Terrence, are you sure you aren't taking this client to some strip club?"

Terrence chuckled.

"It's not funny, Terrence. The last thing I need is for someone to see you in some strip club. I already have enough problems. And you don't need to be going to any strip clubs, touching on some nasty strippers anyway."

"*Sweetie*, this is for the valet. No, I'm not going to any strip club. Give me a break. You really do need some rest."

"I do," Nia snapped.

"Alright, go back to sleep. Get some rest. I'll see you in a few. After we eat and have a few cocktails, hopefully I can get out of there and come home. I'd rather be there cheering you up anyway. Love you."

"Love you too," Nia replied in a whisper and then snuggled back under the blanket.

I could go for a snack...some chocolate, she thought to herself. Nia craved food—preferably sweets—when she was distressed, but intense stress also had an exhausting effect on her as well. She slowly drifted back to sleep. Hours later her phone began to buzz again. She aimlessly felt around the glass end table with her eyes closed until she located her cell phone.

"Hello," she answered groggily. "Hello, hello. Has to be Terrence and that darn phone," she mumbled before drifting back to sleep. But as soon as she fell back asleep, her phone began to vibrate again. Once again, she answered but no one was there. However, this time she could faintly hear voices laughing and talking.

"Terrence, Terrence…can you hear me? Lock your phone. You keep waking me up." *How aggravating! I just want to rest.*

A few moments later her phone began to buzz yet again. By this time Nia had become completely annoyed. She sat up groggily and reached for her cell phone, accidentally knocking a music CD onto the floor. *I swear, if he doesn't stop calling me!*

"Hello, hello," she barked into her cell phone, and then sighed. Once again, she could hear voices; however, this time she could hear more clearly.

"Turn around. Let me see that fat ass. Now drop it to the floor and make it shake!" Nia sprang up. She immediately recognized the voice. It was Terrence.

He must be at a strip club. And I just told him not to go to one. What if somebody sees him there? Ugh, I'm going to kill that boy!

Chapter 62

UNITED STATES SECRETARY OF THE DEPARTMENT OF HOMELAND SE-
curity Conrad Roth sat nervously in his four-door Mercedes-Benz CLS-Class.
He anxiously looked around the indoor parking lot, which was connected to
his condominium, as he began to press the keys on his Blackberry.

Roth was a complex individual. His life was filled with irony. He had worked
hard all throughout the course of his career. Unlike many of his colleagues,
he had come from humble beginnings. He was born and raised in southwest
Detroit. His dad was an unskilled factory laborer and his mom worked in a
local convenience store. His dad worked many hours of overtime to provide
him with the best education. His dad was honest and hardworking, but a man
of few words. He led by example. The one thing he always told Conrad as a
young boy was, "I may not have much else to share, but I can show you how
to be a man."

His dad used every dime he had to send Conrad to Great Pointe Academy,
one of the best private schools in the Detroit area. At Great Pointe, his classmates were all extremely wealthy and didn't readily accept Conrad into their
circle. They taunted him about his poverty-stricken background and flaunted
their expensive cars and electronic toys in his face. He eventually became
immune to their taunts on the surface, but deep inside, they affected him.
His tormenters inspired him to excel in the classroom. He knew he couldn't
compete with them socially, but academically was a different story. He became
obsessed with his studies. He worked tirelessly to show them up and eventually graduated first in his class, receiving an academic scholarship to the
prominent Ivy League school Cornell University.

He entered Cornell University with the same chip on his shoulder that
he had carried throughout his time at Great Pointe. Once again, he was surrounded by wealthy classmates and they too acted like it. Their parents were
influential professionals and business owners and many were Cornell alums.
Although Conrad had repressed his feelings of being left out at Great Pointe,
he really wanted to be accepted at Cornell. Unlike the students at Great Pointe,
his new friends knew nothing about his background and respected his academic prowess. Many of them had slid by academically or simply cheated their
way through school. He spent many spring and summer breaks in their homes
and began to fully absorb their lifestyles and views. The bulk of these friends
and their families were Republicans. Conrad's parents had been staunch
Democrats all of his life, and consequently he was too. But at Cornell he slowly
began to shift his political views.

Thanks to hard work and a thirst for success, he graduated summa cum laude from Cornell and received a law degree from the University of Michigan. He later found his way back home to Detroit and landed a position with local law enforcement, where he worked his way up from the bottom to become the State of Michigan's attorney general. Eventually, his work ethic paid off with an even bigger reward—he reached the White House, which in his mind was the ultimate symbol of success, becoming the assistant to the United States secretary of state. Again, Conrad was well respected by his peers. Subsequently, when President Davis entered office he selected Conrad as one of only three Republicans in his Cabinet.

Conrad Roth tapped the End button on his Blackberry. He went back and forth in his mind on whether or not to place the call.

Chapter 63

NIA SAT FROZEN ON HER SOFA. SHE COULDN'T BELIEVE TERRENCE WAS putting her name in harm's way. The media was thirsty for any kind of dirt they could find on this administration. If someone saw Terrence in a strip club, it would surely spread all over the media within hours like a firestorm.

Damn it, Terrence! I'm so sick of his inconsistency. One minute he's the most thoughtful guy in the world, buying me flowers when I'm upset, and the next minute he's putting my reputation at risk in some strip club. And I don't think I could handle another fiasco right now. Nia shook her head in disgust, as she continued to listen closely to Terrence's inadvertent call.

"Terrence, you're *so* crazy! Don't just put dollar bills in there, put some Benjamins in there, too," the woman demanded playfully and then laughed.

He IS at a strip club! I knew that's why he was getting change in dollar bills.

"Oh, trust me, I got Benjamins. Wait, let me take this cell phone out of my pocket. Now I can make rain!"

"Stop, I can't dance if you keep grabbing me, Terrence." The woman giggled.

What? He's grabbing her. This is getting out of hand! And I could swear I've heard that voice before.

"Okay, now take that thong off, girl," Terrence said. *Pop!*

"Ouch, Terrence. Be careful, don't snap my thong like that."

Nia's jaw dropped. *I know he's not trying to take off her thong. And why is she calling him by name? Is this really a stripper?*

"Whoa, look at that tiny waist and big ole ass! Girl you got a butt like a sister...ass like Serena Williams!"

"So what are you trying to say, only black women can have nice asses, Terrence?" the woman asked sarcastically.

"Nah, it's tighter than any sister's that I know. Now dance."

"*Nia* doesn't have an ass like this. Do you ask her to dance for you, too?"

No this bitch didn't just call me by name!

"Nah...she would never do this. Now stop talking about Nia. Don't spoil the mood," Terrence complained.

"You know I'm jealous of her," the woman wined in a sultry tone.

Who is this? I know I've heard this voice before, Nia pondered in puzzlement.

"Why?" Terrence asked.

"'Cause I want you to want me more than you want her. I want all of your time."

"I'm with you all of the time," Terrence replied in a huff.

"No you're not."

"As much as I can be."

"I just want you to love me like you love her."

"I do. You know I do. Now stop talking so much and dance for me."

Chapter 64

MONTHS BEFORE CONRAD ROTH ATTENDED THE SECRET MEETING OF the super PAC "Recapture Our Excellence" at the Ritz-Carlton, his close friend Tanner Long had shared the super PAC's plans with him. Conrad had been stunned at what he had heard. He couldn't believe what the super PAC was up to, and that Tanner was willing to be involved. Although Conrad was a devout Republican, he was infuriated by the unethical premise of their plan and the disloyalty of Tanner. First and foremost, Conrad was a man of integrity. He knew that spying on the plan was a risky move, but he'd felt compelled to do something. So he'd decided to attend the meeting to find out exactly what they were up to.

Should I really do this? Should I call her and let her know? I should have never gone to that damn "Recapture Our Excellence" meeting to begin with—damn it, I just HAD to put my nose in the middle of Straus's and Adler's plan. But after hearing what they're up to, I just can't stand by watching on the sideline and let it happen. That's not what I'm about. But my name will be trashed with my party. Conrad's mind whirled in contemplation. *I'm a man of integrity. I HAVE to do it.*

He knew the best way to access President Davis after hours was through his chief of staff. He nervously dialed Nia's cell phone number.

Chapter 65

NIA TOLD HERSELF THAT THERE WAS NO REASON TO CONTINUE TO impose such self-inflicted torture by continuing to listen to the call because it was obvious Terrence was definitely not at a strip club—he was cheating, and had been for a while. As she continued to listen in disgust to Terrence's sexual escapades, her cell phone clicked. There was another call trying to come through. She pulled the phone from her ear, wiped her tear-filled eyes, and glanced at the caller ID.

"Conrad Roth, what does he want?" she mumbled. *Should I answer it? I need to hang up with Terrence and this tramp anyway.*

Although she was hurt and devastated, Nia couldn't bring herself to hang up. The moment was surreal. As she pondered whether or not to end the call, her mind churned in denial, and the same kind of curiosity that makes a person want to view a train wreck continued to draw her in. She had to know more. *I can't believe Terrence would do this to me. I just can't believe it. I'll just have to call Conrad back. I have to know who he's with. I just can't talk to Conrad right now.*

She continued to listen.

"Are you going to leave her for me?"

"You know I can't do that right now."

"Why?"

"I've got too much on the line at the firm. I'm too close to making partner. I told you that."

"I know, but I'm soooo jealous, Terrence. I want you all to myself. I don't want her touching you. I don't want you touching her. I want you all to myself," the woman said, continuing to whisper in a soft, sexy tone.

"You know Nia doesn't have time for me. We haven't had sex in months. She doesn't have a sexy bone in her body, anyway."

"Good. Yes, I know how stuffy that bitch is. I'm almost to the point that I can't stand hearing her voice at work," the young woman said in a huff.

As the words rolled off of the woman's tongue, time almost stood still for Nia as she listened. Her eyes opened wide and she leaned forward in a daze.

Chapter 66

I CAN'T BELIEVE SHE'S NOT ANSWERING HER PHONE, **CONRAD THOUGHT,** as he listened to Nia's voice message.

"Nia, this is Conrad Roth," he began to speak with a tremor in his voice. "I hate to bother you so late in the evening, but I have something *very* important to share with you and the president. Please give me a call as soon as possible."

Conrad ended the call and then slumped down in his car seat. Although he knew it was the right thing to do, he also knew that the consequences would likely be disastrous for his career. This presidency had caused a polarization of the country which hadn't been seen since the Civil Rights movement. Conrad had already been hesitant about accepting his position in a Democratic administration, and his worst fears had become a reality. If the Republicans found out that he'd leaked Straus's and Adler's plan, he would be viewed as a traitor and blackballed from the Republican Party forever. He would be completely humiliated. For a man with Conrad's pride, this sort of humiliation was perhaps more than he could handle. He popped open his glove compartment and yanked out a 9mm handgun. *My name and reputation are all I have.* He pointed the gun at his temple, clutching the trigger with his sweaty finger.

Do it, Conrad, he thought.

Chapter 67

AFTER THE WOMAN UTTERED NIA'S NAME, HER WORDS RESONATED IN Nia's mind. Then she shouted, "Maria! That's Maria's voice. I can't believe this!" Nia was not only hurt, she was in complete shock. Maria, the White House staff intern and Nia's workout buddy, had become very close to her. She had taken both Maria and Heather under her wing and treated them like her younger sisters.

As she listened to Maria talk, her brain kicked into high gear. *How did this happen?* She began rapidly reflecting on every conversation she had ever had with Maria, and every interaction Maria had ever had with Terrence.

"Terrence, let's record us," Maria said.

"No, if Nia found the video, she'd kill me."

"Pleasssse," Maria whined.

"Next time."

"Oh, okay. Come here," Maria ordered. Nia heard the sounds moving away from the phone, and then what sounded like bed springs compressing.

"Grab my throat, Terrence!" Maria said. Nia listened in shock. *What the hell?* Maria coughed.

"Don't stop, Terrence. Squeeze tighter!" Maria demanded and then Nia heard the unmistakable sounds of the two having wildly passionate sex.

Nia sat lifeless on the other end of the phone. Tears endlessly flowed down her face. She winced with every moan and groan she heard the two make. *I should drive over there and catch them in the act. Oh, that's crazy. They're not even worth it,* she thought. She began to cry profusely.

"Oh shit!" Terrence yelled.

"What's wrong?"

"I think my damn phone called Nia!" The line went dead as Terrence ended the call.

Meanwhile, Nia continued to weep. "I can't believe this! My staff's trying to sabotage me and get me fired, I might have breast cancer, and now I find out my fiancé is screwing my intern and *friend*!" Nia yelled loudly, sniffling and crying.

Nia then snatched her cell phone from the floor and called Terrence back, but the call went straight to his voicemail. She hit Redial and called back again and again.

"Answer the phone, you coward! And you tell Maria I'll see her in the morning!" she yelled into his voicemail as she sat perched on the edge of her sofa. *Okay, that's enough, Nia, don't say anything that you may regret,* she thought while wiping the tears from her eyes and then ended the call.

She tucked a box of tissues between her legs and began to scroll through her list of contacts. Her eyes were puffy and swollen, making it difficult to see, and thanks to the stress of the moment, she couldn't recall even one of her three best friends' phone numbers. Finally, she located Bev's contact information, but the call went straight to voicemail.

Oh shoot, I forgot Bev's in Africa and it's five o'clock in the morning there, she thought and then tried Valerie.

"Val's not answering. Knowing her, she's probably asleep already. I know Carla's up," she rambled to herself aloud, as she scrolled through her list of contacts and then it finally dawned on her that she hadn't been there for her best friend when she broke up with Jeff Conley.

"Oh, I can't call Carla after the way I treated her when she went through that drama with Jeff Conley. I can't even call my best friend. My whole life is just falling apart. And people think I have everything. There's no way I can go to work in the morning like this," Nia said to herself and then began to weep in self-pity.

"Oh shoot, I forgot to call Conrad back." Nia remembered that Conrad Roth had just called. She tried to gather herself before calling him back, but her scratchy voice told the story. Fortunately, when she tried to return his call she was met with his voicemail.

"Conrad, I'm sorry I wasn't able to get back to you sooner. Please give me a call when you have an opportunity, no matter what the time." Nia then lay in the fetal position with tears continuing to stream down her cheeks until she eventually dozed off.

Chapter 68

THE FOLLOWING MORNING, NIA WAS AWAKENED BY THE SUNLIGHT, which crept through her custom-made blinds and beamed against her swollen eyelids.

"Oh my goodness, what time is it?" she said to herself, as she popped up and scrambled for her cell phone in search of the time.

"Oh my God, it's almost six o'clock!" She realized that she had overslept. She then hurried into the bathroom for a quick shower. Once out of the shower, as she stood over the sink brushing her teeth, she froze as she caught her own reflection in the mirror. She stood mesmerized, staring deeply into her own eyes. It had suddenly dawned on her that what had transpired the night before was far from a bad dream. It was reality and she had to decide how to deal with Maria when she arrived at work. She shook her head in an effort to snap out of her trance and then quickened her pace.

⌒

As she exited the West Wing's second-floor elevator in her designer pumps, Nia's typical swagger was nowhere to be found. The distress from the night before had reduced her normally confident strut to a mere shuffle. Her eyes and face were noticeably swollen. Several colleagues asked her if she was okay, but Nia simply shrugged off the questions, blaming her facial puffiness on allergies.

As she quickly prepared for an interview with International News Network, her phone began to ring.

"Nia, have you heard about the plan?" Greg Connors asked from the other end of the line.

"No, what plan?"

"It's all over the news. Somebody leaked to the media a 54-page plan to oust President Davis that the super PAC 'Recapture Our Excellence' created, and a videotape of their secret meeting. The plan was basically a blueprint to assassinating the president's character. The video was blurry, but you could see quite a few congressmen in attendance."

"Are you serious, Greg?"

"Yes, and you'll never guess who else was involved."

"Who?"

"Tanner," the deputy chief of staff answered eagerly.

"Tanner?"

"Yes, Tanner Long. You couldn't see him in the video, but they actually mention his name in the document."

"Oh my. Maybe that's what Conrad was calling me about last night. I wonder if he knew. I can't wait to talk to POTUS about this. As a matter of fact, notify POTUS of the situation. I'm headed to an interview with International News Network. I'll give you a call later."

Nia quickly scrambled over to the White House Press Room for her interview with the popular all-news network International News Network. As the cameras rolled, Nia got into a groove and thoughts of the disaster from the night before momentarily fled her mind. But halfway through the interview her Blackberry began to buzz. *Oh, I can't believe I forgot to turn this thing off,* she thought, as she peeked down at her cell phone and realized it was Terrence. Then she discretely pressed the End button turning her cell phone off and sending him to voicemail. Nia became distracted. She was ordinarily razor-sharp in interviews, but it suddenly became difficult for her to answer the journalist's simplest questions.

After the interview ended, Nia stormed over to Maria's cubicle.

"Has anyone seen Maria?" Nia asked the other interns who sat nearby.

"No, Nia. You haven't heard?" a young intern asked.

"Heard what?"

"Maria called in first thing this morning and resigned. They asked her if she wanted to speak to you, but she said she would try to call you back later."

Nia's face became red as she was overwhelmed with rage.

"Is everything okay, Nia?"

"Did she say *why* she was resigning?" Nia asked.

"No."

Nia stormed past the group of female interns, headed towards Heather's desk. She wasn't surprised that Maria hadn't shown up for work, but she also wondered what Heather had known about the affair.

"Heather, what's going on with Maria?" Nia snapped.

Heather calmly replied, "She called and said she had a family emergency that would require her to resign. That's all I know. I asked if maybe she could talk to you about an emergency leave of absence and she said she had to resign for good. She said she'd call you back later today. I hope she's okay…poor thing seemed pretty upset."

"Interesting," Nia responded. She immediately got a strange vibe from Heather and didn't believe her story, but didn't want to press it in the office. *Oh, so you do know,* she thought. "Anyway, I need for you to clear up any loose ends left with anything that she was working on."

"Sure, will do, Nia."

Yeah, and I'll deal with you later, Nia thought as she walked away.

Nia had bigger issues to deal with. She turned her attention back towards the super PAC "Recapture Our Excellence" and their diabolic 54-page plan to oust President Davis. As she marched over to the Oval Office, she wondered if the late-night call from Conrad Roth had something to do with it. His message played over again in her head. She realized the drama with Terrence had caused her to miss the sound of distress in his voice. She wasn't sure, but had a funny feeling his call had something to do with the super PAC issue.

POTUS and I will have to give him a call, Nia thought as she approached the Oval Office. "Conrad," Nia said, surprised to see the man barreling down the hallway towards her from the opposite direction. "I was just about to try to reach you again."

"Hi, Nia, I need to talk to you and POTUS ASAP."

"I was just headed in to see him. What's on your mind?"

"I have more details on this plan 'Recapture Our Excellence' had cooked up."

I knew it. Nia'd had a strange feeling that the leak had something to do with the call from Conrad Roth. They both entered the Oval Office and Conrad began to tell his story.

Nia had had no idea that Conrad had tipped President Davis off about Tanner's involvement with the shady super PAC months ago, which, in part, had contributed to his sudden termination. But neither Nia nor the president had had any idea that Conrad had done his own undercover-like investigation and had taken it upon himself to attend one of the super PAC's underground meetings. Conrad anxiously explained that he had attended the secret meeting in an effort to uncover their dirty plan, but had failed to think of the consequences that lay at the end of such a tricky probe.

"I believe you had good intentions, but you just can't take that kind of risk, Conrad. It wasn't necessary. It's one thing to dig for information on others involved, but a person in your position can't attend that sort of meeting. Who knows if rumors will surface later of your involvement with them. It puts the reputation of this entire administration in jeopardy, as well as your own name. We just can't have that," President Davis scolded.

"I guess this means I should be leaving the West Wing."

"No, it doesn't mean that. I do appreciate your efforts and loyalty. But you have to know, I can't publicly back you if it ever gets out that you did this. It raises too many questions and wasn't authorized. We have to critically think through this sort of maneuver."

Conrad had realized that his ill-advised spy tactics were a part of the risk he had taken, but hated to hear it so bluntly from the Commander in Chief.

"Yes, sir. I understand, sir," Conrad replied with his head down and exited the Oval Office.

The president then immediately called an emergency meeting. "Jessica, please get the press secretary in here for me," the president requested. "We need to discuss how we want to deal with this issue in the media. I think we need to stick to what got us here and take the high road."

Chapter 69

SEVERAL MEMBERS OF THE PRESS SWARMED BOTH ADLER'S AGENCY and Straus's corporate office. Straus and Adler were clearly disturbed by the leak. It potentially jeopardized their entire plan. Although their allies in the press simply swept the scandal under the rug, others did not. Several members of the press took their character assassination attempt and spun it back in their direction. Now Straus's and Adler's characters were the ones in question and President Davis's decision to take the high road only fanned that small flame.

The questions about the two cohorts' characters got under Straus's skin. He felt like he wasn't appreciated—he had built a multi-billion-dollar empire that for years had contributed to the good of the country's economy, and now he was being questioned about his ethics.

"It's bad enough they actually let *them* get into the White House. Now they question *me*? How dare these selfish sons of bitches begin to question my ethics. Ugh, what the hell is this country coming to? Bill, I'm as American as they come" the billionaire groaned on the phone with Adler.

"I know, Alex. It's disgusting to see what these liberal bastards have done to the country. They have absolutely no respect."

"Who the hell do you think leaked the plan?" Straus asked.

"I'm not sure, but my bet is Conrad Roth."

"Conrad. You might be right. We should never have let him attend the meeting," Straus grumbled.

"I'll find out though."

"Yeah, we have to find out. But I'll tell ya, Bill, at this point, I say we have to go plan B," Alex Straus said impatiently.

"No, we can't panic, Alex. The leak will blow over."

"But now everyone knows our damn plan. How do we produce a documentary about him now? How do we do this film depicting President Davis as unethical and incompetent if everyone sees it coming?"

"But they won't. I guarantee you that the majority of Americans will never even know that the plan existed. Look, our friends in the press will cover if up for us anyway. It'll appear in a few places, but this thing will *never* hit mainstream media. The only people that'll know about it are the ones that follow this stuff closely. Do you know what percentage of the country that is, Alex?" Adler asked. "Alex, that's nothing more than a mere five percent of the U.S. population, and that demo already knows who they're going to vote for anyway. That's it. We have nothing to worry about."

"I don't know about that, Bill. I think you're taking this thing too lightly. The president may pull this out of his hat later and use it against our candidate."

"That won't happen. He's going to do like he and the rest of the Democratic mongrels do; he'll take the high road."

"I hope you're right, Bill. I hope you're right."

Chapter 70

NIA EXITED THE OVAL OFFICE PONDERING WHAT, OF THE HUNDRED different tasks she needed to accomplish, she should take care of first.

I need to straighten out this issue with my staff right away. Although Greg had taken care of the Somalia relief package and President Davis had moved on about the issue, Ted Thompson, the source of the problem, still remained. Nia knew she had to get to the root of the problem to prevent a complete mutiny by her staff. If she completely lost control, she would surely be in jeopardy of losing her job, as well as her credibility as a leader in the private job sector. Information such as a White House staff member's leadership ability and skill set had a funny way of seeping back into corporate America.

Nia was never one to dance around an issue. She always believed in the direct approach and this situation was no different. She called Ted Thompson into her office and also asked deputy chief of staff Gregory Connors to attend the meeting. Nia and Thompson engaged in a lengthy, and somewhat heated, discussion until he finally let the cat out of the bag.

"I'll just be honest with you, Nia, we've all felt unappreciated lately."

"Oh, you're speaking for your fellow staff members now?"

"I'm just telling you what they've expressed to me and are either afraid of or feel uncomfortable saying. We feel like you've changed and this new chief of staff position has gone to your head," Ted said, pulling no punches. Nia listened closely while jotting notes. Meanwhile, Gregory sat alongside never uttering a word. There was nothing Ted Thompson could say to save his job. Nia felt his purposeful blunder was nothing less than sabotage and was unacceptable. Her only purpose for having this meeting with him was to find out if he was in cahoots with any other staff members, and essentially, to get a confession on record.

"Nia, I take full blame," Thompson blurted bluntly. "Nobody else would step up. Although countless others complained to me and are very unhappy right now, no one conspired with me, if that's what you're thinking. I didn't mean for the situation to unfold the way it did. I simply wanted to get your attention."

Once Thompson had confessed and Nia found out that there were no other conspirators acting along with him, the rest of the conversation was all academic. She let him completely speak his piece and ended the discussion.

"Okay, are you finished, Ted?" she asked.

"Well, huh, I *guess* I am," he responded with a grimace, as Nia stared at him, expressionless.

"Ted, based on the findings from this conversation, you are terminated," she said with a cold stare and then tapped the button for speaker phone.

"Send security in," she ordered and two security agents immediately entered the room to escort Thompson out of the West Wing.

Chapter 71

AFTER ADLER AND STRAUS ENDED THEIR PHONE CONVERSATION, Straus began to panic. He didn't think Adler realized the severity of the situation. He felt like the plan was blowing up in their faces. The entire document was now available for the Democrats to view, as well as the rest of the country—in his mind, it was a strategic nightmare. He began to contemplate if it was time to pull down the lever and unleash plan B.

Straus had always been impatient. Just like any typical billionaire, he was used to getting what he wanted, when he wanted it. Even his family succumbed to his impatient spoiled nature.

The billionaire paced back and forth in his office, mulling over his next move. *Adler doesn't understand. Curry can't win now. Whatever candidate we put against him can't win now and we just can't let that nigger get back in office again, we just can't. If they would have listened to me the first time, we would have won the last election. Now look at where the country's at. He should have never gotten into office. It's disgraceful. I don't even want to let him finish out his term. Oh, the hell with it, Adler will just have to understand. I'm just going to do it. I have to make the call. He'll thank me later.*

Chapter 72

TERRENCE CONTINUED TO TRY TO CONTACT NIA, BUT SHE REFUSED to respond. As difficult as it was, she knew it was over. She knew they could never get back together after what he had pulled. But each call, email, and text message tugged at the strings to her heart. She knew it would take time to get over him and throwing herself into her work was a natural solution.

Her entire focused shifted to her job. Nia was perplexed at how to regain her staff's favor. She was also hurt. She felt betrayed by them. Beneath her assertive, machine-like persona, she was actually very sensitive about the perception others had of her, especially her staff. This, coupled with her issues with Terrence and her health, was all too much to deal with at one time.

Nia found herself more engrossed in her work than ever. Her social life vanished. She began to live on fast food and ceased her workout routine. Although it had taken months to sculpt her body with Heather and Maria, she was quickly undoing all of that hard work. Food was her refuge. Nia's thick build and slow metabolism made it easy to gain weight. She found herself rapidly gaining weight and unfortunately all in the form of body fat. Although she didn't realize it, she had slipped into a complete state of depression.

Late one evening, Nia arrived home to find Terrence waiting in the lobby of her Georgetown apartment. Nia hadn't returned his calls and Terrence desperately wanted to tell her his side of the story, so he showed up unannounced.

"Hi, Nia," Terrence greeted her sheepishly. Nia was shocked to see him, but ignored his greeting and calmly sidestepped him, continuing to walk towards the elevator.

"Nia, I know I'm the last person you want to see right now, but I just want to talk to you one last time," Terrence pleaded, as he walked alongside Nia. "I feel like I have to get a few things off of my chest before I can move on."

Nia stopped dead in her tracks. "Off your chest? What could you possibly need to get off of your chest? I'm the one that should be saying that."

"That's not what I mean, Nia. I mean…there are just some things that I want you to know before we both move on with our lives."

"I've already moved on with my life."

"I'm sure you have. I know how you are…I know nothing fazes you, but I just—"

"You know nothing fazes me? You're unbelievable. Let me tell you something—" Nia began to say, but stopped mid-sentence and began to look around, realizing that the volume of her voice had risen. At that point, the two had arrived at the tenth floor and were approaching the apartment.

"Oh, just come on in, Terrence," she whispered in a huff. After the two entered the apartment, Nia snapped at Terrence, "Like I was saying, you screw my employee and then have the audacity to come here and say you know nothing fazes me? Amazing."

"I'm not saying that. I'm just saying that I know you're such a strong and determined person and I knew you'd be able to move on. Look, I just want you to know, I never approached Maria. She came at me," Terrence said as Nia listened, staring away from him expressionlessly.

"Nia, I just became weak because you were so busy. I barely saw you, and when you were home, you were working. I could count on my hand the times that we've had sex over the course of the past year. So I just got weak and she took advantage of me."

"Terrence, I can't believe you're going to come over and try to play victim. You *chose* to mess around with Maria. Period."

"You're right. It's no excuse. I'm definitely not trying to play victim. And you know how strong I am. When I met you, you were celibate and I accepted that."

Huh, I know he didn't just say that. "You *accepted* that?" Nia snapped.

"No, that's not what I mean. I just mean I was okay with it because that's what you initially wanted. I understood that you were coming off of a bad relationship and didn't want that, and I would have done anything for you. Anyway, when we did start having sex…I'm a man, I wanted it on a regular basis," Terrence explained, as Nia glared over at him.

"Okay, like I said, that's no excuse, but I promise you, she came at me. *She* started sending me messages on The Social Hub. I swear, Nia. I'll even show you the messages with the dates," Terrence whined and Nia continued to look at him apathetically.

"Nia I just wanted you to know that I would never do anything to *intentionally* hurt you. I wanted you to know I didn't approach Maria, she came at me. She preyed on my weakness. She knew our situation. She knew we rarely had time for one another and were like ships passing in the night. Don't get me wrong, I'm not making excuses. It was a terrible mistake. I know I fucked up and I don't expect for you to take me back, but at least now you know I never set out to hurt you. That damn White House just fucked everything up!" Terrence whined. "Before we moved to Washington our relationship was perfect. I always dreamed we'd get married, have two beautiful children, and be happy together forever. Nia, I really believed, and still do believe, that you're my soul mate, but I understand how you must feel. I'll go now. I love you." Terrence headed to the door.

"Wait, Terrence. I just need to know one thing."

"What? Whatever you need to know, Nia, I'll tell you. Ask me anything," Terrence responded sorrowfully with puppy-dog eyes.

"Terrence, this is really important to me. I really need for you to be honest with me when I ask you."

"I will. I promise. Whatever you want to know, just ask me, sweetie."

Nia momentarily gazed into Terrence's eyes and then asked, "Did you ever make a sex tape with Maria, Terrence?"

"No, never," he responded with a look of sincerity. "She would ask me, like— seemed like every time we got together, but I never did. I was always worried about what it might do to you if it got out. I swear I didn't, Nia."

"Hmm, that's all I wanted to know," she said bluntly, then waltzed over to the front door of the apartment and held it open. "Now you can leave."

Terrence looked shocked as he stood sniffling with tear-filled eyes. Nia didn't utter another word; she stood holding the door open, gesturing for him to leave. Terrence finally shuffled dejectedly out into the hallway and turned back to face Nia.

"I love—" Terrence began to utter, but was cut off as Nia slammed the door shut in his face.

Nia had found out the one thing that she desperately needed to know— Terrence and Maria had *not* made a sex tape. This was extremely important to Nia because she feared the repercussions of an embarrassing sex tape getting out in the media. Although she wasn't married to Terrence, the press would have pounced on a scandal involving her fiancé. She was relieved, but mentally exhausted and had reached a breaking point.

I can't do this anymore. This job has ruined my life. It's ruined my health, my relationship with my fiancé, and my friendships. That's it, I'm just going to resign and move to Atlanta, Nia thought as she stood slumped over her kitchen counter with tears streaming down her face. Then her cell phone rang. Nia glanced at the caller ID. It was Kimberly Caldwell. She began to gather herself.

"Hello, Kimberly."

"Hi, Nia. I was just calling to share some rather disturbing news with you. Conrad Roth was found dead outside his home."

"Oh my goodness, that's awful. Was there foul play involved?"

"No, at this point it looks like suicide."

"That's just awful. Conrad was a good man. It had to be the humiliation of the leak."

"Yes, that was a brave thing to do in his position. His career was everything to him."

"I know he was ashamed of the situation, but I just can't believe that he let the pressure get to him to the point that he'd kill himself. And what about his family?"

"That's the saddest part of the story. He should have thought of them first. How have you been holding up under all of the pressure, Nia?"

"Kimberly, not well. Not well at all. I haven't mentioned this to anyone, but, Kimberly, I think I'm going to resign," Nia said somberly. "I just don't think I can do this anymore."

"Nia, I certainly understand the stress our jobs bring and I'm sure the news of Conrad's death doesn't help, but there must be more to the story."

"I think I've just reached the point of burnout."

"I could tell you haven't been yourself lately. Why didn't you say something, Nia? If we're supposed to have a mentoring relationship, then I'm supposed to be here for this very purpose."

"I know, Kimberly, but I just didn't want to bother you."

"But you asked me to be your mentor and it's *my* responsibility to listen to you, first and foremost. And it's *your* responsibility to reach out to me and let me know when you need me. Wouldn't you say that considering resignation is something worth talking about with your mentor?"

"You're right."

"Now, what's really going on, Nia? What's really on your mind?"

"I've just been experiencing some personal challenges," Nia said quietly.

Kimberly calmly responded, "Such as?"

"Well," Nia's voice cracked. "I've just been going through a lot. One of my staff members basically tried to sabotage me and then Terrence and I have decided to go our separate ways." She began to sniffle.

"I heard about the staff member, but of course, I didn't know about your breakup. I'm sorry to hear about that, but I'll tell you this…God doesn't make mistakes. There's a reason that you and Terrence broke up."

"That's true. It's just a lot going on right now. I'm also experiencing some potential health issues."

"Oh, what kind of issues?" Kimberly asked, continuing to subtly draw more out of Nia.

"I'm scheduled for a biopsy next week. My doctor found a small lump that he was concerned with during my last check-up. We have some family history with breast cancer."

"I see. I'll be praying for you, but I'm sure you'll be fine," Kimberly comforted. "And in terms of the staff member, I have so much confidence in you, that I won't insult you with any advice. I know that you know how to handle yourself there. I will just tell you this, as cliché as it may sound—sometimes we have to take a long, hard look at ourselves in the mirror. If we're not satisfied with what we see, then perhaps the problems that we're facing start there."

Kimberly was comforting, but also hit Nia between the eyes with the truth.

"Nia, I don't have all the answers, but I do know who does. In times like this, there is only one way to make it through—prayer."

Nia had always been a God-fearing woman. As a young child, her mom would sit and read the Bible to her and her brother each night, and her grandma wouldn't let her miss church or weekly bible study. So she was no stranger to prayer, but her faith had waivered when her mom was killed, and when she reached adulthood she began to attend church more sporadically. Deep inside, the confusion of the moment that her grade school principal had told her that her mom had been killed in a car accident had left her scarred. That day, as a young, confused, devastated child, she had questioned God. To deal with her mom's death, she had detached herself from her faith. And emotionally, she had been running from it ever since. She would periodically attend church, and even routinely pray, but she was just going through the motions.

When Kimberly told Nia prayer was the answer to her problems, it penetrated her soul. To that point, she'd known something was missing, but she had become used to solving her own problems, or at least she thought she did. The obvious had become not so obvious.

"Okay, you know you can always call me if you just need to chat," Kimberly said. "In our business, sometimes only someone else in the same business can relate to what you're going through."

"Thank you, Kimberly. You're so special. I really appreciate your friendship and support. But I'm fine," Nia said as she tried to fight back the tears. "It's just been a bad..." Nia paused as her voice cracked and tears began to flow down her face. She took a deep breath and cleared her throat. "It's just been a difficult period, but I'm fine. Thanks for listening to me," Nia said sniffling.

"Nia, like I said, working in the White House puts us in a tough position. Life is different for us. But don't ever hesitate to call me to talk. It doesn't matter what you need to discuss...personal life, business, whatever. That's what friends are for. But you have to just turn those troubles over to God and stop worrying," Kimberly said with the warmth and compassion of a mother, as Nia quietly cried on the other end of the line.

"You're right," Nia replied, as she peered over at a beautiful silver frame on the wall that held a picture of her mom and younger brother.

"Why don't you come to my church with me this Sunday?" Kimberly asked with a tone of optimism.

Nia hesitated to respond for a moment. She had no apprehensions about attending church with Kimberly, but just not right then. She just felt like she wasn't in the right frame of mind for it. "Oh, you are so sweet. I would come with you, but I have so much work to catch up with this weekend. I was actually thinking of going into the West Wing."

"And you can..." Kimberly paused, creating a moment of inquisitive silence, "...after you come to church with me," she finished with heartfelt conviction. Kimberly was masterful at the art of persuasion.

"Well, I guess I'll see you Sunday then." Nia sniffed, then grinned and wiped the tears from her eyes and cheeks.

Chapter 73

STRAUS REACHED FOR HIS PHONE.

Where's that damn phone number? he thought.

Adler and Straus had created a plan for use if all else failed, but had vowed to thoroughly think the situation through together before putting it into action. Nonetheless, the billionaire had become so frustrated that he had thrown all of the rules out the window.

"God, please forgive me for this, but I have no choice. It's for the good of the country. God bless America," he mumbled to himself, as he began to dial.

A soft, sweet voice answered, "Hello."

"This is Alex Straus."

"Mr. Straus."

"Young lady, it's time," the billionaire said confidently.

"Are you sure?"

"Yes, I'm positive."

Chapter 74

SUNDAY HAD COME AND NIA TOOK THE LONG, 45-MINUTE DRIVE TO Upper Marlboro, Maryland, to meet Kimberly at her church, Faith Universal. The long drive provoked intense contemplation. She began to soul search. Nia's entire life seemed to have run through her mind. As she became overwhelmed, tears welled up in her eyes. She dreaded the thought of ruining her makeup and tipping Kimberly off that she had been crying, so she gathered herself. *Nia, please don't start crying,* she thought to herself, as she fanned her face.

When Nia arrived at the massive mega-church, she found Kimberly chatting outside. After Kimberly introduced Nia to several members, the two ladies made their way into the place of worship. As soon as they entered the church's lobby, Nia could feel the force of Faith Universal's award-winning choir. The ground rumbled with their every exhale. Once the ladies made their way through the crowded lobby and entered the church's worship area, Nia felt like she had walked into a thick, indescribable energy that filled the air.

By the time the ladies had gotten settled in their seats, the church's pastor had already greeted the congregation and begun to preach. Nia listened closely. His words were powerful. The deeper he got into his message, the more enthralled she became. She began to feel as if he were speaking directly to her.

"Go to Genesis chapter twenty-two, verses one through twelve," the pastor requested. "Physically, we walk this earth together. We have our friends, family, and loved ones, but there is a place they can't go. Spiritually there are trials and tribulations only you will experience. The scope that God has given you, called *vision*, will only allow you to see the world through your eyes. The mainframe that rests in your head that he blessed you with formulates thoughts, and the vessel that houses your soul and spirit is *just* for you. And there are trials and tribulations that *only* you will experience. When these tests confront you in life, no one will truly be able to understand these experiences…what you're going through…because your scope and mainframe are exclusive to you and will dictate how you deal with them. No one can *truly* walk in your shoes. Yeah, your loved ones can empathize and sympathize, but that's it. That is all they will be able to do."

The pastor's voice began to rise. "And you will think that you are alone. And some of you will think that you can overcome these obstacles by yourself. But you can't." He paused. "You will not be able to control the outcome!" he said loudly, causing Nia to quiver in her seat. "It will be bigger than you and all will seem lost. And the only thing you will have to hold on to…" The Pastor, again, paused and stared out into his audience. His eyes seemed to touch everyone in the room, and just as Nia felt them lock contact with her eyes, he finished his thought, "...will be your *faith*." His words pierced her soul and moved her being. She again began to tremble.

"Preach, pastor!" A voice from the congregation shouted.

"But these obstacles are just that...obstacles. Barriers. Just things that stand in your way, and if you have *faith*, you will somehow navigate over, under, and even straight *through* these impediments, because they are nothing more than tests. Tests that will attack your spiritual well-being. Tests that *only* faith will help you endure. So, when you leave this church today, remember, *always* walk in faith."

"Preach, pastor!" A voice from the congregation shouted.

His words spoke directly to what Nia was experiencing, and each time the pastor mentioned the word *faith,* it resonated in her mind. As he came to the conclusion of his sermon, he asked if anyone wanted to be saved. Nia became frozen. She desperately wanted to rush to the front of the church, but was hesitant until the pastor said calmly, "And for those of you that are hesitant to stand and move forward to the front of this church...I need you to step out into these aisles on *faith*."

She felt an inexplicable surge rush through her body and slowly began to stand.

"Excuse me, Kimberly," she said and then stepped out into the aisle. As she slowly made her way towards the pastor with her emotions swelled up in her throat, tears began to flow down her face. Once she arrived at the front of the church, the pastor placed his hand on her forehead and began to pray. She swayed from side to side and within moments, she fell to floor. And from that moment on, the rest of the service became a blur to Nia.

Chapter 75

THE FOLLOWING MORNING, AS NIA DROVE IN TO THE WHITE HOUSE, the sun shone brightly against her windshield. Instead of slipping on her sunglasses to shield her eyes from the blinding sun, she basked in it. As she smiled and squinted to see, the sunrays blazed against her skin, causing it to tingle. She felt exhilarated, like the sunlight was a sign from God—a symbol of rejuvenation and hope. She had gotten to the point that she dreaded to go to work. But that day, she hurried, anxious to move forward and pull her life back together.

She arrived at the White House to find the entire West Wing solemn after hearing word of Conrad Roth's death. President Davis had ordered the U.S. flag to be flown at half staff and then he *personally* emailed a message to the entire staff addressing the incident. Roth's death seemed to have had a significant impact on the staff. Nonetheless, the somber mood provided the perfect backdrop for an apology. Nia called an emergency meeting with her immediate staff to address their issues.

The staff was leery of the meeting with Nia after Ted Thompson was fired. They really didn't know what to expect. But the subdued atmosphere, which had been caused by Conrad Roth's unexpected death, had redirected everyone's focus. She told the staff that she believed she had lost touch with them, and the adjustment to her new role had caused her to act out of character. The honesty and sincerity of Nia's message was well received by the staff, but this was just the beginning of her efforts to mend the fences she had broken over the past two months.

After the meeting with her staff, she turned her attention to her best friend, Carla. *Carpe diem!* Nia thought to herself, bearing a wide grin, as she quickly made her way back to her office and closed the door behind her. As difficult as it sometimes was for Nia to apologize, she knew she needed to express her regrets to her best friend. The two hadn't spoken since Carla called in distress from being caught by the paparazzi with Jeff Conley. Nia felt terrible about not being there for her.

"Girl, I am *so* sorry. I can honestly say that I let my success go to my head. I can't recall ever letting that happen in the past. Please forgive me, Carla. You know we've been friends too long for something like this to ruin our friendship."

"Wellll, I guess I'll give you a pass. You have been my BF since college," Carla said laughing. "Girl, you were just so mean."

"I'm so sorry. I feel terrible," Nia said with a tone of true sincerity.

"Girl, your swag was on one thousand!"

"Like I said, I did get a little case of the big head. So how did it work out with Jeff Conley anyway?"

"I haven't talked to that jerk since. He got back together with his wife. It was all my fault though; I should have listened to you guys from the very beginning. But I can't believe what Terrence did. I'm really surprised at him," Carla said, but was interrupted by a click in the phone line.

"Hold on, girl, this is Bev calling on the other line." Nia answered her other phone line to find both Beverly and Valerie conferenced on one line. Then she conferenced in all three of the ladies on the call.

"I was just telling Nia I was going to hook her up with somebody," Carla said with a giggle.

"That's not what we were talking about." Nia laughed.

"Girl, I was just with Tyrese last week and he told me he broke up with his girlfriend. He is so *PHAT!*" Carla said.

"What?" Nia asked.

"Pretty, hot, and tempting!"

"Carla, please. I don't want to date *anybody* right now. I need a *long* break."

"As hot as Tyrese is, and you talking about you need a break," Beverly joked. "You must be crazy, Nia. You need a break alright. You need to let that fine, chocolate chunk break *you* off."

"Anyway, how are you, Nia?" Valerie interrupted.

"Girl, I couldn't be better."

"I can't believe Terrence would do that, and that intern…what a tramp!" Carla interjected.

"Is he staying with her now?" Valerie asked.

"I don't know. I haven't responded to any of his texts or phone calls. I don't have anything to say to him."

"You don't want to just curse 'im out one good time? It'll make ya feel better. I know it'd make me feel better to drop a few F-bombs on his trifling ass. What you going to do with his stuff?"

"One day I'm just going to box it all up and tell him to come by and get it."

"Are you serious? Girl, you are too nice. You should burn his stuff in the back of his SUV like that scene in 'Waiting to Exhale.' You bought most of his stuff anyway. I just can't stand a broke ninja. Just sorry," Beverly rambled, to the girls' delight.

"You are so crazy, Bev," Nia chuckled, as Beverly's jokes began to annoy Valerie.

"*Anyway*, I'm just glad that intern resigned," Valerie commented. "The last thing you need is drama like that in the West Wing."

"Yes, that's the last thing I need. I really don't need any undue stress right now. I didn't get a chance to tell you guys, during a recent routine examination, my doctor found a lump in my breast," Nia explained with a thickness swelling her throat.

"Oh, goodness, Nia," Carla uttered.

"Yeah, I'm scheduled to have a biopsy in a few days. I'm sure I'll be fine though," Nia said trying to conceal her apprehension.

"I know you will, Nia. Don't you worry. And we'll be praying for you," Valerie said. "Well, you just let me know when the procedure is scheduled and I'm there. I don't care what's on my schedule," Carla said.

"Thanks, girl, but I'll be fine. My grandmother and brother are going to come in for it. They've been dying to come see me anyway."

"Well, like Val said, we're going to be praying for you," Bev added.

Chapter 76

DESPITE THE SUCCESSFUL EFFORTS OF THE MANY REPUBLICANS IN Congress to block much of President Davis's initiatives, the economy was slowly beginning to recover and the president's approval rating had begun to surge upwards. Although Tanner Long's tell-all book had stirred up quite a bit of controversy in the media, the plan of the super PAC "Recapture Our Excellence" to oust President Davis appeared to be in jeopardy. Nonetheless, Bill Adler remained confident that their plan was on course, but his billionaire cohort Alex Straus wasn't quite as sure. Adler had no idea that Straus had panicked and unleashed what they referred to as plan B. Meanwhile, President Davis worked diligently on his "State of the Union" address speech.

While the State of the Union had originally functioned as a means for the president to provide Congress with an update on the welfare of the country, it had later evolved into a presentation for not only Congress, but all of the citizens of America. Just as was the case with all previous presidents, President Davis sought to utilize the State of the Union to lay out his legislative agenda to Congress. But unlike most past presidents, this one had to paint a different picture. He needed to make the American people understand that Congress was stifling his legislative efforts, while also trying to coerce Congress into better cooperation with him. Even for perhaps the most gifted communicator that has ever graced the presidency, it was a daunting challenge.

After working tirelessly for weeks, President Davis had just completed the initial draft of his speech. He always worked on the first draft of his speeches in privacy and then shared the draft with his speech team. They would then assist him in either further building it out, or hammering it down—whichever was necessary. Most often, the team simply found themselves acting as a sounding-board for President Davis because no one could craft a speech quite like he could.

His speeches were always elegant and to the point, but yet incredibly cerebral. But what truly separated his speeches from most past presidents' was his ability to craft and tell a vivid, impactful story.

President Davis, Nia, the press secretary, and the head speech writer had begun to work feverishly each day in President Davis's study to complete the speech. Nia had become instrumental in this process. She brought the element of truth to the table. She always gave an honest assessment and opinion on the group's writings. Although this was the president's top priority, he still had a myriad of other issues to deal with. One of which was a promise he had made during his election campaign—get Osama Bin Laden.

One rainy January afternoon, President Davis was called away from his speechwriting efforts for an emergency meeting in the Situation Room with navy SEAL commander Damion Jordan and Terry Stringer from the CIA's Special Activities Division. The president, Nia, and several U.S. officials including the secretary of defense, all sat quietly as the two surprise guests updated President Davis on the status of the hunt for Bin Laden.

At the close of the meeting, as the president had begun to exit the Situation Room, he invited the SEAL commander back to the Oval Office.

"Nia, I have to make a quick stop by the East Wing. Can you please escort this gentleman to my office?" he asked.

"Absolutely, sir."

Nia shook the well-dressed SEAL commander's hand and ushered him out into the hallway of the West Wing's basement. Damion was striking. He was a tall man with a powerful build and burly chest which virtually engulfed his trendy, skinny necktie.

Nia was normally all business. She encountered attractive men on a routine basis and rarely even noticed, but Damion had caught her eye. She found herself peeking sideways at his perfectly chiseled body as they walked side-by-side through the West Wing. His tightly fitted suit jacket hugged his arms, while his straight-legged pants gripped his toned thighs and round buttocks.

Whew, Bev would lose her mind over this fine, Tyrese-looking hunk of man, Nia thought, as she inconspicuously gnawed on her bottom lip.

"So, Nia, how do like working in the White House?"

"It's been a wonderful experience," Nia replied nonchalantly.

"Seems like it'd be a lot of pressure."

"I'm sure a lot less pressure than strolling through Baghdad in the middle of the night," she said, grinning.

"I guess you have a point. Hanging out in Baghdad at four in the morning *can* be a bit stressful." He smiled.

Emph, nice smile too.

As the two strolled beside one another, Nia tried not to expose her interest, but he got straight to the point.

"I noticed that you don't wear a lot of jewelry...that seems pretty odd since you're such a sharp dresser," he said and was immediately rewarded with a scowl. "Oh, you have to excuse me. I didn't mean to offend you. Because of my job, I notice everything. I can't help it."

"I see. Then I *guess* I should take that as a compliment. I rarely wear jewelry because of my job," she said, glancing over at the commander. "It's not always appropriate with everyone we meet with, so I just forego it altogether."

"Sure. You certainly are a rather snazzy dresser, but I guess I also noticed the lack of jewelry because your ring finger was bare." He grinned. "If you don't mind me asking, does that mean you're single?" he asked confidently.

"Thanks again for the compliment, but I think this isn't the appropriate place to try and pick someone up. Wouldn't you say?" Nia asked rhetorically with a cold glare, as the two rode the elevator alone.

Before exiting the elevator Damion responded, "Please don't be offended; as you can imagine, it's difficult for me to mince words, or opportunities. I'm a firm believer in fate, and as fate would have it, I just met an extraordinary woman that I would really enjoy getting to know better." He smiled with a twinkle in his eye.

Nia was a bit taken aback by his forwardness, especially since they were in the White House. She returned the smile and the two strolled down the West Wing hallway towards the Oval Office, both a bit smitten by their acquaintance.

When President Davis returned to the Oval Office, he went through a brief Q&A with Damion and found himself extremely impressed with the SEAL. "Damion, it's been a pleasure," the president said, as he extended his hand.

"Sir, the pleasure has been all mine," Damion responded, as he stood and shook President Davis's hand. Then as he turned to exit the Oval Office he extended his hand to Nia. "Ms. Taylor, it was also a pleasure to meet you," he said staring into her eyes with a warm smile, as he clutched her palm.

"Same here," she responded.

"Sir," he said, turning back towards President Davis, "I'll give Ms. Taylor my card in case you have more questions for me." He then handed Nia a business card and asked, "Would *you* happen to have a card available, as well?"

"Sure," she replied and handed him her card. *I must admit, that was pretty smooth.*

"Thank you, Ms. Taylor. I'll be in touch," Damion said and exited the Oval Office.

"Sir, he was just a font of knowledge on the Middle East."

"Yes he was, and seemed like a nice guy. When he asks you out let me know how it goes," the president said with a wink.

"Oh, please, sir," Nia said, grinning and shaking her head.

⌇

The speech group had reconvened late that afternoon in the Oval Office. President Davis had done a phenomenal job capturing the attention of the young people in the election campaign, but worried that he was beginning to lose their interest.

"We have to also speak to the young people with our message. They were a big part of what got us here and I don't want to lose them," the press secretary explained.

"I agree," President Davis said. "Do we have any interns that we can pull in here for this session to get a fresh, young perspective?"

"Well, a bright, young intern named Heather Kelly has helped me with some things over the past few weeks. I think she'd be perfect. She's sharp, but not geeky. Our message to the young people has to hit home with the masses… kids like her."

One of the key functions of White House interns was to fill in wherever needed. Consequently, they were frequently moved around the West Wing from department to department. It also provided them invaluable exposure to the almost endless functions of the West Wing.

"Well, let's get her in here," President Davis ordered.

"No problem," Nia replied and then stepped into the hallway, as she began dialing on her cell phone. "Heather, I need you to come to the Oval Office immediately."

"Sure, I'm on my way," Heather replied. She whipped around the corner just moments later.

"Hi, Nia. You said you needed me."

"That was quick."

"I was just down the hallway dropping something off to Greg."

"Okay, we're having a roundtable on the president's State of the Union address in there and we need a young perspective," Nia quickly explained, as she turned towards the Oval Office entrance.

"Sounds great, but Nia, before we go in, can I borrow your cell phone for a moment? My battery died and I want to let my roommate know that I might be late tonight."

"Sure, but make it quick." Nia handed Heather her cell phone and then reentered the Oval Office. A few moments later Heather joined the group, entering the room passively.

The press secretary greeted her. "Heather, thanks for joining us. Now don't be bashful. We need a young perspective in the room."

As always, the intense brainstorming session fueled much debate between the members of the group, and before they realized it, the meeting had moved late into the evening. President Davis insisted they come to a close for the night.

"Okay, that's enough. We need to shut this down and start fresh in the morning," he said.

Although everyone was exhausted, he still wanted to take a look at the annual budget proposal which was due the first week of February. He stopped Nia as the group began to disperse from the Oval Office. "Nia, don't leave just yet. Do you have a few minutes or so to discuss the budget?"

"Sure, no problem, sir," she responded.

"Nia, I thought your grandmother and brother were in town," Heather interjected.

"Oh, Nia why didn't you tell me?" President Davis asked. "You go on home and spend some time with your family. We can talk about it tomorrow."

Nia cut her eyes at Heather and then responded to the president, "Sir, it's really no problem."

"No, I insist. You go spend some time with them. If I had known they were here, I would have sent you home hours ago." President Davis shook his head. "So what brings them to town?"

"Well, sir, I had a medical procedure done earlier this week and they just came to support me."

"Oh, you didn't tell me this. Are you okay?" he asked.

"I'm perfectly fine, sir. Let's just say everything worked out."

"Well that's a relief. You be sure to let me know about things like this. Don't make me worry…I've got enough on my plate," President Davis said with a warm smile.

"Will do, sir." Nia returned the warm smile.

"Now you go home and enjoy your family. And be sure to tell them I said hello."

"Sir, it's no problem. I can stay."

"Nia, that's an order."

"If you insist, sir," Nia said and began to gather her things.

"I'll stay with you, sir," Heather offered as Nia exited the room. "I worked in the Office of Management and Budget while they were preparing it."

"Well, I guess that's fine, if you like," President Davis responded apathetically, never even looking up, as he scanned the budget proposal.

Chapter 77

NIA DARTED THROUGH THE WEST WING PARKING LOT AND HOPPED into her car. She zipped out of the parking lot into traffic on the rainy street and thought to herself, *I better give them a call and let them know that I'm on my way.* Nia wanted to call her grandmother, but found her phone was dead. She plugged it in to charge and reached for the radio, but heard a loud bang and one of the car's wheels began to wobble, causing the car to sway out of control.

"Whoa!" she yelled, as she gripped the steering wheel tightly. Her BMW's tires squealed, as they fought to grip the wet asphalt. She wrestled with the steering wheel, desperately trying to regain control, but the car began to spin. Reflexively, she closed her eyes tight, as the car whirled 180 degrees, screeched to a halt, and stalled, snapping her head back against the headrest. "Ow!" She winced and then realized the car had finally come to a stop. "Uh," she sighed, and then opened her eyes to find herself sitting in the middle of the highway facing the wrong direction with oncoming traffic headed towards her.

Oh shit!

Chapter 78

PRESIDENT DAVIS WAS METICULOUS. HE HAD A REPUTATION FOR BE-
ing almost obsessively compulsive with his attention to detail. However, this
obsession to the particulars was one of the things that had made him so successful. It made him difficult to trip up, which was extremely important because his Republican adversaries, as well as the media, sought desperately to
find his every mistake. He could thank his *original* mentor, his mom, for this
valuable attribute.

As a young boy he had aspired to some day become an attorney. His mom
had fueled this aspiration by staging routine debates with her son. Each week
she would pick a topic and he would be required to study it in great detail in
preparation for their big debate. By the time he was just eight years old, he was
already winning most of those debates.

"Heather, am I just exhausted or did they miss something here?" he asked,
as he pointed to a line in the budget proposal.

"No, sir, I think I see what you're talking about," she responded, as she stood
up. "Sir, I'll be right back, I really have to use the bathroom."

"Humph," President Davis mumbled, as he scratched his scalp and stared
down at the proposal.

"Mr. President?"

"Uh, did you say something?" he asked.

"Yes, sir, I have to go to the bathroom."

"Oh, sure. Just go through those doors and it's off to your left," he answered.
"Ugh, I just can't believe they missed that…"

Chapter 79

NIA SCREAMED AS SHE STARED DIRECTLY AT THE ONCOMING TRAF-
fic. She frantically tried to restart her car. The ignition whined with each
crank, but refused to start. She turned the key in the ignition again and again,
to no avail. The lights of the oncoming cars grew larger and larger. And Nia's
eyes grew wider and wider. Her heart pounded.

She turned the key in the ignition again and again, until finally, the car
started. She quickly gripped the gear shifter and jammed it into drive and then
mashed the gas pedal. Her wheels sputtered violently against the wet pave-
ment. The torque caused the car to jerk. The wheels caught traction and she
sped off in the wrong direction.

Nia twirled the steering wheel toward the shoulder of the road as she mashed
down on the gas pedal.

"Phew!" she sighed after reaching the side of the road. Her car shook from
the force of the oncoming cars as they whipped past her. She sat in disbelief.
"Oh my God, what the heck just happened?"

Chapter 80

HEATHER STOOD IN THE OVAL OFFICE'S WOMEN'S BATHROOM ANX-
iously wiping the lipstick from her lips.

"There can't be any excess," she said to herself and then began to fluff her hair. *Such a cute cut,* she thought.

"Okay, now it's time to play," she whispered to herself. She looked around, quickly scanning the bathroom, and entered a stall, closing the door behind her. She then pulled up her tightly fitted skirt and dug down into the crotch of her panties.

"Ah-ha, here they are," she muttered, as she pulled two small pink pills from her panties. "I don't need these now," she said as she slipped the panties off and stuffed them into her purse. She then stepped out of the stall and trounced back over to the Oval Office's lavish, gold-framed mirrors.

This ecstasy will have him all over me, she thought, as she slipped the two pink pills under her tongue.

"Undo a couple of buttons, and I'm all set," she said quietly, as she pushed her breasts together and blew a kiss to herself in the mirror. "Okay, take a deep breath, Heather." She sighed and headed towards the bathroom's exit.

"Oh my goodness, I almost forgot the most important thing," she murmured. She pulled her iPhone from her purse, tapped the Video icon, and then clicked Record. From that point on, everything the phone captured would automatically be uploaded to her online digital media account.

Now I'm ready.

Chapter 81

NIA SAT IN HER BMW ON THE SIDE OF THE ROAD IN A MOMENTARY daze. *That was crazy! How did that happen? I think I blew a tire and I just got these tires. Let me get out of this car and see.* She exited her vehicle and carefully peeked around each side of the car.

The front tire blew—no wonder I had such a hard time steering. Phew, I could have been killed! Thank you, Jesus! Nia couldn't believe how fortunate she was to have made it through the incident unscathed. She was an excellent driver, but in the back of her mind always worried about being killed in a car accident like her mom.

It's freezing out here, she thought, as a cold chill ran down her spine.

Nia hopped back into her car. She turned up the heat and flipped the switch of her emergency flashers.

"Brrr, it's cold out there. Good thing I have plenty of gas, otherwise, I'd freeze to death," Nia mumbled to herself. "And that's right, this damn phone isn't working. Now what do I do?" Frustrated, she pressed down on her cell phone's power button.

Maybe there's a short in this car charger, she wondered and then began to wiggle the phone charger's cord.

This is ridiculous! I know I charged this phone last night and the only time I used it today was to call Heather. Nia shook her head in disgust.

"Let me check this stupid phone's battery," she mumbled, as she popped the rear cover off of her Blackberry. *Hmm, the battery's gone. That's strange. I wonder who took it out? I know I didn't,* Nia thought, completely perplexed by what she had found. *Let me think, did I let anyone use my phone today?* she asked herself.

"Yes, I did—Heather!"

Chapter 82

HEATHER ANXIOUSLY EXITED THE OVAL OFFICE BATHROOM AND moved into the Oval Office kitchen, which was adjacent. She quickly snatched two glasses from the cabinet and yanked two bottles of Arctic water, President Davis's favorite bottled water brand, from the refrigerator. As soon as she finished filling the glasses, she took a sip from one and inconspicuously released the pills into the water.

"Whew," she exhaled nervously and headed back to the Oval Office. Her jitters caused her long, sensuous legs to wobble as they tried to keep her athletic frame steady. As she began to slowly stroll across the oval, wheat-colored rug, she managed to compose herself. She swung her curvy hips from side to side with each step.

She gazed across the Oval Office at President Davis as her four-inch stiletto heels sunk into the iconic gold, cream, and blue circular seal of the President of the United States of America, which was woven into the center of the rug.

Whoa, she sighed, as she licked her lips. *I can't believe I'm about to fuck the President of the United States.* She became more turned on with each step.

Heather had had a rough childhood. Her dad was a doctor and her mom a homemaker. On the surface, they had appeared to be normal, loving parents, but behind closed doors her dad had tormented both Heather and her mom. Her father had not only physically and mentally abused her mother, he had also sexually molested Heather from a young age. When she turned sixteen, she had run away and moved in with her boyfriend's family.

Throughout all of her hardships, she had remained a stellar student. She was an exceptionally smart child and eventually received a scholarship to Georgetown University.

It was there that she met a woman named Jane Knight. Jane was a popular madam who ran a prostitution ring in the DC area. Her call girl services catered almost exclusively to DC's political figures. Most of her girls were just like Heather: young, beautiful college students who couldn't resist the fast cash she offered. The ladies drew the politicians in like bees to honey. And Jane ran unbiased business—she obliged as many Democrats as she did Republicans.

Jane knew Bill Adler well. Over the years, Adler had amassed a large stable of high-profile political clients. Politicians flocked to him for his highly persuasive, cutting-edge campaign strategies, as well as his outstanding public relations team. But Bill wasn't just a marketing and public relations guru; he was a crafty businessman. Just as sports agents woo their high-priced professional athlete clients with lavish gifts, exquisite dinners, and of course, exotic women, Bill Adler made sure he entertained his political clients. And Jane's services always went over well with them.

Once Adler had coerced Tanner into acting as an inside informant and potentially joining the Republicans as Curry's future running mate, he then convinced him to plant two young interns in the West Wing—Heather and Maria. Adler had hand-picked the two young women from Jane's stable.

Chapter 83

NIA SAT STEWING IN HER CAR, HOPING THAT A POLICE OFFICER OR highway worker would pass by.

That bitch! What the hell is she up to? I have to get in touch with POTUS.

She hopped back out of her car and scanned the area. *I wonder how far the closest gas station is,* she thought. *Damn it, I can't make it very far in this weather with these heels on.*

She stood in the freezing rain desperately looking for help. Then she noticed red lights blazing, off in the distance.

A trooper! I've got to flag him down. Nia began to jump up and down in her pumps, screaming at the top of her lungs.

"Officer, over here!" she yelled while frantically waving at the oncoming squad car.

Whoosh! The squad car whizzed past.

"Ugh," Nia grumbled and moved back inside her car. *Maybe I can get somebody's attention if I wave a flashlight. I could have sworn I had a small one in the glove compartment.* As she leaned over, rummaging through her glove compartment, she was startled by the bright beam of headlights which glared in her rearview mirror.

"Huh!" she blurted, as she popped up. The bright lights made it difficult for her to see. Her heartbeat surged.

"Ma'am, are you okay?" a short, dumpy-looking fellow dressed in an all-yellow jumpsuit asked.

DDOT. Oh thank God, Nia thought, as she realized that the man was from the District of Columbia's Department of Transportation.

"Oh, I'm fine, but I need you to help me with my car. I had a blowout."

"No problem, ma'am. I'll take a look," the pudgy DDOT worker said, as he moseyed back to his large, bright yellow tow truck and began to shuffle through his tool box. Moments later, Nia turned in her car's driver seat, contorting her spine, in an effort to see what was taking the DDOT worker so long to gather his tools.

What the hell is he doing? she thought as she peeked down at her Rolex watch. Moments later the DDOT worker strolled back past Nia to the front of her car and began to work on her damaged tire.

"Finally. Hurry up, little man," Nia mumbled. *I should never have left her alone with POTUS. I wonder what the hell that little heffa is up to. There's nothing she can do though, Secret Service is monitoring his every move. Unless... unless she tries to slip him something. Oh shit, I have to get in touch with him.*

Chapter 84

AGENT JOHN ROBERTS SQUINTED AND BEGAN TO FROWN, AS HE leaned in towards a monitor, watching President Davis and Heather closely. Agent Roberts was responsible for monitoring the president as he moved about the White House. He used a myriad of security cameras that captured virtually every angle of the building. John and his crew not only monitored President Davis, they were also responsible for keeping an eye on the entire First Family.

He noticed a change in Heather's disposition as she glared across the room at President Davis while he sat at his desk, staring at the budget proposal. Agent Roberts snatched the phone up and quickly dialed the Oval Office. Heather flinched when the phone rang.

"Yes, John," President Davis answered on speakerphone.

"Mr. President, is everything okay?" Agent Roberts asked, as he watched the Oval Office closely on the White House security monitors.

"Sure, I'm fine. What's going on?"

"Just checking on you, sir. Let me know if you need us," the Secret Service agent said and hung up. "Agent Castillo, Monarch's guest is acting out of character. Be on alert. I repeat, be on alert," Agent Roberts barked into his two-way radio transmitter.

"Roger that," Agent Rafael Castillo replied while standing in the West Wing hallway, peering through a tiny, inconspicuous peephole which was embedded in the Oval Office's finely crafted door. The Oval Office's plush, gold drapery shielded him from view. Three other agents were stationed just a few feet away. Meanwhile, seven additional Secret Service agents were strategically located throughout the narrow, cream-colored West Wing hallway, which was adjacent to the north side of the Oval Office. Agent Castillo's chest rapidly contracted and expanded. His eyes darted back and forth, quickly scanning the Oval Office. He whispered into his tiny two-way radio transmitter, which dangled neatly against his lapel.

"I have Monarch in my view. I repeat. I have Monarch in view," he murmured. He was edgy, but collected.

"Roger that," Agent Roberts replied firmly on the other end of the radio.

The agents who stood near Agent Castillo made eye contact with him. Each nodded subtlety. The only movement that could be found in the corridor was the dust settling in the air.

"Stand by," Agent Roberts ordered from the White House security office. Castillo, once again, nodded at his agents. He glanced up towards the small, cut-glass chandelier which hung directly above him from the West Wing's surprisingly low ceiling. He then closed his eyes and mumbled a few words of prayer.

⌒

Heather continued to flounce across the carpet until she arrived in front of President Davis's desk. She stared down at him with a sultry look, but he never looked up.

"Sir, here's your water," Heather said, wide-eyed, and then flopped down in a chair just across from the president. She then quickly set her purse on the corner of his desk and inconspicuously propped her iPhone up against it, angling the camera directly at President Davis.

"Oh, thanks, Heather," he replied, as he raised the glass of water to his mouth.

Chapter 85

NIA QUICKLY ROLLED DOWN HER WINDOW. "EXCUSE ME! EXCUSE ME, sir! How are you coming with that tire?" she yelled.

"Oh, it's coming, ma'am. Just give me a few more minutes. Looks like somebody poked a nice little hole in it," the DDOT worker responded without looking up.

Poked a hole in my tire? Heather! Oh my goodness, I have to call POTUS right away, Nia rapidly thought.

"Sir!" she yelled, as she swung her car door open. "I need to borrow your cell phone." The DDOT worker peeked at her over the hood of the car.

"I know you have one because all DDOT workers in the field are required to. Now let me have it!" she demanded.

"Huh?" He stood in dismay, as Nia darted towards him clutching her purse.

"Okay, ma'am, but I'll have to dial the number for you."

"What's your name?" she asked in a rapid fire manner.

"Uh, Donald, ma'am. But—"

"Donald, my name is Nia Taylor, the White House chief of staff, and I need to make a call to the White House on official government business," Nia said, as she whipped her government badge from her purse and thrust it into the DDOT worker's face.

"Uh-oh, I—" the worker stuttered, as he stood holding his cell phone in his hand.

"Now *give* me that damn phone," Nia ordered, gritting her teeth.

"Uh-huh," the man uttered in agreement with his mouth gaping wide, as Nia snatched the phone from his hand.

Chapter 86

HEATHER SAT PERCHED ON THE EDGE OF HER CHAIR, STARING ANX-
iously at President Davis, as he put the glass of water to his lips.

"This is *ridiculous*! All wrong. This entire section is incorrect. What the
heck were they thinking when they did this?" he fussed, then removed the
glass of water from his lips and plopped it down on his desk.

Damn it, take a drink already, POTUS, Heather thought. "Sir, I'm surprised
that there were any mistakes made. They went over the proposal countless
times."

"Inexcusable," he mumbled.

"Mmmm, isn't this delicious?" Heather asked after taking a gulp of the
water.

President Davis looked up. "Uh?"

"The water, sir. Isn't this Arctic water delicious? It's my favorite," she said
eagerly, already knowing that it was President Davis's favorite brand of drinking water.

"Yes, it's my favorite, too," he responded with his eyebrows raised.

Just take a sip of the damn water already.

"I just love it," he added and then, once again, raised the glass of water to his
mouth. Then he took a sip.

Chapter 87

NIA QUICKLY DIALED PRESIDENT DAVIS'S PERSONAL CELL PHONE, BUT was met with voicemail. *Damn it, POTUS! You know it has to be me or your wife, answer the phone.* Then she called the Secret Service.

"White House Secret Service," an agent answered.

"This is chief of staff Nia Taylor. Get me John Roberts immediately!" she demanded.

Seconds later Agent Roberts came on the line. "This is Agent John Roberts."

"John, it's Nia. Where is POTUS?" she asked frantically.

"He's in the Oval Office. Why?"

"Is he with someone?"

"Yes, an intern named Heather Kelly."

"John, I need you to get her away from POTUS ASAP!" Nia yelled.

"Will do!" Agent Roberts responded. Then Nia heard him shout, "Go! I repeat, go! Get Monarch out of the Oval Office!"

Chapter 88

"ROGER THAT," AGENT CASTILLO WHISPERED INTO THE RADIO AND then signaled to the other agents that it was time to enter by pointing towards the Oval Office door. Before Castillo was able to finish his hand gesture, the other agents dashed towards him clutching pistols and submachine guns. *Shuffle, shuffle, shuffle!* The sound of their black, high-gloss dress shoes scuffing against the glassy, marble floor echoed throughout the corridor loudly.

Castillo leaned back slightly in an effort to gain momentum and then drove his shoulder into the Oval Office door. *Bam!* A loud thud reverberated as the impact caused the door's hinges to rip away from the frame.

In the meantime, Agent John Roberts stood frozen in the Secret Service office holding a two-way radio in one hand and a cellular phone in the other, completely transfixed at the Oval Office security monitor.

The 11 agents scattered about the Oval Office in perfect chaos. In what seemed like milliseconds, Heather was surrounded and found herself staring down the barrels of multiple guns. Her jaw dropped and then she ripped open her blouse.

"Help! President Davis tried to rape me!" she yelled and then fell across his desk. Several agents pounced on top of the young woman.

"Freeze! Don't move or we'll blow your head off! You're under arrest," the agents yelled in unison with their guns pressed against the sides of Heather's skull.

Meanwhile, Agent Castillo dove at President Davis. He wrapped his arms around him, causing President Davis to drop the drinking glass. Castillo then whisked President Davis through a hidden door, which was perfectly camouflaged by wallpaper, into a secret passageway.

"Are they in? Are they *in* the Oval Office? Did they get Monarch out?" Nia screamed into Agent Roberts's ear.

By then numerous agents who had awaited Castillo and President Davis in the secret corridor had taken President Davis to safety.

Chapter 89

THE SCANDAL DIDN'T IMMEDIATELY HIT THE MEDIA. THE WHITE House press secretary and the public relations team first went through their crisis management protocol, which took a couple of days. Once the drama unfolded and the media began to cover the story, Nia shared a few of the details with her girlfriends as she rode down Pennsylvania Avenue.

"Well, did he drink it?" Carla asked curiously.

"No, girl, he spit the water out before the Secret Service busted in once he realized it tasted strange," she explained.

"Oh, thank goodness. And what happened to Heather?" Valerie asked.

"She tried to say POTUS and her were already having an affair."

"That's so weak," Valerie said.

"How did POTUS deal with it? Is he gonna prosecute?" Carla pressed.

"Oh, POTUS didn't deal with it."

"Uh…" Carla uttered.

"The First Lady did," Nia and Beverly said in unison and began to laugh.

"What? Girl, stop. You have to be lying," Carla said.

"No, we're not," Nia told her.

"Ahhh!" Carla shrilled in laughter. "Get 'em First Lady!"

"Yeah, when she got wind of what happened, she had the Secret Service bring Heather directly to her in the East Wing."

"I don't care if it *is* the White House and he *is* the president, you don't mess with no sista's man," Carla said with giggle.

"Okay! And you know the First Lady don't play. One hundred percent DIVA," Bev interjected.

"So is she gonna put that little heffa in jail?" Carla asked.

"Nah," Nia replied.

"Good for her," Valerie said.

"Why?" Carla asked.

"'Cause she's too classy," Valerie commented.

"Well, I said no," Nia added, "but actually Heather might get some time. After the First Lady and the Secret Service finished drilling her, she confessed and gave up everybody involved. She was indirectly hired by Bill Adler and Alex Straus, and Tanner is the one that brought her on as a White House intern. I guess this was all a part of their master plan to oust President Davis."

"Girl, SHUT UP!" Carla gasped. "Girl, shut the *damn* front door."

"I'm serious," Nia said. "Girl, it's crazy. Like something out of a book."

"Nia, forget about Tanner's ole, whack, tell-all fable, you need to document this madness and put out your own memoir."

"I don't know if I'll ever put it out, but, girl, trust me, I have a memoir."

"Iiiiiii!" Carla shrilled. "You are TOO…MUCH!"

"Wherever you'd like to go eat," Nia said.

"What?" Carla asked in confusion.

"Oh, I'm sorry. I wasn't talking to you guys," Nia responded.

"Well just who the hell are you talking to?" Beverly asked.

"I forgot to tell you all."

"Tell us what?" the three ladies asked in harmony.

"Well, I have a new friend."

"Iiiiiii!" the three women shrilled in accord.

"You all are *too* crazy," Nia giggled.

"Who? Girl, who is it?"

"His name is Damion Jordan and he's a navy SEAL," Nia said blushing.

"Iiiiiii!" the three ladies shrieked, again.

"You little, sneaky tramp. Why didn't you tell us?" Carla yelled.

"Girl, please," Nia smiled, and then peeked over at Damion as he continued to drive, oblivious to the excitement.

"Now you know you better tell us all about him," Carla said.

"Oh, wait."

"Nah, you wait," Carla replied.

"No, wait a minute. Damion, let me turn up your radio?" Nia asked.

"Sure, go ahead. It's right there," Damion pointed to the volume dial.

"Emph, girl, he *sounds* sexy too!" Carla shouted in Nia's ear, causing Beverly and Valerie to giggle.

"Wait, you all are not going to believe who's on the radio," Nia sniggled.

"Girl, who?" the three ladies asked.

"Just listen," Nia said as she placed her Blackberry close to the radio's speaker.

"Mr. Baisden, my new reality show is called 'Unbeweavable!' And, honey, I'm gone be saving poor women with beat-up weaves all over this country. Trust me, it's gonna be off the chain!" the ladies' beautician André bragged, as he promoted his new reality show on the popular syndicated radio show "The Michael Baisden Show."

"Ahh-ha-ha-ha!" the four ladies screamed, tee-heeing in laughter.